MW01136976

PARENTS WEEKEND

ALSO BY ALEX FINLAY

If Something Happens to Me

What Have We Done

The Night Shift

Every Last Fear

PARENTS WEEKEND

A NOVEL

ALEX FINLAY

MINOTAUR
BOOKS
NEW YORK

This is a work of fiction. All of the characters, organizations, and events portrayed in this novel are either products of the author's imagination or are used fictitiously.

First published in the United States by Minotaur Books, an imprint of St. Martin's Publishing Group

PARENTS WEEKEND. Copyright © 2025 by Alex Finlay. All rights reserved.
Printed in the United States of America. For information, address St. Martin's Publishing Group, 120 Broadway, New York, NY 10271.

All emojis designed by OpenMoji – the open-source emoji and icon project. License: CC BY-SA 4.0

www.minotaurbooks.com

Designed by Omar Chapa

The Library of Congress Cataloging-in-Publication Data
is available upon request.

ISBN 978-1-250-36072-4 (hardcover)
ISBN 978-1-250-42175-3 (Canadian edition)
ISBN 978-1-250-36073-1 (ebook)

Our books may be purchased in bulk for promotional, educational, or business use. Please contact your local bookseller or the Macmillan Corporate and Premium Sales Department at 1-800-221-7945, extension 5442, or by email at MacmillanSpecialMarkets@macmillan.com.

First U.S. Edition: 2025
First International Edition: 2025

10 9 8 7 6 5 4 3 2 1

PARENTS WEEKEND

PROLOGUE

They run. Run with a primal fear knowing that if they slow down, all five of them will die.

It's hard to think in this fog of terror. Earlier this week their biggest fears were a mom finding his stash of edibles, a dad finding those condoms in her dorm room nightstand. A mom finding her fake ID. A dad finding his crumpled exam with the *D* circled in red.

But now, with sand in their shoes, waves crashing, the bonfire burning in the distance, they leave those trivialities behind.

And they run.

They reach the narrow path to the sea cave, link hands in a chain as they navigate the perilous waves and jagged rocks into the hollow.

Huddled in the gloom, they stay still as stone. Thoughts swirling, they wonder what clues the police will find. The group chat? The social-media posts? The video of the horror that brought them here?

Another wave breaks. Another flashlight beam gets closer. Another whimper escapes a hand clutching a mouth.

What clues will they find?

Or will they find nothing but their cold, lifeless bodies?

FRIDAY

THREE DAYS EARLIER

Welcome to Parents Weekend!

Campisi Hall Capstone Group Families:

THE AKANAS

Parents: Ken and Amy Akana

Student: Libby Akana

THE GOFFMANS

Parents: Alice Goffman

Student: Felix Goffman

THE MALDONADOS

Parents: David and Nina Maldonado

Student: Stella Maldonado

THE ROOSEVELTS

Parents: Cynthia Roosevelt

Student: Blane Roosevelt

THE WONGS

Parents: Not attending

Student: Mark Wong

CHAPTER ONE

THE ROOSEVELTS

Blane basks in the morning sun, his skateboard *clack-clack-clack*ing on the campus sidewalk. He marvels at the palm trees and pretty classmates stretched out on towels in the grass, wearing bikinis and pretending to study. He's attended Santa Clara University for only a few months and already decided that he's never leaving California. His hometown, Washington, D.C., with its swampy weather, its status and power infatuation, its boring old marble buildings, has nothing on Cali.

He juts his cruiser to a stop and kicks the back so it flies up and into his grip, a move he's been working on since drop-off day. There's a crowd outside Campisi Hall, a spectacle of some sort. He sees his buddy Mark Wong.

"What's up? Fire drill?"

Mark shakes his head. "I don't know. They cleared everyone out of the dorm. It's like a Secret Service sweep or something." Blane follows Mark's gaze to the four SUVs parked in the lot out front. At the men in dark suits standing erect.

Ugh. How could Blane have forgotten? Parents Weekend starts tonight.

"It's just my mom's advance team." Blane rolls his eyes.

Mark digests this, then his eyes flash. "That's cool as shit, bro. What, is she, like, important or something?"

Blane shrugs. He watches as two stoic men with earpieces glower in their sunglasses. They love the attention.

Blane turns to his friend, offers a lopsided grin. "Watch this." He takes out his lanyard, finds the small device attached to the key chain, then directs the laser pointer at one of the agents. A tiny red dot appears on the man's chest. It takes only a moment before more agents fly out of an SUV.

The din of the crowd rises as the drama unfolds. Then comes the recognition from the detail that this isn't a sniper's laser sight. The lead Diplomatic Security Service agent's glare snags on Blane from the distance, and the guy marches over.

"Oh shit," Mark says, already stepping back as the massive agent stands before Blane, a scowl on his face.

The giant looks like he'd love to take a swing at an entitled college kid, but instead holds out his palm. "This isn't a game," is all he says.

When Blane doesn't hand over the laser pointer, the agent rips the lanyard from his hand. Shaking his head, the agent says, "Your mother's waiting in your dorm room."

Might as well get this over with. "I'll catch you at Benson for lunch," Blane says to Mark.

On the walk into Campisi, one of the kids from the dorm gives Blane a high five like this was the most epic thing that's ever happened.

Inside it's a ghost town. The senior girl who normally works the front desk isn't there doomscrolling, looking exasperated. The foosball table sits to the side, no crowd cheering on a game. The lounge chairs are empty. Blane shuttles down the hallway. Another member of his mom's detail is stationed outside his room.

The agent gives a nearly indiscernible nod, allowing Blane entry. His mom is out of sight, down the narrow hall and in the tiny box Blane calls home. Blane can hear she's on the phone with someone, like always.

He lingers in the corridor a moment, listening.

"I don't know why we're having this conversation," his mother says into the phone. Someone's in deep shit with her, like always.

"Bullshit, Hank. That's bullshit."

Blane realizes it's his father on the line.

"It's spelled out in our agreement. *I* get Parents Weekend."

A heavy silence follows. The temperature is rising, like always. The usual garbage between them.

"Really, Hank? Really? Well I hope they fucking kill me too so I never have to hear your goddamned voice again."

Blane gives it a moment, backtracks, and rests his skateboard loudly against the wall so she'll hear.

"Hi, Mom," he says.

Her back is to him, like she's collecting herself. Then she turns. She's wearing one of her usual power suits, which somehow makes her look even taller than six feet. Her chin-length dark hair is immaculate, like always.

"Honey, how are you?" Her tone reveals none of the tension from seconds ago. "And all I get is 'Hi, Mom'? Get over here and give me a hug."

They exchange a stiff embrace.

Blane catches the faint scent of her jasmine perfume, which transports him briefly to when he was little. Back when Mom sang pop songs, inserting her own silly lyrics, as they drove home from Little League. When she would dance and gyrate as Blane pounded on his toy bongo drums. When she would even watch *SpongeBob* with him, declaring Squidward was her favorite character. Then came her new, powerful job. Then the bounty on her head because of that new, powerful job. Then Blane's terrifying four-day disappearance. Then the divorce. It was as if every stress layered a coat of varnish over her, encasing her in a hard, humorless shell.

He wonders how long it will take for her to critique his hair, his clothes. The mustache the fraternity he's pledging insisted he grow since they say he looks like Goose from *Top Gun*.

Surprisingly, she just says, "I'm excited."

"About what?"

She gives him a hard look. "To spend time with you. To meet your friends. Meet the other parents."

Blane nods, says nothing.

"Is there an agenda for the parents?" She pauses. "Never mind, Paul will know."

Paul is her chief of staff. As smarmy a Washingtonian as you'll ever meet.

"There's a dinner thing tonight with my capstone group," Blane says.

Each freshman dorm breaks the residents into small groups of five to six students. They have to complete a project together by the end of the year, but spend most of the time partying.

"Have you gotten lunch?" his mom asks.

"I'm supposed to meet some friends at the dining hall," he says, hoping she won't gripe.

"That's great. I actually have a few calls this afternoon. So, I'll see you tonight?"

He nods.

"Maybe you can shave that peach fuzz over your lip before dinner."

There she is.

"Can't, it's a frat thing."

She frowns. "At least put on a clean shirt."

Another stiff hug, and he's off.

Alone in the room, Cynthia releases a cleansing breath. Blane's father is such a complete and utter *asshole*. The only reason Hank wanted to come to Parents Weekend in her place was to punish her.

Mitch, the lead on her detail, comes into the dorm room.

"Everything okay?" he says, examining her. He's a trained observer and little gets by him.

She's learned in this job, among these men—even her subordinates or those she trusts, like Mitch—to never show weakness. "Just Hank being Hank," she says.

Her phone pings, she scans the screen. It's a text alert from the university. One thing she's noticed in Blane's few months at Santa Clara: The administration overuses its alert system.

Cynthia reads the text aloud. "It says, 'Bronco Alert: An unhoused man is wielding a knife at the Seven-Eleven on Benton Street.'"

Mitch checks his own phone, presumably the tracker on Blane's device. "Beavis is still on campus, he's nowhere near there." They made the mistake of letting Blane choose his own code name. Blane picked "Beavis" from some idiotic cartoon he and his father think is hilarious.

"Unhoused man?" Mitch says, repeating the alert's message as if he's unfamiliar with the term.

"I forgot, you aren't versed in liberal-speak." She allows herself a smile. "Calling them 'homeless' apparently carries a negative connotation that they're criminals. And we wouldn't want anyone to think the *unhoused* man wielding a knife is a criminal."

Mitch shakes his head.

Cynthia examines the room. For security reasons, Blane's is a single, one of the few in the dormitory. The bed is elevated. Next to it, a miniature fridge, which she decides not to open. On the small desk, there's a box of protein bars, a flyer with Greek letters advertising a "Parents Weekend Blowout." The flyer has a photo of what must be a fraternity house with a giant sign—a sheet hanging from the second-floor window: OUR PARENTS CAN DRINK MORE THAN YOURS.

"Remember the days when you could take a nap whenever you wanted? When you had no responsibilities? When you could bring someone back to your room in the middle of the afternoon . . . ?" Cynthia puts a hand on the bed, pushes down on the thin mattress, testing it.

Mitch holds the hint of a smile. Oh, he remembers.

"Did you see that ridiculous mustache his fraternity's making him grow?"

"It's better than what they had pledges do in my day," the agent says.

Mitch was a frat boy. That tracks.

"Are you the only one manning the hallway?" She holds his gaze.

He checks his phone again, nods.

"Well, if we're going to fuck like coeds, we'd better be fast," she says, turning her back to him, lifting her skirt, and yanking down her panties.

At the dining hall, Blane stabs a plastic fork into his burrito bowl. Mark sits across from him at the long table, a tiny mountain of food on his plate. Mark's a big dude—the pledge master gave him the nickname Tommy Boy from the old movie. It fits, not only because Mark resembles the actor Chris Farley—albeit an Asian Chris Farley—but also because he's a jokester. It's why he and Blane became fast friends. To survive pledging, you need a friend.

Mark takes a big bite of pizza and, with a mouthful, says, "So these dudes, like, have to go everywhere with your mom?"

"Yeah. They've basically lived with us since I was in fifth grade."

"Why? What's the—"

"My mom's high up at the State Department. We dropped a bomb on some official from a hostile government and they put a bounty on her head."

"Holy shit."

"Yeah. She wanted *me* to have a team here and I said, 'No way.' My dad backed me up."

"It'd be kinda cool, though. Girls would think you're, like, mysterious, dangerous."

"It sucks, bro, trust me. DS rotates agents and you have strangers up in your shit constantly. And my mom is always pressed with what we say or do around them. The agents gossip. They tell my mom all kind of stories about the other assholes they protect."

Mark doesn't seem convinced.

Blane doesn't reveal what precipitated the around-the-clock security detail—his abduction when he was ten. The two men didn't hurt him. They bought him Happy Meals and let him watch TV as their bumbling plan to lure his mom into peril came to an abrupt end when burly men in night vision goggles riddled them with bullets. Blane doesn't think about it that much these days. Doesn't feel traumatized or haunted by what happened. It seems more like a dream. But it was pure gold for his college essay.

"The *only* good thing I ever got out of a security detail," Blane adds, "was at Disneyland when I was a kid: We got to cut to the front of the line on every ride."

Mark is distracted. He's looking over Blane's shoulder at something.

Blane twists around and sees Stella walking toward them, her long auburn hair tangled, like she just woke up. She wears a shirt that reads, DON'T TELL ME TO SMILE.

She fast-walks over, takes a seat next to them.

"Sup?" Blane asks.

Stella's expression is just short of panic. She leans in, says, "It's Natasha. She still hasn't come home. And Libby . . . she's freaking out."

Blane looks at Mark, who puts down his slice of pizza.

Blane keeps his voice steady. "You just need to be cool."

"But Libby, she says she's gonna . . . I think we need to—"

Blane puts his hands out, palms down: "Stick to the story like we agreed."

His gut clenches, but he makes sure to smile reassuringly. He warned Stella—warned them all—that Natasha Belov was bad news. Bad, bad news.

CHAPTER TWO

THE MALDONADOS

The ascent is bumpy, but David doesn't mind. It's rare that he gets to fly private, so he can't complain. His wife Nina sits tight-jawed next to him in the luxurious cabin. He decides not to call her on the pouting, lest they get into a fight in front of their hosts, Brad and Jade, who sit across from them in buttery leather seats. Jade is stunning in an overdone way—plunging neckline, contoured makeup, short skirt with tall boots. Brad, with his meaty face and paunch, is much less so. But that's often how it goes, David has learned in his twenty years as a plastic surgeon.

"Thank you again for the lift," he says to the couple.

Brad and Jade raise their champagne flutes in acknowledgment. A leggy flight attendant mistakes it as a signal that they need a refill and ambles over and tops off their glasses.

"I was headed to Frisco for business, so it's no problem," Brad says.

David can't remember the last time he'd heard someone call San Francisco "Frisco"—probably in a movie from the seventies.

With his shirt unbuttoned too low, laying bare his dark mat of chest hair, Brad has that vibe. A relic from another era.

Brad continues: "And after what you did for Jade—for *me*—how could I not?"

David is unsure what he means.

Jade cups her breasts with her hands. "They're perfect, absolutely perfect. All my friends are asking about the *artist* who sculpted these masterpieces."

David doesn't need to look over at his wife to know the expression on her face. He simply smiles. His father taught him to always accept a compliment.

"The best part," Brad says, "is that they're so damn upright." He removes something from his shirt pocket. It takes David a moment to realize that it's a vial of white powder. Brad sprinkles a jagged line on his wife's chest, leans over, and snorts the coke.

David can't help but look at Nina. Her eyes are wide. David and his wife aren't prudes, but they're not drug people, either. When David looks back, there's already another line on Jade's chest. Brad gestures for David to take it.

"Oh, thank you," David pauses, trying to formulate his excuse, "but Jade is a patient and it wouldn't be appropriate as her physician to—"

Before he finishes the sentence, Nina has leaned forward and buried her face in Jade's cleavage.

Jade arches her back, laughing as Nina does the line.

"*Now* we've got a party!" Brad says.

Nina peers at David as she wipes her nose with her index finger and thumb, then falls back into her seat.

"What's your business in San Francisco?" David asks, if only to restrain his astonishment at what just happened. To contain the anger rising in his chest.

"The usual bullshit with one of my tech companies," Brad answers. He swallows another glass of champagne. "Jade said you're visiting your kid?"

"Yes, college Parents Weekend. Our daughter, Stella, is a freshman."

"Where? Stanford?"

The question always irks David. Santa Clara is a small but elite school without the brand recognition.

"SCU, a private school about an hour from Frisco," David says, using Brad's lingo and hating himself for it.

Brad shrugs and holds up his flute to signal to the flight attendant. "Top you off? Or get you something else to drink? She makes a mean Old Fashioned." Brad looks toward the flight attendant, his eyes fixing on her ass.

"You two don't look old enough to have a college student," Jade says, reclining back in the seat now. "The benefits of marrying a master surgeon," she adds, like it's an afterthought.

Nina smiles, but it doesn't reach her eyes. "I guess," she says. It's true, Nina is a beauty, but not by the scalpel. She practices yoga, eats healthy, and seemingly drinks gallons of water every day. With her glowing skin and bohemian style, she has the air of an aging-gracefully, girl-next-door fashion model. She's never said so, but she's always disapproved of David's chosen profession. These days, she disapproves of everything about David.

She still hasn't forgiven him, and probably never will.

His mind flashes to that night. Naked in the back seat of his Range Rover. The anesthesiologist frantically tugging up her scrubs, tears streaming down her face, her husband standing outside the vehicle in the woodland near where she and David parked. The husband saying he called Nina and told her. Then—

Brad's voice mercifully breaks the memory. "You guys in the club?"

"Club?" David asks.

"The mile-high one." Brad cocks one of his thick brows.

David offers a polite smile. "Can't say that I am."

"There's a small bedroom in the back. Feel free to . . ." He makes a clucking sound with his tongue.

David turns to Nina, who is downing another glass of champagne and seems out of it. Even after the coke, there's no way she'd want David to touch her, much less join "the club."

But then his wife surprises him. "Will you be joining us?" she says to Brad and Jade.

Brad's Adam's apple bobs up and down.

What in the fuck? David glares at his wife. "Nina's a kidder," he says.

"Damn," Brad says, "this was just getting interesting." He leans forward, slaps David on the ball of his shoulder.

"I'll take that drink," David calls out to the flight attendant.

Later, Nina doesn't know whether to be annoyed or satisfied that David hasn't spoken to her since they landed and escaped that awful couple. Not a word in the back of the town car waiting for them at the airstrip. Not at the rental car place. Not now, waiting for their daughter to meet them in front of the fountain at the center of campus. That's David's specialty. The silent treatment. A Maldonado inheritance passed down generation after generation, from father to son.

To be fair, she was acting out. But what does he expect?

Still jittery from the cocaine, she downs a bottle of water. Nina was a party girl in college, but usually just booze. She tried coke two times and never liked it. She's remembering why. The brief euphoria is dwarfed by the anxiety. The need to chatter, an urge she's had to fight, given David's cold shoulder. And honestly, it's his fault she acted that way.

She stops herself from the internal rant. This weekend isn't about them. Isn't about their marital problems. It's about Stella.

"Are you going to give me the silent treatment all weekend?" she asks.

David ignores the question, stares out at the campus church, a sand-colored Spanish-style structure with a bell tower. David is a lapsed Catholic with all the guilt that carries.

"Can we at least try to get along for Stella?" she continues.

David turns to look at her. It's a beautiful day, seventy degrees, warm for March. The sun is beating down on them, highlighting his thinning dark hair, the lines etched in his face. He's still damned handsome, but this afternoon he's showing his age.

David looks like he's about to let loose on Nina for her behavior on the plane. But then his eyes jerk to something behind her. Maybe it's their daughter, arriving in the nick of time.

No, his face is drained of color. Something's wrong.

Nina whirls around. That's when she sees him. She rubs her eyes in an almost cartoon-like gesture to make sure it's not the coke playing tricks on her. But it's *him*.

How?

Why is he here?

David grabs her by the hand and yanks her away.

CHAPTER THREE

THE GOFFMANS

"Dean Pratt?" Alice pokes her head into her boss's office. She doesn't want to bother him. The dean has been in a mood all week. Parents Weekend always stresses him out. Alice understands. These aren't just helicopter parents. They're UH-60 Black Hawks who are spending a fortune on the private institution and expect their money's worth. They want face time with the head of the school to discuss their "ideas" or to gripe about this or that. Dean Pratt has three associate deans assigned to handle such matters and who, frankly, are better at front-of-the-house. But on Parents Weekend, there's no escaping the parents.

The dean looks up from his desk. Gives Alice one of those stares over his reading glasses that reminds Alice of her father. The dean is about the same age as Alice's father was when he left the family and never looked back.

"Yes," is all the dean says in that get-to-the-point tone of his. He'd once cut Alice off mid-sentence, barking, "I don't need to know how the sausage is made." He'd later shortened it to just "sausage" whenever Alice went on for too long. So Alice rehearses nearly every encounter with the man.

"Natasha Belov's parents called again."

The dean exhales loudly. "She still hasn't turned up?"

Alice shakes her head. It's not the first time a student has gone AWOL. They always reappear, usually returning from an impromptu road trip or a bender, oblivious that anyone was looking for them.

"What does Chief McCray say?" The campus has its own police force, called CSS, that's accustomed to the shenanigans of college kids.

"He said she's missed all her classes this week. No one's seen her since Tuesday."

"Missing classes isn't all that unusual for Ms. Belov," the dean points out.

Natasha's on academic probation and has been called before the student disciplinary board for alcohol and weed offenses on more than one occasion.

"The chief said they're searching the Panther Beach area." The last place she was seen, drunk or high and out of it. No one reported the girl missing until yesterday.

The dean sighs again. "I think we should have Dean Schwartz meet with the Belovs. He'll walk them back from the ledge. Can you tell him to come to my office right away? And tell Professor Turlington I need to see him about another matter."

"Of course."

"And call Dean Morris, ask him where he's at on my speech. I have to give it tomorrow morning, for goodness' sake. He always waits until the last minute." Pratt shakes his head in disapproval.

Alice nods. "I look forward to your speech," she says timidly.

The dean's forehead wrinkles like he's confused. Like why

would he give one lick about Alice's opinion on his opening remarks for Parents Weekend? She's his admin—his *secretary*, as he calls her, using the outdated term. Not someone who needs to worry about matters of substance.

"I'm a parent this weekend," Alice reminds him.

"Oh, that's right. How's your son's freshman year going?"

The dean always refers to him as "your son" because he doesn't remember Felix's name. They're well into the school year, and it's the first time he's asked about Felix. He undoubtedly disapproves that Alice isn't paying tuition—one of the few perks of her job, but a big one.

"He's doing great. Thank you for asking."

The dean nods, turns back to the papers on his desk. He's done with her.

"Oh, and Alice," the dean says, catching her before she's out the door.

Alice turns, waits.

"That file I mentioned still hasn't turned up. We need to be more vigilant about security. Last week, I saw two students in the lobby and no one was at their desks."

"Yes, sir."

Back at the reception area, Alice is pleased to see her favorite student sitting in the concourse.

"*Fe-lix*," she says. She looks back to make sure the dean's door is still closed—mindful of his comment about unattended students.

"Hi, Mom."

"I didn't expect to see you until the dinner tonight," she says.

"I was in the neighborhood."

Felix is tall and slender, with long-lashed dark blue eyes and a gentle smile. He hands her a chocolate bar. A KitKat, her favorite.

"You didn't need to do that. And you know I'm trying to watch what I eat."

"Oh, if you don't want it . . ." he says playfully, pulling it away.

"Hand it over, mister."

Some of the students are rude or entitled, but not Felix. He's her precious boy. It's been the two of them against the world for so long. Her heart swells with pride seeing him on campus, just one of the gang, as if they were affluent like the other families. As if they didn't live in a dumpy apartment on the outskirts of Santa Clara.

As if his problems in high school didn't exist.

"Is everything all right? Do you need something?"

"Can't I just say hi to my mama?"

She beams at that. She loves it when he calls her *mama*, for some reason. Loves it more that he knows that and makes a point to say it.

Before she can ask him about his day, a couple bursts through the tall wooden doors. The man is in his fifties. His suit is expensive-looking but badly wrinkled, his demeanor intense, almost frenzied. The woman with him is more subdued, as if she's in a daze, medicated.

"Can I help you?" Alice says.

"We're Natasha Belov's parents," the man says. He has an Eastern European accent. "We need to speak to the dean right now." A wildness fills his eyes. He's clearly frantic about his missing daughter.

From behind the couple, Felix mouths, *I'll see you tonight*, as he slips out.

The dean releases a groan into the phone when Alice tells him the Belovs are there.

"Bring them to my office in ten minutes," he says.

It's a mistake to make them wait, but Alice doesn't say so.

Those ten minutes are excruciating. Alice watches the couple as they touch foreheads. She catches a few whispered foreign words that could be a prayer. With every passing minute, her heart breaks a little more, then her phone finally buzzes, signaling the dean is ready.

CHAPTER FOUR

THE AKANAS

Amy emerges from the Starbucks bathroom to find her husband holding his venti black coffee—always black, for efficiency more than taste. The drive from LA to Santa Clara is a long one, desolate, mostly small agricultural towns with few bathroom-stop options, so she decided against a drink of her own. They walk back to the Volvo and she notices a driblet of coffee trickling down Ken's hand.

The barista overfilled. Amy hates the vexing errant drip that's impossible to stop once the lid's seal is compromised. You'd think Starbucks would have solved that problem by now.

"You should have them give you another cup," Amy says.

Ken opens the car door. "It's okay. I have napkins."

Amy doesn't push it. They don't call her husband No Drama Akana for nothing. To his face, it's Your Honor—chief judge at the LA Superior Court—but Ken has heard the nickname, and Amy thinks he secretly likes it. And it fits. Ken is unflappable. Maddeningly so at times.

Ken buckles his seat belt, waits for her to secure hers, checks his mirrors. Then they're off. He keeps the radio on low, an easy-listening station, just loud enough to drown out the silence between them. Silence that has grown only more pronounced since their daughter Libby left for college, leaving their house feeling cold and empty.

Back in law school, Amy and Ken—he went by Kenny then—would talk late into the night. About the law. About their dreams. About their future lives together. It stayed that way as they progressed in their careers, got married, and had two children.

Timmy's cancer didn't just kill their beautiful little boy, it ravaged his parents. These days, the only thing that brings Ken happiness is Libby. And when she left for college, he and Amy became one of those couples who have nothing to talk about. Ken doesn't even consult with Amy about his cases anymore. Since becoming a judge, he says it's inappropriate to discuss his docket. That's an excuse. Ken hasn't cared about her opinion on the law, or much else, for that matter, since she stopped working. It's not like she wanted to give up her career. But after Timmy's diagnosis, one of them had to be available for the endless medical appointments, post-op care. It wasn't even a choice; she had to be there for her son.

Now, Amy has nothing.

She shouldn't think this way. She has the memories. And, of course, she still has Libby. Their golden girl. So smart, so hard-working, an effervescent smile always blooming on her face.

Amy looks at the GPS on the dash. "Two more hours." She blows out a breath. "We'll be cutting it close for the dinner."

"Beautiful day, at least," Ken says. He sips from his paper cup, and Amy can't help but fixate on the bead of brown liquid bleeding down his hand.

Then comes the familiar silence. It lasts nearly the entire drive.

Amy finally sees a sign for another Starbucks—cultural landmarks in America. "Can we make a bathroom stop?"

"We're almost there, you can't make it?"

She shakes her head.

He takes the exit and both head inside. Checking his phone, Ken frowns. "I got a campus safety alert."

"I saw it, texted Libby," Amy says. "She's fine."

Ken nods. He's been on edge since his last case—the biggest of his career—dominated the news. An A-list movie star named Rock Nelson charged with beating up his starlet girlfriend. A case that made the Johnny Depp–Amber Heard trial seem tame, complete with TMZ cameras in Ken's face and crazed fans outside the courthouse holding up JUSTICE FOR ROCK signs. And, of course, the online vitriol.

After the pit stop, they return to the car. Ken says, "Are you kidding me?"

"What?" Amy asks.

"We've got a flat."

Amy walks over to the driver's side, bends down to look at the tire. It is indeed flat. But that's not the eerie part.

Three of the four tires are flat.

Libby sits on her dorm room bed, hugging her knees. "Just don't ask my dad about the case, okay?"

"I got it. You already told me," her roommate Deepa says. "But can I just say it's so cool your dad is No Drama Akana." She points her thumbs to her shirt, which has a cartoon caricature of Libby's father dressed as a Hawaiian warrior, standing in a Superman pose.

"Change your shirt," Libby says. "He'll hate it. And it's kinda racist."

Libby shouldn't be dreading her parents' visit. But the truth is, spending time with them is draining. It has been since Timmy's diagnosis, when Libby took it on herself to become the perfect child. One who got straight As, who won public service awards, who was the star of the track team. One who didn't drink or smoke or curse or complain. Anything to allow her parents to focus singularly on her little brother. But nothing she did could purge their devastation, nothing she did would save Timmy.

She thought Perfect Libby might die with her little brother. But the movie had already been cast, and there was no changing it now. She even has a catchphrase: *Everything's amazing!*

And for a time, in the euphoria of those first days on campus, everything *was* amazing.

Amazing new friends. Amazing campus. Even amazing classes.

But now she can't sleep.

She can barely keep food down.

She needs to get it together before this dumb capstone dinner.

Everything's amazing!

"Oh my god," Deepa says, eyeing her phone. She bolts upright on her bed.

"What is it?"

"It's Natasha. They found her."

Relief floods Libby, but she can't let Deepa know why. "About time." Libby's voice, remarkably, remains steady. "She's going to be in *so* much trouble . . ."

"No, she's not," Deepa says. "She's dead."

CHAPTER FIVE

THE KELLERS

Sarah Keller looks over at the last of the travelers threading into the tiny tunnel leading to the plane. JFK Airport's distorted speaker squawks a last call for Boarding Group 5.

There are two kinds of people in this world: those who arrive at the gate two hours early and constantly check to confirm they haven't lost their boarding pass—the Sarah Kellers—and those who pride themselves on making it just under the wire—the Bob Kellers. On cue, she sees her husband through the throng of fast-walking travelers. Bob is hard to miss. He's heavyset and wears a concert T-shirt that's faded and frayed. And today he's carrying their nine-year-old twins, one slung over each shoulder.

She can't help but smile. Her fellow agents at the FBI, with their starched white shirts and conservative demeanor, never quite know what to make of Bob.

"Hurry, we're gonna miss the flight," she tells him.

"We've got plenty of time, G-woman." Bob sets the twins down. Heather and Michael are getting too big for such antics.

But if she's being honest, she likes that they're young for their age. And it's her husband who keeps them that way—Bob sprinkles Peter Pan dust wherever he goes.

The kids are giggling now. Keller notices that Michael is holding something behind his back.

She gives him the wide-eyed mom look that says he'd better come clean. Michael reveals a Hudson's bag that is stuffed full.

"I assume that's filled with healthy snacks . . . ?"

"Daddy said 'Airport Rules,'" Michael tells her.

Keller narrows her eyes. When they were young, before kids, Airport Rules was their term—their justification—for having too many cocktails when they were traveling, no matter the time of day. Vodka and soda at 7 a.m.? Airport Rules. A fourth beer? Airport Rules. Now it apparently means candy and potato chips and god knows what else.

She herds them to the gate, hands out their boarding passes, and they march through the tunnel to the plane.

Keller is slightly annoyed about the snacks. But it's hard to get mad at Bob.

The flight attendant greets them with a *nice of you to finally join us* expression, asks to see Bob's boarding pass. She perks up when she sees he's in first class.

"There must be a mistake," Bob says when she directs him to the front of the aircraft, the fancy section—the seats that recline flat, the full video setup, the plastic cup of champagne he's handed. Bob turns and looks at Keller.

"An early birthday present," she says.

For once, Bob is speechless. Until he sees Keller and the twins head toward the back, the economy section.

"Wait. You just bought one first-class seat?"

"I only had enough miles for one."

"I'm not going to sit up there while you're in the—"

"Airport Rules," Keller replies. "Right, kids?"

Michael and Heather hold conspiratorial grins as Keller ushers them to the rear of the plane. The upgrade isn't really about his birthday. It's because this trip—this move—to his hometown is going to be difficult for her husband.

The back of the aircraft is as expected. Overhead bins full. Too many people packed into too little space.

The businessman sitting in their row audibly sighs when he sees them. He closes his laptop, removes his papers from the middle seat.

"Sorry," Keller says, "you almost made it without a seatmate."

The man mutters something under his breath.

Keller couldn't get three seats together so she booked the middle and window seat next to the cranky passenger and the aisle seat in front of them.

Keller is about to ask if the businessman would trade for the seat in front when a baby in that row starts wailing.

The businessman clenches his jaw. "My secretary booked me in coach by accident. Let's just say she'd better be updating her Indeed profile." He looks around for support. And gets none.

Keller takes the middle seat. She doesn't want this sour man any nearer to her kids than necessary.

The flight attendant makes her final rounds, tells the man to stow his laptop for takeoff, and he grumbles some more.

The baby wails for the next three hours. The poor mom, early twenties and overwhelmed, stands in the aisle, bouncing the child in her arms.

Keller can feel rage emanating off Asshole Businessman.

The new mom can see it as well and a tear escapes her eye. Keller is about to get up to help, but then sees Bob walking down the aisle, a midflight constitutional.

His eyes widen at the scene before him: line for the bathroom; glaring Asshole Businessman; crying lady holding crying baby.

Bob lightly musses Michael's hair. He's asleep. He can sleep through anything.

"How's *your* flight going?" Keller asks with an exaggerated smile.

Bob grimaces, like it's amazing. "You should come up and check it out." Then he stops. Grins. "Never mind, they don't let *you* people up there."

"Watch it . . ."

The baby starts up again and the mother is falling apart. An older woman waiting for the restroom is consoling her.

"Jesus Christ," Asshole Businessman says, too loud.

"Whoa, buddy." Bob stares down at him.

"Unless you want to trade seats with me, I'm not your buddy," Asshole Businessman says. "And do you mind not looming over me?"

Bob holds eye contact with the guy. Keller doesn't like the look in her husband's eyes. Bob is the nicest person you'd ever want to meet, but he has a line you don't want to cross.

He stares at the man a long time, then breaks away. He looks at the woman with the baby. Her face is streaked with tears and exhaustion.

Keller decides it's time to help. She tells Asshole Businessman she needs to get out of her seat and he huffs.

Keller kisses Bob, sidles past him, and approaches the young mom. "Hi, I'm Sarah. This is my husband. Bob is something of a baby whisperer." Keller gestures for her to give the baby to Bob. The mom seems reluctant at first, but then carefully hands the baby to Bob, who starts to sway and bounce. And if Keller hadn't witnessed it so many nights with the twins, she wouldn't have believed it: The baby actually stops crying.

Keller and the older woman try to comfort the mom in the tiny area next to the bathroom. She's on her own, she says. Going to California to live with her parents. She hasn't slept in what feels like days. She's losing it, says she's a bad mom, her son deserves better. Then she begins sobbing again.

It's then that Keller decides. She looks over at Bob, who is already nodding, knowing what's coming.

Keller puts her hands on the woman's shoulders and looks her in the eyes. "You need some sleep. How about you follow my husband? He's going to trade seats with you."

When wheels finally hit the tarmac in San Francisco a small eternity later, Bob is crowded in the middle seat in front of Keller. Asshole Businessman is already standing, yanking his bag from the overhead. A flight attendant asks him to remain seated until the seat belt light is off, and he refuses, gets too close to her face.

"Sir, please sit down."

Keller's had enough. She stands, yanks out her badge, shoves it in Asshole Businessman's face. "You think the flight is bad, wait until you see the airport holding cell."

The man sits quickly and looks at his lap.

Her husband twists around and gives her an admiring look, the one that fills her chest with something warm. She's simultaneously filled with sadness. Bob looks spent, and the trip is off to a rough start. And it's not going to get any better for him. But he still manages to give her a crooked smile, conjure some humor in the situation, and she loves him even more for it. She hears a text and she opens it. It's from Bob:

Agent Badass

CHAPTER SIX

THE MALDONADOS

Stella sits in the back seat of the rental car, eyeing her parents. They're acting even stranger than usual. The last few times she spoke with him, her father wouldn't shut up about flying to Parents Weekend in a private jet. Yet he's barely said a word since he ran up to Stella, yanking Mom by the hand, and rushed them both off campus.

And Mom, she's acting cuckoo. Usually she's the yoga/Zen one.

"What's up with you two?" Stella finally asks.

"Nothing. Just tired from the flight," her dad says.

"Private jet didn't live up to the hype?" Stella jabs him. Stella likes to jab him. "Where's this hotel? We've been driving forever." Most of the hotels are only a few minutes from campus. They're on 92 West, miles from Santa Clara.

Her mom looks at the GPS. "Looks like fifteen more minutes."

"What? Where did you guys book?"

"Half Moon Bay," her father says.

"Why would you—"

"It's the only place nearby with a Ritz."

Of course. Her parents both grew up poor, so they have chips on their shoulders. Like they have something to prove and can't possibly stay at the Embassy Suites like ordinary parents.

Stella's annoyed, but she says nothing. That's the approach she's learned works best, the one that gets under their skin. Under Dad's skin, anyway. Mom doesn't deserve the silent treatment. Actually, Stella reconsiders, she *does* for letting him get away with everything. Her parents think she's an idiot. That she doesn't know about it all. But she's not stupid.

Her mom does a strange juddering movement like she's forcing herself to focus. Shaking off whatever fight they're in. Forcing herself to *be present*, as she always says to Stella.

Be present. Give me a fucking break.

Stella has enough going on in her life without their bullshit. Her phone's dead, but she puts in her earbuds anyway to signal she's done talking.

The road twists like a corkscrew and Stella's ears pop as the rental Audi heads up the coastal range. She's been to Half Moon Bay only once, with a group of friends from SCU. The boys all planned to go "chasing mavericks" at a famous surf spot but chickened out when they saw the giant waves.

At last, they stop at the guard shack on the narrow road that leads to the Ritz. The area is surrounded by a massive golf course where men with white hair and loud pants putter around in carts. The guard waves them through without checking ID. He can tell they're the type to stay at the five-star hotel. Profiling isn't always wrong. Under the covered front entrance, men in crisp white shirts and dark slacks jump to attention. They unload the bags. Cup the bills Dad palms them.

At the check-in desk, everyone clicks their heels at the rich people arriving. Stella studies her mom again. What's up with her today? She seems so *not* present.

"Are you sure you're okay?" Stella asks her mom as her father chats with the young woman checking them in.

"Why don't we go for a walk while Dad gets the room situated?"

"I need to charge my phone," Stella says.

Her mother doesn't reply and floats through the lobby. Stella shakes her head and follows her across the marble floor, arriving at an outside terrace perched atop cliffs that plummet down to the beach. Couples sit on Adirondack chairs, sipping cocktails and gazing at the ocean.

Stella catches up to her mom. They're quiet as they walk along a path, following the arrows on small signs planted in the grass that say BEACH ACCESS. Her mom holds the railing, looking a little unsteady, as they descend the steep concrete stairs.

Her mother slides off her flats and walks toward the water. Stella leaves on her sneakers and trudges through the sand after her.

No one else is on the tiny strip of beach, which is shaded by the cliffs.

"Mom, what's going on? You're both acting so—"

"We're fine. Dad and I . . . we just had a tiff."

As they stroll, her mom tells her about the repulsive couple on the jet. Asks how things are going. Does Stella like her classes? How are her professors? Has she given more thought to a major?

Stella lies, says everything is peachy.

Her mother turns to her, looks her in the eyes. Stella notices her mom's eyes are spider-webbed with red. Like she's been crying. Or maybe she had one too many glasses of wine on the flight. "How are *you* doing, Stella?"

I'm not fucking good, Mom, she wants to say. But "fine" is all that escapes Stella's lips.

"Fine." Her mom repeats the word so it's loaded with sadness.

Stella feels a pang of sadness herself wondering when this gulf between them emerged.

"Are you coming to the dinner tonight?" Stella asks, throwing Mom a bone. She seems like she needs one. Maybe they both do.

"We're looking forward to it."

Stella says nothing.

Her mom stares out at the ocean. "Stella . . ."

"Yeah."

"Do you know a student named Cody Carpenter?"

Stella blinks in confusion. What's *this* about? "I don't think so. Why?"

"Oh, he's just the son of someone we know. We thought we saw him on campus when we picked you up."

Stella shakes her head.

"Probably just someone who looks like him," her mom adds.

"Yeah, the boys with their dumb shaggy haircuts and attempts at facial hair make them all look alike," Stella says.

Her mom smiles. A weak smile. One that says some shit is going on.

They make their way back up to the resort and find the room. It's a nice suite, lots of space. Elegant furniture. Her father is on the balcony, talking on the phone.

Stella spies a socket on the desk and plugs in her phone.

Mom sits in a wing chair, a faraway look in her eyes. Stella finds a bottle of water in the minifridge and hands it to her mother.

"Thank you."

It's strange. Her mother used to take care of her whenever Stella was sick, bringing Gatorade or soup or Nyquil. It's the first time Stella has ever looked after her mom.

Stella's phone starts to ping over and over, downloading a barrage of messages. Her heart seizes as she skims them.

Natasha died

Natasha's body was found

Omg natasha drowned

Tributes from people who didn't know Natasha are filling her Insta feed. The university's president has sent an email blast to all parents:

Dear Santa Clara University Parents,

With profound sadness, I share the news that third-year student Natasha Belov, 21, has died. We join with Natasha's parents, Ivan and Iza Belov, in their grief and remember the gift of Natasha's young life . . .

Another text pings, one from Libby Akana:

We need to talk now

Stella takes a deep, steadying breath.

Her mother is slumped in the chair across the room, dozing. On the balcony, her father is still talking intensely into the phone.

Stella texts back:

no, you need to STFU

CHAPTER SEVEN

THE GOFFMANS

Alice lays her new blue blouse on the bed, admiring it. The garment cost $112, the most she's ever spent on an item of clothing. She's been saving since Felix told her about the Parents Weekend dinner for his capstone group. She shouldn't be so nervous about tonight, but she can't help it.

In her years working in the dean's office, she's encountered many SCU parents, and $112 is nothing to them. They shop in fancy boutiques instead of the outlets where Alice found the blouse. Still, the girl at the store said it brought out Alice's eyes—dark blue, like Felix's—and not to worry, she'd fit right in at the dinner.

Despite her nerves, she's excited. After everything she and her little man have had to deal with—the tiny apartment, the tight budget, the aftermath of Felix's abusive father—they *made* it. Felix is in college. She raised him well; she feels proud of herself for this. Also, it's been so long since she's been out to dinner. Out anywhere, really. She saved up not just for the blouse but to make sure she could pay her share of the check. Felix told her that SCU covers the dinner itself, but not drinks. He was so sweet and said he'd use his summer job money to buy his mom a cocktail, but she'll have none of that. She already feels guilty that he doesn't have a meal plan and doesn't get to eat with his friends at the dining hall. But her job only covers tuition, not room and board, and just paying for his space in Campisi Hall has stretched her thin. Felix deserves the real college experience—not living with his mom. Let's just hope she won't need a meal plan herself soon—one funded by the welfare department.

Whoever said money doesn't buy happiness is probably right, but Alice bets they had money. It might not buy happiness, but it must take the edge off.

She shouldn't think this way. She should be grateful. Her mind jumps to Natasha Belov's parents. They have money but they'd spend every penny to bring their daughter back.

Alice feels a chill skitter down her spine. An hour after Natasha's parents burst in to see the dean, their daughter's body was found. The chief of police brought the news himself. The search team located Natasha in one of the sea caves at Panther Beach. It appears to be an accidental drowning. The caves are dangerous—misjudge when the tide will rise and you're a goner. Last year, the Santa Cruz fire department rescued four tourists from the caves. A father also drowned trying to save his son, who'd been hit by an errant wave walking the path to the caves and dragged into the ocean. It's not a place to be after midnight, after partying.

The dean spent the rest of the afternoon in his office with the door closed, presumably dealing with the fallout.

Alice knows the news will put a damper on Parents Weekend. She hopes it will make the parents look past the small things—

messy dorm rooms, grades that aren't up to expectations, grooming deficits—and hug their kids tighter.

She takes a shower, trying to wash the afternoon's gloom away. In the steamy air, she practices what she will say at the dinner: *What a pleasure to meet you. Felix has said so many great things about your son.* To prepare for tonight, she read a book about how to be a better communicator. The bottom line is she just needs to ask a lot of questions, steer the conversation away from herself. That's easy enough. She's a quiet person, a trait she passed down to her son. She loves to avoid talking about herself. How to diplomatically explain she's a mere secretary. Also, if they find out she works for the dean, they might want dirt. Yes, she'll ask a lot of questions. Listen intently to the answers and ask follow-ups.

After drying her hair, she carefully removes the tag to her new blouse and slips it on. Examines herself in the mirror. *You're good enough. You're going to do great.* The book said self-affirmations help, but Alice can't help but think of the old skit from *Saturday Night Live.*

She passes Felix's room and notices something that wasn't there before: his stuffed laundry bag. He must've come by the apartment.

She smiles, remembering his gift of a KitKat. She didn't dare eat it today. The new blouse is already dangerously close to being too snug.

Alice walks to her dresser and hesitates, her hand on the top drawer. Then she pulls it open and extracts the manila folder she snuck out of the office. Dean Pratt has mentioned the missing file twice. There's no way Alice can turn it over now.

CHAPTER EIGHT

THE ROOSEVELTS

Cynthia sits in the back of the SUV, the privacy glass shielding her from the two agents up front. She gazes out the side window at the sunset, the stunning streaks of orange and pink. Blane is right about one thing: It is beautiful here. Three hundred days of sunshine a year, he always says. Low humidity. Her East Coast boy has been seduced by California. Not just the weather, but its mood, its character, its vibe—his persona now resembling that of Spicoli from *Fast Times at Ridgemont High*, a movie Cynthia loved as a teenager. The movie means she was carefree once, right? If she was, Washington stomped it out of her. She feels a stab of melancholy thinking about her ex, Hank. Theirs isn't a unique story. As her career went north, his tumbled south, and all the predictable problems ensued, including his affair. They might've had a chance. They'd loved each other once. But Blane's abduction was the last straw. She's never said so aloud—and to his credit, Hank hasn't either—but her job, her ambition, her meteoric rise precipitated it all. At times, the guilt consumes her. But she won't let it conquer her.

"Where's this dinner?" she asks her chief of staff, who's perched in the seat next to her, thumbing his phone.

"A place called The Hut."

Charming.

"Who will I be meeting?"

This part isn't just for security, the checks her team runs on guests at scheduled events. It's to give her a leg up, a trick the senior U.S. senator from Virginia taught her years ago. Investigate the guests so you're prepared to ask them questions about their boring lives. As Winston Churchill's mother once said when asked to size up two competitors for prime minister of England, "When I left the dining room after sitting next to Gladstone, I thought he was the cleverest man in England. But when I sat next to Disraeli, I left feeling that I was the cleverest woman." The secret to Cynthia's success is her ability to make everyone in the room feel like the cleverest.

Her team has done workups of the families from Blane's capstone group. Paul digs through his briefcase and pulls out a file, opens it like he's handling oppo on a political adversary.

The first page of the dossier shows a guy in his late forties or maybe early fifties. He's handsome, dark eyes, strong jaw. Maybe this dinner won't be torture after all.

Paul says, "Dr. David Maldonado. A plastic surgeon from New York."

Cynthia turns to Paul, puts her index fingers on the sides of her eyes, pulls the skin tight. "Maybe he can slip me some Botox."

Paul frowns. "His wife's name is Nina. She teaches yoga."

The wife is attractive, in the way of clean living and organic vegetables. She's not smiling in the photo, though.

"No concerns. A normal affluent family. Their daughter Stella got into some trouble as a teen—shoplifting, that kind of stuff, but nothing serious."

The next page shows an anxious-looking woman with slightly frizzy brown hair. She looks kind, like the sort of woman you'd ask for directions if you were lost. Paul explains that Alice Goffman is the admin assistant to the dean of the university. Her son Felix is a scholarship kid. Single mother. Lives in a rundown apartment on the edge of Santa Clara.

Cynthia nods as Paul turns the page. "Is that the judge from the Rock Nelson trial?" she asks, placing a finger on the photo. She doesn't keep up with pop culture but there was no escaping coverage of that trial. The late-night shows, which Cynthia watches mostly because they skewer politicians and are a good barometer for public sentiment, took a particular liking to the judge. They gave him a nickname, but Cynthia can't remember it.

"Yep," Paul says. "Judge Kenneth Akana. Obviously no red flags there. Though he's received threats of his own from Rock Nelson supporters, so our team reached out to his detail."

"A kindred spirit," Cynthia says dryly. "This is going to be the most fucking protected Parents Weekend in history."

Paul raises his brows. "Judge Akana apparently isn't bringing his detail, now that the trial's over. Our team thinks that's fine. Our guys won't let any crazies get within a hundred yards of the place."

Next up: photos of Akana's wife Amy, a lawyer turned stay-at-home mom—dark-rimmed glasses, enviable bone structure—and their beaming daughter Libby. He closes the file.

"That's it?" Cynthia asks.

He nods. "Nothing of any concern. That said, given what happened with the air strikes last week, the team is recommending you skip public appearances until things calm down." In response to an attack that killed three U.S. service members, the military bombed the shit out of militias affiliated with the government that put the bounty on her head.

"I didn't come all this way to sit in a hotel room."

Paul gives a resigned nod, like he expected this. In true Washington form, he was just covering his ass.

Cynthia would love to skip all the small talk and pretending to be interested in these people. But if her ex found out she missed the Parents Weekend dinner, it would prove the asshole right. And she's *not* proving Hank right.

She peers out the window again. The sky is an extraordinary shade of purple now, though this area is not particularly quaint: strip malls and a Jack in the Box.

"One last thing," Paul says. "Again, not a concern, but we did get a hit we thought you should know about."

Cynthia is intrigued. She nods for Paul to continue.

"Mark Wong's father."

"Blane's friend?" she says. "He and Blane are pledging that fraternity together. Blane was voted pledge class president and Mark is VP." Her son was quite proud that the other pledges voted him their PCP.

Paul's eyebrows knit together. He plainly wasn't cool enough to be part of Greek life and almost certainly spent college as a virgin, so it's lost on him.

"The father has a sheet. But don't worry, he's not coming to Parents Weekend. He appears to be estranged from his son."

Cynthia turns to her chief of staff. "A sheet?"

"He did a ten-year stretch inside."

"Inside *prison*?" In Washington she's surrounded by criminals every day, but none ever sees the inside of a cell.

"Yes. For multiple counts of sexual assault."

* * *

Back at the dorm, Blane checks himself in the mirror. His 'stache looks good. Who cares what Mom says? And if he shaves it, his pledge master will make him pay. The last pledge who disappointed had a dinner of Pledge Apples—raw white onions—followed by two hundred push-ups. No thank you. Blane "Goose" Roosevelt is keeping the 'stache.

He did find a clean shirt—borrowed from another pledge. In the mirror's reflection, he catches Mark, who's tapping on his phone.

"Sure you don't wanna come to the dinner? You don't need to have parents there to come. No one gives a shit."

Mark doesn't talk much about his family. Blane knows why.

"Nah, but meet you after?"

"Cool cool cool. It's gonna suck anyway. Free food, though . . ." The Hut isn't some fancy place, but it's still cost-prohibitive to most students.

"Check you after."

"Shit." Blane notices the time on his phone. "I gotta jump. My mom will be pissed if I'm late."

He musses his hair one more time in the mirror, nods in satisfaction, grabs his skateboard, and leaves.

Riding the board through campus, his mind drifts to lunch and Stella and Libby's beef. Libby's such a damned Goody Two-Shoes. And all the rest of the drama. He's going to put it out of his head. Deal with it later.

A fraternity brother spots him and stops in his tracks, standing erect. Blane gives him a salute as he skates by—shouts "Sir, yes sir" in military fashion—in his Goose persona.

The brother gives an exaggerated salute back. "At ease," he yells as Blane flies past.

Blane has always been social. Always been part of teams—football, lacrosse, soccer—but he never would have guessed how much he'd love the fraternity. Sure, the hazing sucks and it's not even Hell Week yet. But it's part of the process. The bonding of a band of brothers. And it's nothing like the movies. Just silly shit. This isn't the fucking eighties and nineties. And while some of the blue-hairs on campus stereotype him and his boys, it's all bullshit. They respect women. When a pledge got handsy with a girl, the frat booted him out. And they hate racists. When a brother made a racist comment to Mark—called him Tommy Choi instead of Tommy Boy—they excommunicated the dick.

He sees The Hut up ahead. It's only a thousand feet from campus. A shack-like structure on the same block as the frat house and other run-down places rented to students. He's looking forward to a juicy burger and a cold craft beer. Nah, better not use the fake ID in front of Mom.

As he nears the restaurant, the breeze in his face like he loves, he hears his name from behind. He turns and looks and that's when he goes flying through the air, after the wheels hit a patch of gravel.

On the ground, it takes a moment to confirm he's okay. No broken bones. A few scrapes. He looks around to confirm no one saw this embarrassing plunge. Or caught it on their phone. He does *not* want to end up on PrankStool. That would serve him right for all the prank videos he and Mark have posted on the site.

A hand reaches down.

Holy *shit*. He blinks. Takes the hand. Feels himself being yanked upright.

"Dad?" he says, confused. This is Mom's weekend. They were just fighting about it on the phone. "What are you doing here?"

CHAPTER NINE

THE AKANAS

Ken and Amy hurry into the restaurant. Between waiting for the tow truck and finding a garage to repair their slashed tires, they're more than an hour late for the dinner and Ken's feeling anxious about it. He despises tardiness. In his courtroom, he fines lawyers $100 for every minute they're late for an appearance. Few have been late since he started the practice. Lawyers respond better to the stick than the carrot.

Ken looks around The Hut. It's a small place and it's packed for Parents Weekend. He searches through the crowd, hoping to catch a glimpse of his daughter's beaming smile. But he doesn't see Libby.

He feels the skin-prickling sense of eyes on him. The media frenzy has died down since the Rock Nelson verdict, but he still draws attention. He wouldn't admit it out loud, but it was fun at first, getting recognized. Though it quickly grew unsettling. The stares, the requests for selfies, which he always politely declines.

And some of Rock Nelson's fans were intense. He wonders how real celebrities deal with it all.

Amy points to a sign that says that the capstone dinner is on the patio. They make their way to the covered outdoor dining area and it's even more crowded. Loud with chatter and laughter. Parents and students drinking beer and playing Jenga and other games on the long tables.

Ken spies a table with a sign for CAMPISI HALL. As they approach, the other parents smile. A few stand to shake hands.

That's when Ken notices it. Everyone at the table is a parent.

Their kids are nowhere to be seen.

CHAPTER TEN

THE MALDONADOS

David wonders when his daughter started hating him. He looks down at the series of texts he's sent her over the last hour, the escalation of the anger in each message matching the feeling rising in his chest.

We're at the restaurant.

Where are you?

You know the dinner started at 7?

Seriously, Stella?

Disrespectful to your mom and other parents.

Nina must read the tension in his face. She says softly, "They're just kids. Let's make the best of it."

He swallows the irritation. Placing his phone face down on the table, he turns his attention back to the other parents.

"Since our kids are all running late," he says to the group, "I say we be college kids for the night."

The other parents eye him suspiciously.

"I'm getting us a round of shots," he declares, swinging his leg over the cafeteria bench.

It takes a moment but there's a groundswell of support. A *this will teach 'em* nod of heads.

"I'm in," the tall woman—he remembers her name is Cynthia—says. She gets up from the table, then takes the lead and walks out of the patio toward the bar. David notices one of the serious men standing in the back of the patio say something into his sleeve.

Cynthia already apologized for the intrusion of her security detail but said her job—she's some honcho at the State Department—requires her "goon squad." No one needs to worry, she assured them all.

David reaches the bar and discovers Cynthia has already ordered eight shots of tequila.

"All right, all right, all right," the bartender says, mimicking some movie star.

"Kids, right?" David says.

Cynthia widens her eyes. Her look says, *You have no idea.*

"Remind me, who's your child?" Cynthia asks.

"Stella Maldonado."

"I'd like to say I've heard more about her, but my son, Blane, isn't a fountain of information."

"Same," David says.

"Sometimes to get Blane to respond to my calls or texts I have to change the Netflix password," she says.

"Nice. I'll have to try that one."

She's an attractive woman, this person with a team of bodyguards. It's not so much her physical appearance, which is almost corporate. It's the confidence. Which is normally what people say they admire about David. The self-assured way he struts into the exam room, promises his patients he will erase the ravages of time, correct the imperfections, make them more perfect.

"Blane's pledging a fraternity, so I assume him ghosting me tonight has something to do with that," she says. "Maybe he pulled your daughter into the trouble."

"Oh, if anyone's pulling people into trouble, I wouldn't count Stella out."

The bartender places the shots on a tray.

David is surprised when Cynthia picks up a glass. Gestures with her chin for David to do the same.

"Pregaming, as the kids call it." She taps her shot glass with his. And they both kick back the tequila sans the salt and lemon wedges on the tray.

"Our little secret," she says, holding David's eyes for too long.

It's then that David remembers when his daughter started to hate him. The time she visited him at work and noticed his anesthesiologist give him a look just like the one this woman's giving him now.

That pain on Stella's face, that dagger to his chest, made him vow to be a better man. If only he were stronger, had broken it off with the anesthesiologist that night instead of luring her to the park for another tryst. But he is so weak. He always has been. He's tried to analyze it over the years. Why can't he be satisfied with the life he has? With his beautiful wife? Why does his sex drive rage like that of a man recently released from prison? Why does he need the attention, the stimulation of something new, something exciting, something forbidden?

Why is he tempted to give this confident woman his cell number? Why does he fantasize about sneaking out while Nina sleeps beside him, going to Cynthia's hotel room?

And the biggest question, the one he hates facing the most: Why is he such a pile of garbage?

CHAPTER ELEVEN

THE GOFFMANS

Alice stands in the buffet line, examining the food stuffed in the metal pans over flickering burners. It's bar cuisine—mini burgers, grilled cheese sandwiches, street tacos—and it looks tasty. Alice is starving, but she waited until nearly everyone else at her table filled their plates to get in line. Only one other parent—Libby Akana's mom, the judge's wife—is in front of her. Alice chides herself for not remembering the mother's name. The book she read stressed the importance of remembering and saying people's names and even gave tricks to commit names to memory. People love hearing their names.

"This is a lot of food," Libby's mom says.

"Yes, my Felix would've cleared it out. He has a hollow leg."

"I'm sorry," Libby's mother says, "can you remind me of your name?"

"Alice Goffman," she says, pleased she's not the only one bad with names.

"I'm Amy."

There's an awkward silence as they move down the line.

"Felix has said great things about Libby," Alice says.

Amy offers a fleeting smile. Then: "I wonder where on earth she is."

Alice detects apprehension in her tone. "Where they *all* are." She tongs a small amount of salad onto her plate. "I'm getting a little worried."

It's been only a couple hours. But Felix knows she gets anxious. It's completely out of character for him to leave her hanging.

"I'm sorry," Alice adds. "I'm being one of *those* parents." She looks over at the others, who are having a second round of shots, seemingly without a worry in the world.

"The kids will turn up," Amy says. "They were probably walking over together and got lured away to a party. You remember college."

Alice didn't go to college, but she's worked for SCU long enough to agree. It happens; kids this age do all kinds of crazy things. In her years working in the dean's office, she's seen it all. Good kids in disciplinary meetings, reprimanded, expelled. But not her Felix. He's a good boy.

"I wouldn't want to be Libby," Amy Akana says. "My husband is a freak about punctuality."

Alice smiles. "I saw him on TV. I loved it when he scolded that one lawyer who was late."

"Yes, his fifteen minutes of fame has been *interesting*." Her voice carries an undercurrent of annoyance. Or maybe resentment, Alice isn't sure. "Don't worry," Amy continues. "They'll show up soon." She rests her hand on Alice's arm reassuringly.

"Sorry," Alice says again. "I work for the university and we just had a student die this week, and it's obviously gotten to me."

"I saw the message from the dean. I heard she drowned, right? Tragic. And heartbreaking for her parents."

Back at the table, Stella's dad—his name is David, Alice reminds herself—is telling a story. He's classically handsome, the kind of man used to holding court. She supposes it comes with being a doctor. She tries asking a question but it's drowned out, leaving her feeling invisible.

She sips her wine, ignoring the tequila shot David put in front of her. She'll find a way to discreetly pour it somewhere. It's so darn loud in here, but she thinks she hears the chime of her phone. A wave of relief crashes over her. No one calls her after business hours except Felix.

Fishing the phone from her handbag, Alice smiles when she sees Felix's photo pop up on the screen. She feels the other parents looking at her. They're pretending not to be worried, but they must be. How could they not? None of the kids have shown up for this dinner and aren't answering calls or texts.

"Felix, honey, where are you?"

There's no answer. She hears movement in the background, but nothing coherent. It's like he butt-dialed.

"Felix?" she says, louder than she intended.

No reply.

Then the line goes dead, severing the link to her son.

CHAPTER TWELVE

THE KELLERS

They pull up to the modest home in San Jose. Even in the dark she can tell the yard is in need of care, and the house seems dated for the high-end neighborhood. Keller thought New York housing costs were out of control, but they're nothing compared with the Bay Area, where professionals are often forced to live in group homes or even on houseboats. Bob claims it wasn't always that way. At one time, this was a solid working-class neighborhood where kids played in the street and his parents—both musicians—held big parties for the neighbors, who got a kick out of their unconventional lifestyle. They bought the place for a song. Now the cheapest homes on the block sell for $1.5 mil.

Keller appraises her husband. It's only nine at night, but he looks tired, drained. Sure, it's three hours later in New York and it's exhausting traveling with kids. But that's not it.

"Are you okay?" she asks, watching him stare at the house like memories are flooding his system.

Bob smiles, but it's empty. "Who, me?"

"The nurse warned us that he looks quite different," Keller says, preparing him.

Bob's father has cancer. The meds he's on swell and disfigure the face. The nurse had offered to Zoom them to prepare Bob—and the kids—but Bob's father refused.

"I'm ready," Bob says.

She knows he's not.

Bob twists around to the back seat, where Michael and Heather are out cold. "Maybe I should go in and check things out before they . . ."

"I've already talked to them about their grandpa," Keller says. "They'll be fine."

Normally, Bob is the sunlight they all bask in. She hasn't seen him down like this since his old dog died.

"Thank you," is all he says.

"For what?"

"Don't play dumb. It doesn't suit you."

When they got word that Bob's dad had less than a year to live, Keller applied for a "hardship" transfer—a temporary placement at the Bureau's San Jose office. The resident office, a satellite of the San Francisco field office, doesn't handle many financial-crimes investigations—her specialty in New York—so she'll be doing whatever shit work no one else wants. Keller has received some notoriety as an agent at different points in her career, including solving the infamous Blockbuster-video murders. Keller's former boss and mentor—who's now the deputy director—pulled some strings to get her approved for the hardship. He warned that there was some grumbling about special treatment.

"With 'fame'"—it had been a phone call but she could hear the air quotes in Stan's voice—"comes resentment and jealousy."

To his credit, Stan, a buttoned-up man who thinks FBI agents should be invisible to the public, never held her passing fame against her. And the agents are right to gripe—she *did* get special treatment. Stan also warned her that a transfer at this point in her career could change the trajectory of her rising star. But she had no choice: Bob needs her, for a change.

"You don't have to thank me," Keller says. "I want to spend time with your dad. I want the kids to spend time with him."

"I suppose it will be good for the twins to learn about the origin story of this cool slab of sexy," Bob says, puffing out his chest.

Inside, Bob's father sits in a lounge chair. He starts to get up but Keller rushes over to help him back into the seat. Though they've been warned about his appearance, it's still a shock. Once heavyset like Bob, he's frail. His swollen face is nearly unrecognizable. But, bless the twins, they rush over, not missing a beat, and chant "Grandpa!"

Keller steals a look at Bob. He's got his poker face on, but she knows him. It's hitting him hard.

"Hey, Pops!" Bob says.

"Bobby!" Pops beams. He's been living alone since Ruth died, before the twins were born.

"You keeping my boy outta trouble?" Pops asks Keller. He's insisted on Keller also calling him Pops since the first day Bob brought her home.

"I'm trying."

"Grandpa, wanna see my drawing?" Michael says, yanking off his backpack to find his sketch pad.

"You bet I do."

Keller reminds the kids to give Grandpa some space. She and Bob lug the suitcases to the basement. Bob's childhood bedroom.

Bob is purposely averting his gaze. He's the most enlightened man she's ever met, but he's weirdly macho about anyone seeing him cry.

Keller looks about the room. The walls are covered with posters: Pearl Jam, Joan Jett, Alice in Chains, Blondie. An eclectic mix of artists, including many Keller has never heard of. A mixing board and an elaborate sound system occupy a large table in the back next to shelves and shelves of vinyl records. Before he took a break from his career to stay home with the kids, Bob was a sound engineer at a recording studio. Between the musicians' unorthodox hours and Keller's unpredictable travel schedule, he gave it up for the family. At the time he said, "No one gives a second thought when a woman gives up her career to stay home with the kids, so why do people keep asking if I'm okay?"

"You think your equipment will be safe with the kids?" Keller asks. The twins will be sharing this room for now. Getting the hardship detail was difficult enough, finding affordable temporary housing impossible. So they'll be staying with Pops. Just as well. He looks like he may need around-the-clock care soon.

Bob doesn't respond. His back is to her. He opens the lid to the record player.

"You okay?" Keller asks again.

He doesn't turn around.

"Come here," she says. When he doesn't move, she pulls on his shoulder, forcing him to face her. Tears fill his eyes and she takes him in her arms.

Before she finds the right words, the twins bounce into the room. Bob turns away again. Wipes his face with his shirt.

"This is our room?" Heather says.

"Cooool," Michael adds.

Bob turns back. A big smile now. "Wanna know the best part?"

"What . . . ?" the kids say together with wonder.

Bob removes a black vinyl disc from a sleeve and puts it on the record player. The familiar grainy sound of the needle comes through the large speakers. Then, over the opening guitar riff to AC/DC's "Back in Black," Bob—holding an imaginary instrument—shouts, "Air guitar contest!"

The four of them strum imaginary Gibson SGs and Bob does his funny Angus Young duckwalk, and then he lifts the kids one at a time and spins them around and around as they shriek with delight.

And in that moment, Keller nearly loses it herself.

CHAPTER THIRTEEN

THE MALDONADOS

"What's the problem now, Nina?" David says. They're crammed in the back seat of an Uber on the long drive back to Half Moon Bay.

Stella was right, Nina thinks. It was stupid to pick a hotel so far from campus. Particularly after David bought everyone shots and they had to leave the rental car parked near the restaurant. Nina stares out the window at the blur of pine trees flanking the dark road.

David's had too much to drink, and now he's spoiling for a fight. Nina should let it go. But *she's* spoiling for a fight too. "I didn't say anything."

"You don't have to, Nina. I'm so fucking tired of this."

She feels the heat of anger settle into her core. "*You're* tired of this."

"What the hell's that supposed to mean?" he says, lowering his voice for the benefit of the Uber driver.

"You spent the entire dinner flirting with that woman." Nina took an immediate disliking to Cynthia Roosevelt, the tall woman with the security detail. It's not that she was unfriendly or insufferable. It was the way David looked at her.

"I wasn't flirting."

As usual, his denials have no energy, no conviction.

"You're just mad at Stella," David says. "Don't take it out on me."

He might actually be right. It hurts that they came all this way, and their daughter couldn't be bothered to show up for dinner. But Stella likes to punish them.

At the same time, Nina feels a tingle of worry under her skin. After all, Stella didn't seem angry at them earlier today at the hotel when they checked in. Only mildly annoyed, like she's been constantly since she turned fourteen. Nina could kick herself for asking if Stella knew Cody Carpenter. Maybe that's it. If Stella knows the boy and what happened, that would explain her sudden decision to head back to campus early—her transparent lie about needing to turn in her Critical Thinking assignment. But that doesn't explain why the *other* kids were no-shows at the dinner. The one boy's mom, the dean's secretary—Alice—seemed like she was about to burst into tears when the kids didn't appear by the end of the dinner.

But Nina knows her daughter. Despite the distance that erupted during Stella's teenage years, they're inextricably linked.

Where are you, Stella?

Back at the hotel, she steps out of the bathroom and is surprised to see David in shorts and a T-shirt, his right foot propped up on a chair as he ties his HOKAs. He snatches the key card from the night table.

"Where are you going?"

"For a run."

"What? It's nearly midnight."

"I need some air."

Running. A David specialty. Running from anything he doesn't want to deal with. She shakes her head. She feels something rise from deep within her body—is it hatred? Disdain? Maybe it's time to start facing the fact that they're not fixable.

"Tell Cynthia I said hello." Maybe she shouldn't have said that. But it felt satisfying after he flirted with that woman all night.

"Fuck you, Nina."

The lobby of the Ritz is hushed. David can't endure silence anymore. The long stretches where they don't speak. Nina's disapproval of Every. Single. Thing he says. Every. Single. Thing he does. The worst part is the sinking feeling that there's nothing he can do to fix them. That it's time to call the game.

David walks down the hallway where the restaurant—it has amazing views, he can tell even from here—is closing up. Staff quietly setting tables for breakfast, the lights dim. The bar is closed as well, which is probably a good thing. He asks a hostess how to get to the outside terrace, a running path. She insists on escorting him, leads him to an elevator that goes to the ground floor, walks him to the terrace. At these types of places if you ask directions, they're trained not to direct you but to escort you.

Outside, his heart is thumping. Pulse tripping in his neck. Anger juicing through his veins. It's partly from the booze. Tequila makes him aggressive.

For the record, he wasn't flirting with the tall lady with the security detail. Between his bitter wife, the anxious admin lady, and the boring-ass judge and his wife blathering on about their perfect daughter Libby, someone had to lead the conversation.

And what the *fuck*, Stella? He can't believe his daughter skipped dinner. Was she punishing him? Will she ever forgive him? Will he ever feel this weight lifted from his shoulders? All he wants is to be happy.

Adirondack chairs line the hotel's terrace, curving around the firepits. Like the lobby, the area is nearly empty. He can see a couple in the glow of firelight at the far end.

He starts jogging on the path, the only light coming from the hotel. It's not a high-rise, more like a compound, an exclusive country club, rambling along a bluff overlooking the ocean.

In med school, running was the only thing that leveled David out. Helped him cope with the sleep deprivation, the stress. He ran so much back then he shot his knees, so he needs to take it easy. He finds the steps that lead down to the beach. A sign says the beach opens at sunrise and closes at sundown, but there's no one here to enforce that.

The wind is blowing hard tonight. As he runs in the sand, the moon dips in and out behind clouds, its slash of silver reflecting and disappearing in the choppy water. When he was younger, David might've gone for a swim. To hell with the risks of a strong current or sharks, he would've dived in. Probably with a pretty girl next to him.

Is it wrong that he misses that? Misses the admiring gaze of a woman? Misses feeling wanted? Women have always been his Achilles' heel. But he tried to be faithful after he got married. Really tried.

And he *wasn't* flirting with the tall woman tonight. Fuck Nina and her accusations.

He's sweating now. Beach running is harder than he anticipated, the soft sand dragging down every one of his footsteps. Getting older sucks. He doesn't care what anyone says, there's nothing good about it. He'd trade every bit of wisdom he's obtained to be in his thirties again. That was the prime age. Not rich, but enough money in the bank. Washboard abs without much effort. No kids.

He feels guilty about the thought. He wouldn't trade having Stella, his fiery, funny, secretly sensitive daughter. She may hate his guts right now, but she's one of the best things he's ever done.

Picking up his pace, he listens to the waves. He normally jogs to music. But in the heat of storming out of the hotel room, he forgot his phone.

He sees a figure running toward him.

His teenage brain hopes it's a woman in a bikini. Wishful thinking. What's wrong with him?

As the person gets closer, David realizes it's not a woman; the silhouette is a male form. David feels a tingle at the back of his neck. Something is off.

His heartbeat explodes when the man charges toward him.

David can hold his own, but in the shadows he thinks the man is clutching something in his fist. It could be a cell phone. It could be a weapon. A gun, a knife.

His instincts scream at him to turn and run with everything he has.

So he does.

CHAPTER FOURTEEN

THE GOFFMANS

"Chief McCray," she says timidly into the phone. "It's Alice Goffman from Dean Pratt's office. I'm sorry to call this late."

Alice hears some shifting around. She imagines the chief of campus police sitting up, clicking on the bedside lamp.

"Hi. Everything okay? Does the dean need—"

"It's not official business. I'm worried about my son."

She tells him about Felix not showing up at the dinner. About *all* of the kids standing up their parents. Not even responding to texts.

"I know it seems like I'm overreacting, but it's not like Felix. He knew I was nervous about the dinner. He wouldn't have left me alone. My son is a considerate boy, he wouldn't . . ."

"When's the last time you talked to him?"

Alice tells him about Felix's visit to the dean's office.

"You haven't seen him since?"

"No." She's pacing the apartment now. Her eyes land on the

laundry bag. "He must've come home after stopping by the office. His laundry is here."

"But he's not responding to texts or calls?"

"I got a call from him at the dinner, but he didn't say anything. It was loud at The Hut, but it seemed like a butt-dial."

"And you said none of the other kids in his capstone showed up for the dinner?"

"No."

"Well that could explain it."

"What?"

"The frats are all holding parties—get-away-from-your-parents events, stuff like that. They probably went as a group."

Alice is quiet. She knows how she'll sound.

"Tell you what," the chief says. "I'll call the watch commander. See if they can check Felix's entry swipes or if the cameras at the dorm show anything."

She closes her eyes, feeling grateful. "Thank you. I know it's a bother. But I just—"

"Not at all. We're all on edge after Natasha Belov's death, and it's better to be safe than sorry."

The chief is already taking some flak for how his office handled the missing person report for Natasha, though it wasn't his fault. The chief followed the Clery Act protocol—contacted the Santa Clara police and Natasha's parents right away. But everyone assumed Natasha was just being the wild young woman she was, which delayed the search. Not that it would've mattered, since she apparently got trapped in that sea cave and drowned two days before she was even reported missing.

"I'll get back to you soon. And don't worry, Alice. He'll be okay."

"Thank you," she says, then disconnects.

She considers going to bed. But there's no way she can sleep. She tries Felix's phone again. It goes right to voicemail. Alice peers in the refrigerator. She can't eat. She could watch some TV, but decides to do some anxiety cleaning. She starts with the refrigerator, taking everything out, wiping down the shelves. Then she scrubs the counters.

After the small kitchen is spotless, she grabs the Clorox and heads to the bathroom. On the way, she eyes Felix's room, the laundry bag at the entry, feels a twinge in her chest. Felix likes to take care of himself, insists on doing his own laundry, but this will be a nice surprise. She tugs the bag out and over to the tiny laundry area. She dumps the clothes on the floor and begins separating the items.

That's when she sees the hoodie. It's too small for Felix. Pink.

And the front is stained with what looks like blood.

CHAPTER FIFTEEN

THE AKANAS

Ken sits in the car in the dark campus parking garage. He can feel his wife examining him.

Amy finally says, "She's okay."

"It's not like her." Worry burrows deeper into his chest with every minute Libby doesn't respond to their calls or texts.

Amy is quiet. Ken knows she's scared too.

"You have her roommate's number?" Ken asks.

"Yes. But I swore I'd never call unless it was an emergency."

"What did she say earlier?" He's trying not to overreact. But something's off here; he can feel it.

"Nothing. Just that she'd meet us at the restaurant. Told us to be careful, since I mentioned what happened to the tires."

His worry tunnels deeper.

Amy dials their daughter again and puts the phone on speaker. It doesn't ring, just skips to Libby's bright, happy voice: "This is Libby! Leave a message! Or, better yet, send me a text!"

Amy leaves another message to call her: says they aren't mad, just worried.

That settles it. Ken says, "Call Deepa."

Libby's roommate's phone goes to an automated message too.

"I'm sure she just lost track of time," Amy says. "Maybe they had too much to drink. It's only been a few hours and—" She stops midsentence. "Where are you going?"

Ken's already stepped out of the car. He stoops and looks inside. "To her dorm."

"Ken, wait."

He slams the door.

Amy jumps out. "Can we talk about this?"

He stops, looks at his wife. "I know her. Something's wrong."

"If *you're* wrong, she's going to be humiliated. Charging into her dorm like she's in middle school."

"It's a risk I'm willing to take," he says. "You don't have to come." It's an idle threat; he won't leave her alone in a parking garage this late. He sees the acquiescence on her face.

They trudge down the stairs of the structure. The stairwell reeks of beer and urine.

The campus is well lit and students mill about. Ken never understands why their generation insists on doing everything so late. They don't even leave the house until ten or eleven at night. It would be much more efficient and logical to start earlier.

He lets his "judge" thoughts flow through his mind unedited. It helps him keep calm. If ever he needed to be No Drama Akana, it's right now.

Amy is silent. As they reach the heart of campus, Ken recognizes Campisi Hall from drop-off day. Libby's energy was infectious as they loaded her things into the giant bin on wheels. When they went inside her small dorm room, she hugged her new roommate.

Libby and Deepa hit it off right away. Both neat. Both prelaw majors. Both responsible. Soon after, Libby told her mother that she was trying to venture out of her comfort zone, open herself up to different crowds. She'd been hanging out with a group from her capstone lately. The crew that skipped tonight's dinner.

Ken and Amy stop at the front entrance to Campisi. The dorm requires a key card but it's an easy system to bypass. They simply wait until students leave the building and catch the doors before they shut. Ken and Amy get a few sideways glances as they walk down the hall, maybe because the students recognize him from TV or maybe because it's weird for parents to be roaming the dorm so late on their own.

They find the room. The door still has small laminated stickers with LIBBY and DEEPA written on them. Ken can hear a television inside. Or someone watching a show on a computer. Please be Libby. He knocks.

The TV goes quiet. The door opens a crack.

"Hi, Deepa. We're so sorry to bother you, but we can't seem to get hold of Libby. Is she here?"

Deepa's eyes flash. It takes her a moment, like she's processing, then she opens the door. Invites them in.

"You didn't see her at the dinner?" Deepa asks.

Ken shakes his head. "She didn't show up. None of the kids did. They probably lost track of time or something. But she's not answering her phone."

Deepa blinks several times.

"What is it?"

"Last I saw her, she was on her way to the dinner." Deepa pauses, walks over to Libby's side of the room.

"But I know why she's not answering her phone."

"Why?" Amy says, finally speaking.

Deepa points to Libby's desk. On it sits an iPhone. Its face is cracked and screen black.

"It's, um, broken. She borrowed mine since I wasn't going out tonight. She wanted to be able to reach you in case you couldn't find The Hut or something."

"How did her phone—" Ken stops himself. "We called your phone too. No answer."

"I know. I've been texting her. Using my computer." She looks over at the laptop on her bed.

"Do you have Find My Phone?" Amy asks.

Deepa shakes her head. "But my mom does. She likes to make sure I'm in the dorm at night."

"Can you call your mom?" Amy asks. She holds out her phone for the roommate to make the call.

"Um, yeah, sure." She takes the phone.

There's something in the way she takes the device that causes Ken's Spidey sense to tingle. He's seen many a witness in his courtroom lie by omission.

"What is it you're not telling us, Deepa?"

The roommate appears conflicted. "Before Libby left for the dinner . . . she and Stella . . ."

"Libby and Stella what?" Ken says. Stella Maldonado is in the capstone, her dad was the guy so full of himself, the plastic surgeon.

"They had an argument. Stella showed up—she was angry. I stepped out so they could talk. When I came back Stella was gone. Libby's phone was broken. Libby was stressed, running late to the dinner, and asked for my phone. Said she'd bring it back right after."

"Do you know what they were fighting about?" Ken asks. The headache that's been creeping up his neck now feels like an explosion in his skull.

Deepa shakes her head. "All she said was Stella freaked out and stomped on her phone."

Twenty minutes later, Amy is fighting to keep the panic from consuming her. She's also feeling guilty that she didn't listen to Ken. It's not like him to overreact; she should've given him the benefit of the doubt. Judge No Drama Akana isn't one to act like the sky is falling.

"Please slow down," she says, gripping the handle that hangs over the passenger window. Ken is racing to the coordinates Deepa's mom sent them. It's an unusual location: Rancho San Antonio County Park. Amy's never heard of it, but the internet says it's a public park with miles of hiking trails.

Ken doesn't slow down. "I told you something was wrong."

"We don't know that," she says, but he's right. "Crashing the car isn't going to help."

"I think we should call the police," Ken says.

She's not going to fight him this time. "Let's get to the phone first."

He huffs, shakes his head like she doesn't get it.

She searches on her phone for the campus police number. It's late but they might have a night shift. Or should she call 911? She's fighting her familiar companion, a force that took hold after Timmy's diagnosis: *despair.*

She's about to dial when she sees strobing lights ahead. A sign directs to a parking area for Rancho San Antonio. Ken drives faster, juts to a stop.

Amy sees the tall woman from the dinner—the mom with

the security detail. She has a huddle of large men near her in the blue lights.

Then Amy sees a campus police car.

And her heart free-falls.

CHAPTER SIXTEEN

THE MALDONADOS

Amid the throbbing of his pulse in his ears, David hears the man racing behind him, getting closer. He doesn't dare look back; if he loses even a nanosecond, his assailant will catch him.

He sees the railing to the stairs that lead up to the resort. His pursuer must see the exit too because he tries to cut David off.

A seizure of terror rips through him, but he keeps running.

The moon dips through the thick layer of clouds and David spots a makeshift path up the steep bluff some twenty yards away. A downed tree leans against the sandy cliff, where someone carved handholds into the side of the bluff. David sprints for it, his breathing ragged.

He should stop, turn and fight. But the man is clutching something in his hand, David is certain of it, and if it's a weapon, he'll have no chance.

He reaches the tree and starts to clamber up the trunk. He makes it to the top, pulling himself up the makeshift ladder of holes in the rock face. Dread spreads through him when he hears the man huffing close behind him. What does he *want*? Why is he chasing him?

David climbs higher, his pounding heart nearly ripping a hole through his chest. Near the top, he thrusts his right arm over the bank. It's overgrown with weeds and brush and seems unstable. He grips the foliage and starts to yank himself up, but the sandy cliffside crumbles under his weight. The weeds pull loose and the last thing David remembers is the man shouting something as David falls backward to the earth far below.

CHAPTER SEVENTEEN

"Stella, this is Mom." Nina tries to keep the annoyance from her voice. "Please check in. We're not mad, we know you probably got caught up with your friends, but please call when you get this. It doesn't matter what time."

Nina presses the red end-call button on her phone. What a shit show. From snorting coke on that appalling couple's plane to mentioning Cody Carpenter to her daughter to the endless fighting with David. Nina has always been superstitious that way: do a wrong, get a consequence. And this is her consequence: alone in a hotel room, her daughter doing a disappearing act, and her husband on a run, likely planning their divorce.

She opens the mini fridge and takes out a chocolate bar, likely a fifteen-dollar one, but she doesn't care. She rips it open and takes a big bite. She can't remember the last time she ate chocolate, and it's delicious. She eyes the miniature wine bottle, but decides against.

She's already performed her nightly routine: her skincare regimen, the multitude of creams, the hydrating lotion for her legs, brushing her teeth until her expensive toothbrush automatically stopped itself at the optimal number of minutes.

She pulls back her comforter, throws the extra pillows on the small sofa, clicks on the television. The host, the cute one with the dimples, from *Access Hollywood*, tells her about the hotel's movie selection.

She sits on the bed, checks the time. David has been gone for a while. Longer than his usual run, but he's angry. Even factoring in sulk time, though, he should be back by now. She picks up her phone, sends him a text.

She hears a ping from the other side of the bed. His phone sits on the nightstand. He left it when he stormed out.

There's a knock on the door. She has a sensation—relief, maybe?—that he's returned. He must've forgotten his key card as well.

"David?" she calls through the door.

"Ma'am, I'm the night manager."

Nina peeks through the peephole and sees a nicely dressed man. Next to him a woman in a hotel uniform. Her pulse hitches.

"Hold on, please," Nina says. She pulls the white robe tight, pondering whether to get dressed before answering.

"Please hurry, ma'am," the voice says, "it's an emergency."

SATURDAY

CHAPTER EIGHTEEN

THE KELLERS

Saturday morning begins with a shadow hovering over them on the uncomfortable mattress in Bob's sister's childhood bedroom—Bob and Keller's bedroom for the unforeseeable future. Keller opens an eye and sees the twins looking down at Bob.

"Daddy," Heather loud-whispers. "You said we're going to the beach today. You said to wake you up early."

Michael chimes in. "You said . . ."

As every parent knows, to a child, "you said" is an ironclad contract, an unbreakable vow, a blood oath that shan't be broken.

Bob grunts something but his eyes are still closed.

Imitating a child's voice, Keller says, "You saaid," in his ear.

An hour later, everyone is beached up—well, the best New Yorkers could do on short notice—cutoffs, old T-shirts. They'll have to buy sunscreen at the CVS, buckets and shovels at one of those beach shops.

"You're sure this is okay?" Keller says to Bob. "We just got here. And don't we need to keep an eye on your dad?"

On cue, Pops shuffles into the kitchen wearing a robe.

"Never say no to the beach, right, Pops?" Bob says.

"That's right. Ocean and sand keep you young."

Pops isn't looking so young this morning.

Keller eyes her husband. "You sure it won't be too cold?"

Pops scoffs. "It's gonna be seventy-five degrees out today. I thought you were from New York?"

She grew up in New Jersey, but she gets the point. "I mean the water—won't it still be cold?"

Pops bobbles his head like, *maybe yes, maybe no.*

"Make you something for breakfast?" Keller asks.

Pops says, "I can fend for myself. Nurse Ratched comes at nine on Saturdays, so you kids go have fun." The home care service has a nurse visit every few days. "I told Bobby I don't need them coming so often. I'm not an invalid."

Bob and his father have obviously discussed the beach already.

Pops looks at the twins. "You have fun at your air guitar party?"

They both nod, wide-eyed.

Keller says, "Sorry if we were too loud."

"No such thing," Pops says.

"Oh, that reminds me," Bob says, "I brought you something." He disappears out of the kitchen and returns quickly. He hands Pops an old record in its sleeve.

"I found it in that vinyl shop I took you to in SoHo. It's a first press, super rare."

Pops examines the Rolling Stones album and nods approvingly.

"Thank you, Bobby," he says, and he looks a little choked up. "You remember that Stones concert I took you to?"

"It was my first concert, Dad. That's like asking if I remember when I lost my virginity."

Pops grins. "I remember worrying that might never happen."

"Boys . . ." Keller says, trying to stifle any questions about what "virginity" means from the twins.

Pops turns to the kids. "Let's go to the garage and see if we still have any of your dad's old beach stuff."

Keller walks over to Bob and gives him a hug. It's interrupted by the chime of her phone. She checks the screen. The caller ID says Richard Peters. He's the assistant special agent in charge of the San Jose office. Her new boss. Strange that he's calling from a personal phone. On a Saturday. Maybe she needs to fill out more paperwork before starting on Monday.

"Sarah Keller," she says in her FBI agent voice.

"Agent Keller, it's Richard Peters," he says, outmatching her formality.

"Hi . . . Good morning . . ."

There's a long pause.

"I hate to start you off this way. But I need you for something today."

"Of course. Whatever you need." She suppresses a sigh.

"We got a call from the chief of campus police at SCU," Peters continues.

Keller listens.

"Seems a group of college kids have gone missing and our campus liaison who usually handles such things is on parental leave. Had the baby yesterday."

Keller's been there. "Missing? For how long?"

"Not long, and it will likely be a waste of our time. But there are some extenuating circumstances so we need someone on the ground ASAP."

"Of course," Keller says, wondering what "extenuating circumstances" would cause the FBI to get involved in a missing persons case.

Peters fills her in and gives her the name of her point of contact at the university.

She breaks the news to her family. Explains that she's the new person at the office, which means the less desirable assignments, the weekend work.

Bob has already quelled the whines from the kids with talk of ice cream and pizza and burying them in the sand.

When Keller tells him the assignment, he gives her a rueful grin: "Paul Blart, Campus Cop."

CHAPTER NINETEEN

Keller arrives at Santa Clara University, pulls Pops's old Buick into a space on the top floor of the concrete parking structure. The university's police force—called Campus Safety Services—is housed on the lower level, the station house literally built into the parking garage. Life as a cop. On TV, the Bureau's offices are always sleek—clusters of good-looking agents working in high-tech facilities where information on perps and clues pops up on giant screens at the tap of the quirky tech person's keyboard. The reality is that most offices have the look and feel of the DMV. The typical agent isn't an underwear model, either. And the technology, well, calling it outdated is charitable. Even the New York field office, one of the most sought-after assignments in federal law enforcement, is drab and no-frills. So it should be no surprise a campus police force is tucked in the bottom of a parking garage, the entrance covered by a faded red awning.

Keller displays her badge to the receptionist and she's quickly swept into a conference room with a smattering of campus officers who wear bright-colored uniforms. An authoritative man—the only Black man in the group, who wears plain clothes but has the unmistakable carriage of a career cop—sees Keller and comes over. Jay McCray gives her a firm handshake, says he's the chief. He then introduces her to two shift supervisors and a fit-looking man with the Santa Clara city police. It's a strong turnout for a Saturday morning.

"Veronica picked the wrong week to have that baby," McCray says, referring to the Bureau's campus liaison who Keller is filling in for. "As she'd tell you, we welcome the Bureau's help on this, all egos checked at the door."

The others nod. It's sincere, and it was nice of him to say. Another thing TV gets wrong is the trope that local law enforcement hate when the Feds arrive. They know the Bureau has massive resources they do not.

Keller eyes the whiteboard in the back of the room that's already becoming a crime wall. Pinned at the top are four computer printouts—photographs of the missing students, probably from their student IDs.

Under the photos are tiny magnets for posting clues as they come in. Nothing's hanging there yet.

"Here's what we know," Chief McCray says in clipped cop speak. "The capstones for the freshmen hosted small-group dinners for Parents Weekend." The chief gestures to the photos on the whiteboard. "These four were set to meet their parents last night at nineteen hundred hours." McCray pauses. "None of them showed."

"So they've been missing for less than fifteen hours," Keller says. She doesn't need to add the rest: They're college kids, probably sleeping one off as they speak.

"I hear you," the chief says. "If we were talking about one

student, even two, for less than twenty-four hours, you wouldn't be here. But this is different. Four kids gone, completely off the grid. No contact with their parents and their phones are off or disabled. I've worked a lot with this generation, and that's highly unusual. And there are extenuating circumstances."

Those words again: extenuating circumstances.

"My ASAC mentioned that," Keller says.

McCray nods. "Two of the students have parents who present unique security profiles. One of the parents is high up at the State Department, another an LA judge. Both have had threats." McCray pauses again for effect: "So, we have what I'd call an 'oh shit moment.'"

Keller nods.

"Not to mention we had a student die this week," McCray adds. "Poor kid got trapped in one of the sea caves at high tide. So the pressure is on."

Keller blows out a breath. "You've reached out to the phone companies?"

The chief nods. "All the devices stopped pinging around the same time, twenty-thirty, somewhere at Rancho San Antonio."

"I'm not familiar," Keller says. "Sorry, I don't know the area well. I'm on temp assignment from the New York field office."

"It's a public park that has miles of hiking trails, some that lead to the summit of Black Mountain."

"So, we may be dealing with an impromptu camping trip?"

"Let's hope," McCray says. "But something feels off. No vehicle associated with the students is parked in the Rancho San Antonio lots. And while cell service can be spotty out there, it seems likely that at least one of them would have checked in with their parents. We're working only with the quick, critical missing cell phone data reports. We've requested more detailed cell data that will hopefully give us more on the route they took, whether they were all together, and where exactly their phones went silent. It's a Saturday and the phone companies have protocols when there's no warrant, so it's taking longer than I'd like."

Keller nods. "My office can request location data from Google. It's more accurate than cell pings."

"Excellent."

Keller isn't sure that calling in the cavalry is necessary, not yet, anyway. But she understands. The situation is weird; her gut tells her this isn't just a simple prank or spontaneous off-the-grid camping trip. And the university is under additional pressure since it's Parents Weekend.

"This park, how large of an area are we talking about?" Keller asks, thinking about a search.

"Rancho San Antonio? Massive. Thirty miles of hiking trails alone. We've got teams searching by foot and by drone."

The chief explains they've also pulled access control data, which will show any time the students used their security passes to enter the dorms and other buildings. They also have a team gathering video from all campus CCTV cameras. And his team is working with the resident director of the dorm to search the students' rooms. There's a BOLO out to all area law enforcement for the students.

Keller nods. McCray knows what he's doing.

"Tell me more about the kids of the parents with security details," she says.

The chief exhales loudly.

"Blane Roosevelt," he points to a photo on the whiteboard. The student has longish hair and an impish grin. "His mother, Cynthia Roosevelt, is the assistant secretary of state. Apparently she has a bounty on her head from a foreign entity."

"A bounty?"

He nods, fills her in on his discussions with Roosevelt's detail, explains that eight years ago Blane Roosevelt was abducted by civilians trying to get to his mother. "It didn't work out for the perps," McCray says. "A special ops team rescued the boy and took them out. They're obviously looking into any connection to that mess, but Cynthia Roosevelt's detail is skeptical."

Keller examines the crime wall again. It must've been traumatizing for this kid, but you wouldn't know it from his photo.

"Libby Akana," McCray continues, this time pointing to a photo of a young woman with long dark hair and a beaming smile. "Did you follow the Rock Nelson trial on TV?"

"Can't say that I did."

"You can google it, but it was a big celebrity trial. Her father is Ken Akana, the judge in the case. He got some threats after the verdict against the movie star."

Keller nods, says, "You seem to have this under control, Chief McCray." She's not trying to flatter. It's true.

"Call me Jay."

"What can the Bureau do to help?" Keller still isn't sure if she's here to lead or merely provide support, and it's better to respect the team that's been running point. Particularly when they know what they're doing.

"If you can talk to Assistant Secretary of State Roosevelt," he says the title with exaggerated enunciation, "that would help. She doesn't want to deal with the local yokels."

"Is she here?"

Chief McCray shakes his head, displays a cellular phone, cheap and plastic and of the burner phone variety.

"Roosevelt's security lead gave me this," he says, frowning. "They're waiting on your call. Said the number is saved on the device." He hands it over.

Keller finds the contacts. There is indeed only one number saved. She maneuvers the toggle so it highlights the number and clicks.

A stern voice answers. "With whom am I speaking?"

"Special Agent Sarah Keller," she replies. "With whom am I—"

"Listen carefully," the man interrupts.

Keller is tempted to protest, but she's of the get-more-flies-with-honey school, at least in the beginning of an investigation. She listens as the voice instructs her to walk out of the police station and head across campus and over to the Bronco Suites, about a seven-minute walk. She'll receive further instructions, so keep the phone nearby.

Someone's been watching too many movies, Keller thinks as the line goes dead.

CHAPTER TWENTY

As instructed, Keller treads across campus toward the Bronco Suites.

The sun is shining, the sky an unbroken swath of blue, and Keller admires the campus as she strides under the palm trees among the Spanish-style buildings that seem more fitting of a resort than an institution of higher learning. She eyes the giant cross; SCU must be a Catholic university. Keller attended one herself—Notre Dame—but the campuses bear no resemblance to each other. Though it's in an aggressively Midwestern town in Indiana, Notre Dame has the feel of a New England college: old stone buildings, manicured grounds, statues of old white men. Keller's father attended Notre Dame for both undergrad and law school—a Double Domer. A career lawyer in Big Law, her father expected her to follow in his footsteps and attend law school. He expressed his extreme disappointment when she announced that she was joining the Bureau. She shakes the thought.

There is one thing she misses about Notre Dame, though. On nights when she was stressed with school or life, she would go to the Grotto, a small cave made of boulders filled with twinkling candles. It was remarkably peaceful and calming.

This school has its own peacefulness about it. Students laughing and basking in the golden rays. Except for the damned skateboarders, she thinks as one barrels toward her. He's distracted, wearing earbuds, trying to look cool, and she's afraid he won't see her. Grown-ups are invisible in places like this. But he makes a sharp turn in the nick of time, oblivious that he nearly plowed down a federal agent.

She makes her way to El Camino Real. The campus bleeds into the town of Santa Clara—no barriers or markers separate them. She can see the sign for the Bronco Suites, a small economy lodge, across the street.

She makes it to the hotel lobby, which has a front desk with a single employee and the remnants of a continental breakfast on a table to the right. Keller hears the chime of a phone and it takes a beat for her to realize it's the burner. They know she's here, which means they're watching her. She glances around and doesn't spot the detail.

The voice on the phone, the same one from earlier, says, "Take the elevator to the parking garage."

"Should I call you 'Deep Throat'?" Keller asks.

He doesn't laugh. Instead, the phone goes dead again. Maybe he's too young to catch the reference. And honestly, Keller's too young to be dropping Watergate references.

She spies the elevator bank and follows the instructions. The door spreads open and two burly men in suits wait inside. One of the men pushes the button for L3.

When the doors open to the garage, there's a line of four identical black SUVs, all idling. One of the men from the elevator walks her to the fourth SUV, opens the passenger door.

Keller peers inside, sees a stately woman in the back seat. The woman gestures for Keller to get in, which she does.

"Welcome to my life," Cynthia Roosevelt says dryly.

The bevy of SUVs then tears out of the mouth of the garage, each one close on the rear of the next. Then, one by one they split off in different directions. Decoys, in case anyone is watching. Keller now realizes that they met underground to evade drones or satellites. Sent her to a hotel as if she were simply staying there, in case she had a tail. Cynthia stares ahead, annoyed.

A voice from the back, a third row in the SUV, startles Keller.

"I'm Paul, Secretary Roosevelt's chief of staff."

A thin arm threads through the gap in the bucket seats and Keller shakes his hand. "Sorry for the theatrics, but our team thinks that it's necessary until we get a better handle on the situation."

Keller catches Cynthia rolling her eyes.

"Stan says you're one of the Bureau's best," Cynthia Roosevelt says at last.

"You know Stan?" Keller should've assumed that this went through HQ.

Roosevelt gives her a sharp look. "They say you've handled high-profile cases—including one involving college kids."

Keller nods. Doesn't elaborate on the Pine family case from five years ago. She helped uncover what happened to an NYU student's family, murdered while vacationing in Mexico.

"You're from the New York office," Roosevelt says, not a question. "You got here fast."

"I'm temporarily here on assignment," Keller replies, again without elaboration. If she's going to get any information, she needs to take charge, which could be a challenge here. Cynthia Roosevelt is accustomed to running the show. "I know this must be difficult," Keller says. "I hope this turns out to be a—"

Roosevelt waves away the preliminaries with a hand. "What do we know so far?" Her tone is calm, but Keller hears an underlying thread of fear. Roosevelt may be a high-powered official, but right now, she's first and foremost a mother.

"It's early in the investigation and there are no solid leads. Yet. But we're pulling CCTV, phone records, interviewing their friends. And talking to the parents . . ."

Taking the hint, Roosevelt nods for Keller to continue.

"So let me start by asking: Does your team think it has anything to do with your 'situation'?"

Roosevelt exhales, like this is a waste of time. Her chief of staff leans in from behind them. "The government levied a strike against militias associated with the administration behind the bounty this week. But there's been no chatter. No indication they're involved here. Still, out of an excess of caution, we're operating under elevated security protocols."

"You've been under protection for some time," Keller notes.

"Nearly a decade."

"Have they made any prior attempts on your life?"

"Not for several years. There was a plot to lure me to Dubai, but our team quashed it. Nothing else since."

"I understand that Blane, when he was a boy, was taken. Is there any reason to believe—"

Roosevelt cuts her off with a sharp shake of her head. But she grows pale, her hands gripping each other tightly. It seems as if this second possible abduction of her son is almost more than she can bear, and she's doing everything she can to hold it together. "The men who took him weren't affiliated with any government. Just two idiots who thought they could cash in. They were wrong."

Keller debates pushing this line of questions, but decides to wait.

"My people are certain," Roosevelt says, "it has nothing to do with what happened to Blane."

"Is there anything other than the strike that suggests they'd come after you or your loved ones now?"

Secretary Roosevelt shakes her head. Her hands are still wound so tight they must be losing circulation.

"Have you received any demands?" Keller continues. "I know kidnappers will often threaten their targets not to alert the Bureau and there's pressure to handle it privately, but that would be a mistake."

"No contact. Nothing."

Keller scrutinizes the woman. She believes her.

"Has Blane ever gone off the grid before? To clear his head, get away for a little while? Or go on an adventure he didn't want you to know about?"

"Blane is no angel. He's certainly never met a party or pretty girl who couldn't lead him astray. He's like his father that way." She pauses. "But he's never just disappeared. He knows better because"—she gestures to the agents in the front seat—"because of my 'situation,' as you called it. He knows it would cause alarm. That's why I had my team track his phone's location last night. It's unlike him to simply ignore me."

"What do you know about Blane's friends?"

At this, a manila folder slides through the gap between the seats. The chief of staff says, "This has standard background checks on all of them. We worked it up for the Secretary's visit for Parents Weekend."

Keller clasps the file, doesn't open it. The SUV takes a curve fast. They appear to be driving to nowhere.

"You mentioned Blane's father. Is he here this weekend?"

"No. We're divorced."

"Have you spoken to your ex-husband, asked if he's heard from Blane?"

"I spoke to Hank yesterday afternoon," Roosevelt says. "I've been trying to reach him all morning, but he takes pleasure in ignoring my calls. If you get hold of him, please tell him he's an asshole."

"I take it you two don't get along?"

Roosevelt doesn't reply.

Keller probes further. Most people fear crime from strangers, but you're most likely to suffer at the hands of someone close. Cynthia Roosevelt doesn't hold back about her ex-husband. He's a novelist, she says, one who spends more time online virtue signaling than writing. Roosevelt uses the word *woke* several times with derision.

"Spend ten minutes reading his Twitter posts—or X posts, whatever it's called now—and you'll get a portrait of Hank."

"Do you mind if I ask why you divorced?"

"How much time do you have?" She shakes her head again. "We got married too young. He had early success with his first novel, but nothing since. His publisher dropped him and he teaches writing at a community college. Between working on the Great American Blank Page and posting on social media, he likes Maker's Mark. Oh, and he had a thing with his teaching assistant. For a writer who hates clichés . . ."

"Do you think he and Blane maybe just went off together or something?"

Roosevelt shakes her head. "Blane wouldn't leave without telling me. And for all his faults, Hank wouldn't . . ." She stops. "And that wouldn't explain where the other kids are."

"If this has nothing to do with your security situation or your ex, can you think of any reason Blane and his friends might disappear?"

She shakes her head. Then, as if thinking out loud, says, "He's pledging a fraternity, so I suppose maybe it's some hazing thing or something like that. You know how boys are. But that still wouldn't explain the other students."

Keller's phone chimes. It's a text from Chief McCray:

Pls. ask her if she knows this person

"Excuse me for one moment," Keller says. She clicks the link that appears in the next text, which opens a video. It shows a college kid on a skateboard. He's zipping on the sidewalk just like the boy from earlier. He then almost comically goes flying in the air, tumbles to the ground. Keller notes the time stamp: 6:55 p.m. yesterday. Right before the parents' dinner.

A figure comes into the frame. He helps the kid off the ground. It's then that Keller recognizes that the skateboarder is one of the students from the crime wall photos. Blane Roosevelt. The man helping him appears in frame, but for less than a second. The CCTV video then freezes on the man's face.

"Do you know this person?" Keller displays the screen to Secretary Roosevelt.

"That's my ex. Wait, Hank's here? That doesn't make any— What the hell is he doing *here*?"

"That's what we're going to find out."

CHAPTER TWENTY-ONE

Keller returns to the station house. It's getting crowded. More CSS campus officers. More Santa Clara local cops. More agents from Cynthia Roosevelt's detail. An electric buzz charges the air. She fears there will be too many cooks in the kitchen, or whatever that expression is.

She finds Chief McCray—Jay, she reminds herself. Briefs him about the talk with Secretary Roosevelt: There's no indication that the missing kids are connected to the bounty on Roosevelt's head. She's received no ransom demands. But there is this matter with the ex-husband's unexpected appearance on campus. Right before Blane's disappearance, no less.

"Did she give you the father's cell number and carrier?" the chief asks.

What did law enforcement do in the days before everyone voluntarily carried a tracking device?

Keller gives him the number so they can track Hank Roosevelt's location, see if he's still in town. She knows divorce does strange things to people, so it's possible the father knows where Blane is, but it's unlikely that he'd take three *other* kids.

"I'd like to talk to the other parents," Keller says.

The chief nods again. "They're coming in. We have a room set up. I've made clear you're point on the interviews."

"Nothing so far from the search at Rancho San Antonio?" Keller knows the answer.

McCray shakes his head. "But we've got more CCTV." The chief gestures her over to an officer who's concentrating on a laptop screen at the conference room table.

"Show her," the chief says.

The officer taps on some keys and the screen pops to the front of what looks like a dormitory. Students flow in and out.

Girls wearing pajama pants are scrolling their phones. Boys wearing T-shirts with Greek letters on them are screwing around. Her thoughts cut to Cynthia Roosevelt speculating that maybe this is a fraternity pledge prank or something. She mentions it to the chief.

"I wouldn't take it off the table. The fraternities can be"—he pauses, searches for the word—"*creative* with their pranks and whatnot. We forbid hazing, of course. But you know kids."

"Here they are," the officer at the computer says, pointing to the screen. The time stamp is 6:54 p.m., around the time Blane was seen on his skateboard heading to the dinner. A girl pushes out of the dormitory. She has golden brown skin, wears a shirt that reveals her midriff, and has a confident—almost confrontational—stride.

"Stella Maldonado," the police chief says.

"She looks angry," Keller says, examining the young woman's body language. There's not a clear image of her face, but there's no mistaking that she's furious.

The tech fast-forwards the video. A heavyset student strides out of the same building. He appears to call out to Stella.

"We're trying to get an ID on him," McCray adds.

"You don't need to," Keller says. She opens the file Cynthia Roosevelt's chief of staff gave her. "Mark Wong. He's in the same capstone group as the missing students."

McCray calls over a campus officer, tells him to get over to Mark Wong's dorm room, try to confirm his location.

"You're thinking what I'm thinking?" Keller asks McCray.

"Our four missing kids may be five."

They both turn their attention back to the computer. The tech pulls up additional footage. Another young woman, another one of the photos on the crime wall, appears on the screen. Libby Akana, the judge's daughter, looks like she's been crying. She's rushing somewhere.

"It's like they were all summoned," Keller says, thinking out loud. "Any video on where they went?"

"We lose them when they exit campus."

Keller doesn't know what to make of it. She needs to talk to the parents. But until they arrive, she needs to make good use of her time. In a missing persons case, every second counts. Bad news doesn't get better over time.

"What's near the spot they're last seen?"

"The Hut, off Franklin."

"Where they were supposed to go for the dinner?"

"Yeah."

"Any frat houses nearby?"

The chief says, "There's one on that street, the main house for Alpha Kappa."

"Blane's mother said that's the one he's pledging." Keller decides then that she's going to the frat house. She considers asking

Jay to accompany her, but hesitates. She likes this police chief. He exudes confidence despite what Cynthia Roosevelt may think of him and the local cops. But he needs to man the fort. Maybe one of his officers can take her, they'll surely know the grounds. Frat houses are probably on their regular beat for noise and underage drinking and the like, though maybe they don't have jurisdiction off campus. Also, the students may instinctively shut down when they see the university involved. Keller's father, for all his deficits, taught her a few things. One is about local counsel. He practices law in courts across the country and he told her that he'd never appear without a local lawyer by his side. Someone to advise on local customs, someone trusted by the judges and lawyers in the community.

One of their own.

That's what Keller needs.

She eyes all the bodies in the station again. That's when she spots her. The twentysomething young woman with the SCU sweatshirt, standing at a photocopy machine. The woman catches Keller's glance and smiles.

"You," Keller says.

It takes the student a moment to realize Keller is talking to her. She looks behind her to make sure.

Keller waves for her to come over. The woman still appears skeptical. She points to herself, mouths, *Me?*

When Keller nods, she hurries over.

"You're a student?" Keller asks.

The girl's eyes flash more with excitement than nervousness. She holds out her hand to give a firm shake, the way Annie was taught, which Keller likes.

"Annie Hafeez."

"Intern?" Keller asks.

She nods.

"You know the frats?"

"Ah, yeah, I'm in a sorority and we all hang out."

"How about Alpha Kappa?"

"Yeah, sure."

"Can you take me to their house?"

Her eyes flash again. "For sure. Which one? They have three houses."

"The one near The Hut."

"Hangover."

"Pardon?"

"Hangover. That's what everyone calls the house."

Keller almost asks why, but decides it's obvious.

"Show me."

The chief, who has been quiet throughout the exchange, tilts his head to the side, silently asking Keller whether this is a good idea—involving a student.

Keller gives a firm nod. "I need local counsel."

CHAPTER TWENTY-TWO

THE ROOSEVELTS

"You need to find Hank," Cynthia says, trying to mask the desperation in her voice.

The head of her detail twists around from the front of the SUV. "We don't have investigative authority. DS's jurisdiction is protection-focused. The Bureau is the agency that—" Mitch stops, almost certainly because of her derisive gaze.

Cynthia could give one shit about investigative authority or the jurisdictional dick-measuring of the seventy different federal law enforcement agencies and their alphabet soup acronyms.

Mitch continues: "Since the divorce, we disabled the tracker on your ex-husband's phone. I can see if there's a way to reactivate it remotely. But the Bureau is all over this. I've asked around. This Agent Keller, she's good."

Cynthia had the same impression. She liked that the agent didn't cower to Cynthia. Didn't suck up either. A straight shooter, a rarity in Cynthia's world.

"Find him," she says. "Hank may know where Blane . . ."

Cynthia lets the sentence fade. Her heart thrums at the thought of Blane. She can't go through this again. She takes in a deep breath, trying to quell the panic rising in her chest.

"You're sure this has nothing to do with Blane's abduction?"

Mitch nods. "The director said that every agency involved back then assured him."

"How can they be so sure?" She shakes her head. Most of the half-wits running the federal government are walking embodiments of the expression *Often wrong, never in doubt.*

"I need to use the restroom," she says as they continue their drive to nowhere.

"The safe house isn't cleared yet."

"I don't know why we had to move. The house last night was fine." She shakes her head. "When will the new house be cleared?"

Mitch looks at his watch. "About an hour."

"*Oh*, about an hour. So I suppose I should just pee in a Gatorade bottle. That's what you all do on long shifts, isn't it?"

Mitch doesn't reply.

"Better yet," Cynthia continues, "let's stop at the Seven-Eleven, you can run in and get me some adult diapers."

"Cynthia," her chief of staff says from the seat next to her. "Everyone's doing everything they can to—"

"I don't want to hear it. Just find my son!" She needs to calm down. Regain control. You don't think straight when you're erratic. She needs a clear head. "Pull over there," she says, pointing to a run-down gas station.

Wisely, Mitch and the other agent up front don't question her, and the SUV pulls under the awning. Cynthia reaches for the door handle.

"If you can give us five to check things out," Mitch says.

"What? You think my friends are staking out a dirty roadside bathroom?" She'd taken to calling the hostile government that put a bounty on her head her "friends," which somehow made the situation less terrifying.

"Secretary Roosevelt," Mitch says. "Please."

She tightens her lips to a seam. "Tell them to make it fast."

At that, Mitch says something into his wrist microphone and two agents in another SUV that has arrived from out of nowhere jump out of their vehicle. One goes inside the gas station's small store, the other around back to a separate structure that must be the bathroom.

The first agent returns with a key tied to a piece of wood.

The door to the SUV finally opens and she's escorted to the structure adjacent to the store.

Cynthia goes inside and shakes her head at the disgusting scene. The floor is wet, like the toilet has a leak. Soggy paper towels and toilet paper smear the tiles. The walls are scrawled with graffiti.

No way she's using the facilities here. She didn't really have to go, anyway. One of her mentors, the senior senator from Virginia, had once given Cynthia a wise piece of advice: "The woman's bathroom is your sanctuary. There are no men, no cameras, and no one will judge you if you cry."

Cynthia goes inside the stall, shuts the door. She closes the lid to the rancid toilet, steps up, and sits on the tank, her feet resting on the seat. And she lets out a long, primal scream. It's audible to no one. Her mouth is wide open, her face hot and contorted as she roars at the sky without making a sound.

CHAPTER TWENTY-THREE

THE KELLERS

On the walk to a frat house called Hangover, Keller assesses her student guide, Annie Hafeez. The young woman has a twinkle in her eyes, an overcaffeinated energy, and hasn't stopped talking since they left the station house. Keller would ordinarily think it's nervous chatter, but she suspects this is just Annie's way. Keller is instinctively drawn to people like this, people who think the glass really is half full, who see the best in others, who are comfortable in their own skin and like nothing more than to chat and smile.

"You said your name is Agent Keller," the intern says. "What do I call you? Like, Agent Keller or Special Agent Keller or FBI Agent Keller or—"

"Sarah works," Keller says.

"Sarah," Annie repeats. "What an old-fashioned name."

The young will do nothing but make you feel your age.

On the walk, Keller learns that Annie is studying business because it was the only major that would make her parents happy. She graduates this year and has no idea what she wants to do. She's not dating anyone serious and doesn't care. She's got two siblings who have serious boyfriends, but whatever.

"I told my dad, *no*, I don't have to move home after graduation if no one's asked me to get married." She shakes her head seemingly endeared by her father's traditional way of thinking. "I told him I don't need a man"—she offers a wicked smile—"or a woman."

Keller smiles in spite of herself.

Annie continues: "He said my grandparents are rolling over in their graves. And I said Nani told me, right before she died, not to live my life the way other people expect me to. She made me promise." The young woman sets her jaw, like she's proud of her oath.

"What brought you to intern at the campus police?" Keller asks. "I interned for a police department when I was in college."

"It was here or the dining hall. And no way I'm cleaning up after those slobs. But I've found it interesting, everybody's nice." She thinks a moment. "What's it like being in the FBI?"

"I can't complain. Well, I can, but I won't," Keller says. "It's been an interesting career. But it's not like on TV."

Annie raises her hands like she's holding a handgun, pretends to stalk around. "You're not, like, busting down doors and capturing terrorists or stopping bombs from going off or flying to some small town to stop a serial killer?"

"Not usually. Mostly it's analysis. I work in financial crimes so it's a lot of data crunching, following a money trail."

They walk briskly through campus and turn onto Franklin Street.

"Do you know any of the missing students?" Keller asks.

Annie shakes her head. "I don't know many freshmen."

Keller reflects on the days when a three-year gap seemed like a chasm.

Annie points to a squat house that looks like the other dilapidated ranches on the street. Keller wouldn't have a clue it was a frat house but for the throng of young men, most shirtless, on a side patio. A few of them are playing some type of game at tables made of large slabs of plywood. The others are scuttling about picking up trash and setting up what looks like a homemade bar constructed of Home Depot lumber.

"There must be a darty today," Annie says. "They're never up this early."

"Darty?"

"A daytime party—a darty. There's also the 'dusky' for a dusk party, and a—"

"You know any of those guys?" Keller cuts in.

Annie surveys the shirtless masses, shakes her head. "I've seen some of them around, but don't know them."

Keller watches as two guys appear to be trying to hoist up a tarp that will shield the outdoor patio from the street.

"Pledges," Annie explains. "They're basically servants for the brothers until they're initiated."

Keller and Annie step onto the patio. Keller flashes her badge, if only for the amusement of seeing the fear in their underage-drinking eyes. One of the boys drops the tarp in an effort to conceal a keg.

Keller points to the boy who looks most afraid. Or maybe the least hungover.

"Do you know Blane Roosevelt?"

"Yeah. I mean, he's in my pledge class."

The other boys start buzzing around.

"When's the last time you saw him?"

The kid blows out a breath. "I'm not sure. A couple days ago, I think."

Another student, this one wearing a cowboy hat and, yes, shirtless, moves in closer. "I saw him on Wednesday night. The night we got our Bigs."

Keller furrows her brow.

Annie says, "Bigs are like, ah, mentors. All the pledges get one."

Keller looks at the half-dozen pledges. "Any of you see Blane since then?"

This prompts a shirtless ensemble shaking their heads.

Keller makes a show of examining the area. "I really need to find Blane. I'd hate to start checking IDs if someone's not telling me something."

There's murmuring. Then a pledge steps forward. "I saw Blane last night."

"What time?"

"Ah, like six or seven."

"Where?"

"Here. He asked if his Big was around."

"Name?" Keller enjoys watching them squirm for some reason.

"His Big? It's Shaggy."

Keller looks around at all the boys with their floppy hair. It's a nickname that would work for any of them.

"Shaggy lives here?"

The pledges are all nods now.

Keller points toward the door, and they nod again, which she takes as consent to enter the premises. Consent is an exception to the warrant requirement, though she'd be on shaky ground if she saw anything illegal inside the frat house. But right now she doesn't care: She's focused on finding the missing students, not whatever paraphernalia lurks in the common area of Hangover.

Keller looks at the boys one last time. It's funny, they're legal adults, but Keller can't help but think of them as boys. She says: "You all respect girls?"

"Oh yeah, of course," one of the more assertive boys says. Nods all around again.

"If I hear one whisper otherwise, I'll be back, and things won't go well for you."

Keller signals to Annie to wait there as she goes inside to find "Shaggy." She's already involved the intern more than she should.

From behind, she hears a burst of laughter. This will be a story they tell later at their "darty."

In the living room of Hangover, two students look up at her curiously from the television screen. They have game controllers in their hands. They say nothing and simply shrug off the sight of a strange woman in their home.

The kitchen is cleaner than expected. The benefit of having a group of pledge servants. They probably forced them to clean for Parents Weekend.

A girl walks toward her from the hallway.

"Shaggy's room?" Keller asks, nonchalantly.

The girl looks over her shoulder. "The one with the *Fight Club* poster on the door," she replies.

Fight Club came out before these fraternity bros were even born, but whatever. Keller finds the door, stares at shirtless Brad Pitt with a cigarette dangling out of his mouth, understanding now why these boys are averse to covering their torsos. She knocks. No answer, but she hears rustling inside. She pounds again.

The door rips open aggressively. The young man's face softens when he sees it isn't a pledge bothering him.

Keller stands corrected: The name "Shaggy" fits this boy uniquely.

She holds up her badge.

Shaggy's eyes widen, then he slides out a crack in his door into the hallway, shuts it behind him.

"You're the FBI, no shit?"

"Yes."

"Sick."

With those stimulating preliminaries out of the way, Keller asks, "You're Blane Roosevelt's Big?"

"Goose? Yeah, he's my boy. What's—"

"Goose?"

"Just nicknames we . . ." He stops himself. Keller's expression must say she gets it.

"Can I come in?"

Shaggy grimaces, scratches his head. "Do you, ah, have a warrant?"

"Never mind," Keller says. She appreciates his television understanding of his rights. And she's already pushed the Fourth Amendment to its limits today. "We can talk here: When was the last time you saw Blane?" She can't bring herself to call him Goose.

"Last night. Is he in some kind of trouble?" Shaggy rubs the sleep out of his eyes.

"You haven't heard? He's missing. So are three other students from his capstone group."

Keller realizes that the campus alert hasn't gone out yet.

"I just saw him literally last night . . ."

"What time was it?"

He thinks about it. "I was about to get dinner, like, seven or seven thirty."

"You're sure? This is important."

He nods, more confident.

"Where did you see him?"

"Here."

Keller nods for him to continue.

"Yeah. He came rushing in. Said he needed to borrow the Machine."

Sweet mother. "The Machine?"

"My van. We call it the—"

"Was he with anyone?"

"Yeah, Tommy Boy."

"Tommy— I need a real name."

Shaggy looks at the ceiling like he's trying to conjure the name.

A pledge walks by. He's carrying a caddy full of cleaning supplies. Oh the rituals of boys.

"Yo, Urkel. What's Tommy Boy's name? Like, his real name?"

The pledge says: "Mark."

"Mark Wong?" asks Keller.

"Yeah."

This confirms that the missing four are actually the missing five.

The pledge continues down the hall. Keller hears him utter a loud groan when he sees the state of the bathroom. A voice from the other room says, "I want to be able to eat off that floor, Urkel."

Keller turns back to Shaggy. "Did Blane say where he was going, why he needed your van?"

He shakes his head.

"And you just gave him the keys?"

"Goose is my boy, of course."

"Did he bring it back?" Keller says.

Shaggy shakes his head like he doesn't know. "I park it on the street out front. If it's not out there, then . . ."

"What's the make and model of your van, the color?"

"It's hard to miss. It's painted like the Mystery Machine from *Scooby-Doo.*"

Of course it is.

"I need your plate number."

There's that dumbfounded expression again. "Ah, I don't— No, wait. I have a picture of the Machine on my phone. Hold on." He opens the door only a crack, squeezes through the gap. He returns to the hallway in the same awkward way.

"Here's one," he says. "I can AirDrop it." He holds out his phone, taps it on Keller's. And she sees the photo pop up. The scene looks like Halloween. A group of students dressed up like Fred, Daphne, and the others from the cartoon series stand in front of a green-and-turquoise hippie van. She confirms the license plate is visible in the shot.

"We painted it for the party," he explains.

"Do you have any idea where Blane and Mark went? Where they might be?"

"You checked their phone location?"

Crime shows. Keller doesn't answer.

"Goose loves the beach. Or maybe they all just went camping. Somewhere with no cell service. We went to Death Valley last year and my mom freaked when she didn't hear from me for a few days."

Keller hopes that's what's going on. The students are camping at Rancho San Antonio Park, out of range of a cell tower. Everyone is freaking out unnecessarily. But she has a gnawing in the back of her mind that tells her it's something else. Something worse.

"Has Blane borrowed the van before?"

"Just once when they all went to a concert in the city. Kanye." He looks around the hallway conspiratorially. "They kept it on the down-low 'cause Kanye's problematic."

"You said Mark was with Blane?"

Shaggy nods.

"Did he say anything or tell you where they were—"

"Nah. I actually sent Tommy Boy outside. Told him he shouldn't be in the house."

"Why? I thought he's a pledge too."

"He's on probation."

"For what?"

Shaggy bites his lower lip like he's mulling how much to say. Then, in a more serious voice he says, "We take allegations seriously."

"Allegations?"

"You'll have to ask Griffey. He's frat president. I don't know the deets."

Keller exhales, not sure if she's up for another talk with a bro.

When she returns to the patio, Annie is in the midst of the weird game at one of the plywood tables. A frat kid throws what looks like a die high into the air and they all wait for it to bounce on the table. Annie nimbly kicks the die when it ricochets off the tabletop. The pledge next to her tries to kick the die on the rebound but misses, and it flies onto the concrete. The boy who missed then downs whatever is in the Solo cup on the table.

Annie notices Keller, says her goodbyes, and comes over.

Keller says, "I need to speak to the frat president. He apparently plays something called 'drone soccer' on Saturday mornings. Do you know what that is and where . . . ?"

"For sure," Annie says, waving to the frat boys as they leave Hangover. "And I've got some intel for you from the pledges."

Keller knew she liked this young woman.

CHAPTER TWENTY-FOUR

Keller and Annie make it back to campus quickly, Keller hurry-walking, with Annie struggling to keep up. It's late morning and more students are rousing.

"So what's this *intel*?" Keller says, repeating the term Annie probably learned from Netflix documentaries or true-crime podcasts.

Annie looks over her shoulder as if to make sure no one hears her gossiping.

"The pledges aren't worried about the vanishing act. Blane and Mark are apparently big partiers. But one of the guys said Mark is on probation."

Keller doesn't reveal she already knows this. "For what?"

"An allegation."

It's the same vague term Shaggy used.

"What's that mean? Like a formal report of something?"

Annie shakes her head. Pulls up something on her phone. "There's this app called Rizz SCU. It's where students post anonymously about stuff. Campus gossip, memes, things like that." She displays her phone to Keller, warning: "They can be really mean."

Keller reads the first few entries in the thread:

I fucking hate Greek life

One of the girls that lives with me is such a bitch

Spotted: Tuba Boy walking near library

"Someone said Mark did something?"

"That's what the pledges said, though I couldn't find the post. And apparently it said something about Mark's dad."

"His dad?" Keller doesn't like playing dumb with her new young friend, but her job demands it. She knows from the file Cynthia Roosevelt's chief of staff gave her that Mark Wong's father is a predator who groomed and molested teenaged girls on the swim team he coached.

Annie shrugs.

"Does the school follow up on these reports?"

Another shrug.

Keller asks Annie if she can search the site again for any posts mentioning Mark Wong or the other missing students. The intern's eyes light up.

"For sure, as soon as I get to the office." Annie starts explaining in detail how she'll methodically go about the search, how she'll also scour other sites, the Wayback Machine for historical posts . . .

Keller tunes her out while she reads a text from Bob. He sent a photo of the kids on the beach. Heather's hair blows in the wind and Michael is wearing orange plastic sunglasses:

Too cold to go in water

But fun day

Keller feels an ache in her heart. Her father was one of those people who put his job before family, and she vowed to never—

Another text from Bob interrupts her thought:

How goes the investigation G-woman?

👍

She notices Annie peeking a glance. That the intern is spying is confirmed when Annie says, "You mad at someone?"

"No, why?"

"The thumbs-up emoji. You know it's considered rude?"

Keller chuckles. "I didn't know that. Your generation— I'm never going to break the code."

"You sound like my dad. Let me give you some rules," Annie says with an earnestness that is charming. She explains it is "one, not two, spaces after a period" when you type something; "no punctuation in texts"; and "stop turning off the closed-captioning on Netflix."

Back at the station, Keller finds Chief McCray, debriefs him on what she's learned. He does the same. It's still a lot of nothing. But now they have a vehicle to look for. And someone is bound to notice a van painted like the Mystery Machine.

"Any of the other parents here yet?" Keller asks.

He nods. "Judge Akana and his wife are in the conference room."

"What about the others?"

"I talked to Alice Goffman, Felix's mom, last night, but asked her to come in for another interview. She should be here soon," McCray says.

"How about Mark or Stella's parents?" Keller's already referring to these kids like she knows them. She reminds herself she most certainly *doesn't* know them and should check herself.

"They're a little trickier," McCray says. "Mark Wong's father, he—"

"Has a record for sexual assault, I know," Keller says, finishing his sentence.

"He's been out of the picture since he went to prison. He's served his time, lives at a halfway house in East Palo Alto, but our understanding is that he and Mark are estranged."

"How about the mother?"

"It appears from university records that she's deceased. A year ago."

"Kid can't get a break. Any other family?"

"None listed in his file."

"Stella's parents?"

"We've been trying to reach David and Nina Maldonado, but haven't had any luck. Emergency contact is the father, but he's not answering his phone."

"That's odd."

"Maybe, maybe not," McCray says. "It's still early, and Alice Goffman said the Maldonados didn't seem concerned about their daughter's disappearing act last night. They said their daughter can be 'mischievous.'"

"Let's hope that's the explanation for all this."

McCray doesn't say anything, but she sees skepticism etched in his face.

"The Akanas—you spoke with them last night as well," Keller says. McCray had already told Keller about the interview: about the couple going to their daughter's dorm, Libby's roommate telling them that Libby and Stella had a dispute of some sort, Stella allegedly breaking Libby's phone.

McCray nods.

"They're here, so maybe they've thought of something else?"

"Or maybe the judge wants to make sure we're doing our jobs." McCray says this as if Judge Akana was a handful last night.

Keller smiles. "Let's go find out."

In the conference room, Judge Akana sits upright, his eyes intense. His wife is strangely calm, like she's trying to keep it together. She keeps closing her eyes, taking deep breaths, in and out.

After some preliminaries, Keller confirms what they already told McCray last night: that they were running late for the dinner, that they spoke to Libby that afternoon, nothing seemed out of the ordinary. She was her usual cheerful self.

"I understand your tires were slashed?"

Judge Akana nods. "You're getting CCTV from the Starbucks and surrounding area?"

McCray chimes in: "We've requested the footage. Without a warrant and on a weekend, it can take a little time."

Judge Akana frowns. "You need a warrant for anything, you go to Judge Henry in the Northern District. He'll get you whatever you need."

"Good to know."

"How about geofencing?" Akana asks.

He's a man used to being in charge of his courtroom. And he's familiar with the latest in electronic tracking technology, likely because of his criminal docket. Tech companies store massive amounts of location data, a digital record of every place a person goes with their phone. A geofence filters that data to show all phones present in a specific area within a certain timeframe. Keller asked her ASAC to have the San Francisco field office request geofence data showing every phone located at Rancho San Antonio Park within the hour of when the students' phones went dark.

"Judge Akana, I know this is difficult, but rest assured we're pursuing all avenues for electronic data," Keller says.

He nods like he accepts this, but then says he turned Libby's broken phone over to the Santa Clara PD and wants to confirm the Bureau has it for analysis.

"Santa Clara PD is working with the Bureau's forensic team," she assures him again. "They're going to retrieve anything they can from the device."

Akana nods.

"Was Libby having any problems?" she asks.

A shake of the head from the judge.

"Do you know why she and Stella Maldonado were fighting? Why Stella might break your daughter's phone?"

Again, a shake of the head. All the while, Mrs. Akana has said nothing.

"How about you, Mrs. Akana?"

"Please, call me Amy," she says. "Libby is doing great, she told us everything at school is amazing."

Maybe it was, Keller thinks. Or maybe her parents are oblivious.

"The slashed tires, can you think of anyone who'd—"

"Other than fans of Rock Nelson, you mean?" says the judge.

"Were there any fans in particular that you can think of?"

"My team is running that down, but no."

"Anyone else have a grudge? Some other defendant you sentenced?"

"My team has identified no plausible threats. I get my share of hate mail and hostility from the bench, but I'm miles from home, no one knew I was coming to the Bay Area."

"It could be just vandalism," Keller says. "The area isn't immune to that."

Frustratingly, the couple seems to have nothing new to offer. But Keller senses Mrs. Akana is holding back.

In the hallway outside the conference room, Keller is about to get McCray's take, but the chief has his attention focused intently on his phone.

Before she can speak, he looks up. "We located the Maldonados. This could be the break we've needed."

CHAPTER TWENTY-FIVE

BLANE ROOSEVELT

Blane is in that twilight area, half asleep, half awake, and unsure why he doesn't *want* to wake up. Perhaps it's the familiar ache in his head from too much beer, the feeling of a hand clasped around his brain, squeezing. But dread is also blanketing him. He feels it even in this fugue state.

He's hot, sweating, but in this quasi-dream he can't move, can't rip off his shirt, push the bedspread to the floor. His thoughts frolic from place to place, time to time.

For a moment he's eleven years old, playing with his WWF figures, shutting his door to block out his parents screaming at each other. Then he's at Panther Beach that night, half baked, stars twinkling overhead.

Then it's back to his parents, them sitting him down, telling him he'd have two houses, two bedrooms, two Christmases now.

He knows his parents' story from various versions he's heard over the years: meeting at Harvard, opposites attracting. Mom needing a creative writing class to satisfy some course requirement she found absurd for her international politics degree; Dad being the star of his program, selling his first novel six weeks after they graduated. Though he didn't make much money from the book, it was everything a trust-fund creative could ask for: literary awards, speaking invitations, hanging with those types. They moved to D.C. to support Mom's job, where she rose quickly in the government. A Washington golden couple if there ever was one.

Then the downward spiral.

Finally, Blane realizes he's awake. It's pitch-black. Then he remembers. About last night. About their phones being taken from them. About his hands and feet being bound. About the tape covering his eyes and mouth.

He yanks at his arms violently, trying to free himself. Oh god oh god oh god.

He hears movement, a groan to his left. He realizes the others must be here too. Lined up like sardines.

He tries to shout through the tape sealing his mouth. It's muffled, but the panic echoes in the small space where they're confined.

Someone, one of the girls, responds with a gagged scream-turned-moan. She's only a few feet away.

No no no no no.

The muted pleas, the sounds of terror continue until they all are too exhausted to continue or realize it's futile. There's no one to help in this sensory deprivation tank.

He rolls to his right, feels another body.

He manages to scooch over, hands behind his back, closer to the mass. He bumps his shoulders to the figure to elicit a response.

But the body is still. Then a crushing memory hits him: the image of Mark rushing one of their captors. The *pop* of the gun, Mark hitting the ground hard.

This can't be happening.

But it is.

CHAPTER TWENTY-SIX

THE KELLERS

Keller regards David Maldonado, who has a bandage on his head but still somehow looks kind of dashing sitting up in his hospital bed. His wife stands at the perimeter. She's fidgety and seems to be bridling panic. Keller isn't sure if it's because of what happened to her husband or because her daughter remains missing.

The air is filled with anxiety. Hospitals do that. So do real-time investigations. And Keller rushed here by herself rather than deal with questions of whether McCray or Santa Clara PD should venture miles from their jurisdiction since San Mateo County and Half Moon Bay law enforcement had already responded to the incident.

"I know you've been through this with the police, but it would help if you walked me through what happened," Keller says.

"That's fine," Dr. Maldonado says. "But first, the kids, they still haven't turned up?"

His wife Nina blurts, "We haven't heard a word from Stella. Do you think something's happened to them?"

"That's what we're trying to find out," Keller replies. "We need you to tell us about last night."

David tells her. About the dinner for Stella's capstone group from Campisi Hall. The kids skipping out. The return to the hotel. David going out for a run. He doesn't say so, but Keller suspects from the way he tells it—from the fold of his wife's arms across her chest—that there was an argument in there somewhere. Probably what precipitated a jog so late after a night out for dinner and cocktails.

"When Stella didn't show up at The Hut, you weren't concerned?"

Dr. Maldonado shrugs. "Stella can be . . . tricky. It isn't the first time she's ghosted us."

Keller stores that away for more questions later. Pacing is key in an interview. "So, you're out on a jog and someone attacks you?"

"Not so much an attack. But he just shows up from the shadows, like in some horror movie. He had something in his hand. I thought it could've been a knife, but it was dark. So I wanted to get the hell out of there, and I ran."

"And he chased you?"

"Yeah. He cut me off at the stairs to the hotel, so I found this opening where you could scale the cliffside. That's when I fell."

"Did you get a look at him?"

Dr. Maldonado shakes his head. "It was dark."

"Do you have any idea who it might be?" Keller sees Maldonado and his wife tap eyes. "This isn't the time to hold back." Keller doesn't add that it could relate to their missing daughter, but they get it.

Finally his wife speaks: "You tell her or I will."

Dr. Maldonado blows out a breath. "There was an incident back in New York."

"An incident."

His wife chimes in again. "Call it what it is, David. An affair."

"It wasn't like a love affair and—" He stops himself. "It was an affair. *I* had an affair," he concedes, more for his wife than Keller.

Keller is curious where this is going. The trajectory suggests the man on the beach wasn't a random assailant, perhaps a jilted spouse, but she lets him talk.

"I was out with her late one night."

"Her."

"Zoe Carpenter, an anesthesiologist at the hospital."

Keller shows no judgment on her face. Judgment can make an interviewee shut down.

Dr. Maldonado continues: "We were parked in the woods at a park near her house."

Keller can almost feel Mrs. Maldonado's glare burning into him.

"Zoe's husband must've had a tracker on her car or something. Or maybe he followed her." He swallows. "Next thing we know her husband is pounding on the window."

Keller continues to show no reaction as her mind plays the movie in her head.

"I thought, 'Oh, this is bad.' But I had no idea . . ."

"What happened?" Keller asks after a long silence.

"He had a gun. I thought he was going to kill me. Kill us both. He was ranting. Crying. He'd been drinking. He'd already called Nina." David flicks a glance at his wife, then back to nothing. "It started raining. He was growing increasingly agitated. I tried to talk him down. Tell him I'm sorry."

This elicits a noise from his wife's throat.

"And then he just puts the gun under his chin and . . ." He doesn't need to say more.

Keller swallows, imagining the grisly scene.

"But it gets worse," Dr. Maldonado says.

"Worse?" Keller says, failing to conceal her bewilderment. How could it possibly get worse?

"While we're waiting for the police, I get out of the car to get some air. Zoe is in shock, nearly catatonic. Her husband is lying there in the grass, his head . . ."

He's quiet for another long moment. Keller can't take it anymore: "What was worse?"

"Across the knoll, I see a figure. A kid on a bicycle."

Oh no. Keller feels her pulse in her neck, anticipating where this is heading.

"Apparently when her husband rushed out of the house upset, drunk, and got behind the wheel, their son followed after him on his bike."

"He saw," Keller says.

"Everything," Maldonado says. "And he's just standing there staring at me. Even in the dark from the distance I could see the hatred."

Another stretch of silence. Then he says it: "I saw that same stare yesterday when we got to campus."

"Wait, you're saying the son, he was at SCU?"

"It was him. Standing there with that same glare. I thought I was imagining it. Maybe it was another kid who looked like him. But Nina saw him too."

His wife is nodding. An exhausted nod.

"And you think that's who went after you last night?"

"Who else would it be?"

"Is this the first time you've seen him since his father died?"

Nina Maldonado speaks now. "I saw him a couple times in New York. Once outside my yoga studio. Another time at Patsy's

Pizzeria. And we were getting harassing calls, hang-ups. But then it stopped."

"What's his name?"

"Cody Carpenter."

"Does Stella know him? Did they go to the same high school or—"

"Stella went to private school in the city," David Maldonado says. "Zoe lives in Englewood and her son went to school there."

Nina adds, "I asked Stella yesterday if she knew Cody. I thought it could be a crazy coincidence that maybe he went to Santa Clara."

"What did she say?"

"That she doesn't know him."

"And you believe her?"

The wife hesitates, thinks, then says: "Yes."

"Was there anything unusual about Stella yesterday? Did she say or do anything that seemed out of the ordinary?"

Nina Maldonado ponders this. "She did leave the resort abruptly."

"What do you mean?"

"She drove up to Half Moon Bay with us, she was annoyed we'd booked a place so far from campus. She and I walked on the beach. Like I said . . . she seemed slightly annoyed with us, but that's not unusual."

She peers at her husband for a moment and continues. "Stella was supposed to hang out for the afternoon and then we'd all go to the dinner together. Then she gets a bunch of texts, insists she has to get back to campus right away. Something about needing to turn in a paper for one of her classes or risk a bad grade."

"Did you believe her?"

"I mean, not totally. But she clearly wanted to get back, so we got her an Uber."

"Do you know what time that was?"

"No, but the app will have the time." Mrs. Maldonado examines her phone. "She left here at four fifteen."

Keller thinks about this. This was more than two hours *before* the kids all stormed out of the dorm, possibly summoned by someone. She makes a mental note to check whether Stella really had an assignment due. It's more likely the texts were about whatever she and Libby Akana were fighting about. Keller imagines Stella Maldonado charging into Libby's dorm, smashing her phone.

Nina Maldonado's eyes are filling with tears, like she's coming to terms that her daughter isn't voluntarily missing. She glares at her husband: "This is your fault."

Keller places a hand on her shoulder. A gesture of sympathy, but also one that says this isn't the time; it isn't going to help them find Stella.

Keller needs to move fast. Track down Cody Carpenter in case he has anything to do with the missing students. It seems unlikely. But so does the Maldonados seeing this kid three thousand miles from New York.

"Do you have his mother's contact information?" Keller asks. "It may be the fastest way to confirm it was him, that Cody's in California, how to find him."

"If you get me my phone," David says, eyeing the nightstand that's out of reach amid the tubes and monitors.

"You still have it?" his wife says, more hurt in her tone. "You said you deleted—"

"This isn't about us. It's about finding Stella."

Keller thanks them both. She wonders how they got to this point: the infidelity, the secrets, the bitterness.

In the hallway she takes a deep breath and makes a call that she knows is going to devastate another woman, another mother.

CHAPTER TWENTY-SEVEN

Keller's calls to Zoe Carpenter go to voicemail. Understandable. No one answers an unfamiliar number. She leaves a message. Says the magic words that ensure a quick response. "I'm with the FBI. It's about your son."

Meanwhile, Jay McCray has confirmed that Cody isn't a student at Santa Clara University. And he's determined that the boy attends UC Santa Cruz, about forty-five minutes from SCU. The chief knows the head of Santa Cruz's campus police and has already reached out. McCray will meet Keller at the campus.

On the drive, Keller catalogues what the investigation has yielded so far. CCTV footage showing Blane Roosevelt's crash on his skateboard, his father appearing in the frame. Seven minutes later, Mark Wong pushing out of the dorm. Shaggy placing Blane and Mark at the frat house shortly thereafter. The boys borrowing the Mystery Machine.

Keller flashes to the footage of the other students—Stella, then Libby—rushing out of the dorm separately, around the same time. Were they all going somewhere together? Is that why Blane and Mark needed the van? And where was Felix Goffman? Do any of them know Cody Carpenter? Or is he a red herring?

She reaches Santa Cruz forty minutes later. The campus is nestled in the mountains and has a bohemian vibe. Meadows and sprawling trees line the drive to the main campus, as do signs for a nature preserve. Girls wearing braids and looking like characters from a sixties hippie movie sit under the immense eucalyptus trees.

She's met by Jay McCray and his Santa Cruz police chief counterpart in the parking area. They all make their way to the dormitories. Keller isn't dialed in to campus procedures and protocols, but it's clear they plan to enter Cody Carpenter's dorm room without a warrant. Just like they did at Santa Clara. She assumes the university requires consent to searches as a condition to living in the dorms.

On the walk, Santa Cruz's chief says, "I checked our databases and talked to my squad. We've had no issues with Cody Carpenter. Last we have him is swiping in on Thursday night."

"It only swipes when they go into the dorms, not out, right?" Keller says. It might be a stupid question, but she doesn't like to assume.

"That's right."

"Witnesses place him at SCU's campus Friday afternoon," Keller says. The Maldonados thought they saw him when they arrived. "So, unless he found a way to enter the dorm without his security card, he hasn't been back to his room since yesterday."

"Sometimes the kids hold the door for each other," McCray observes, which elicits a nod from Santa Cruz's chief.

They get some looks coming into the dormitory. Keller's in plainclothes, but they're met in the entryway by two uniformed campus officers. The students pretend not to be watching, but they are.

They find Cody's room. Unlike the doors to the other rooms, which are decorated with stickers and mini erasable whiteboards and photos hanging from strings, Cody's door is plain.

The chief of Santa Cruz bangs on the door hard three times. Announces that they will enter.

When no one answers, he uses a key card to open the door.

It's quickly apparent no one is in there. Keller examines the room. Two beds, one stripped down to the bare mattress. Laundry day, perhaps. But then she notices that the storage containers under the stripped bed are empty. The desk on this side of the room has nothing on it.

The other side appears lived in, the bed unmade, a tangle of sheets. On the desk there's a stack of books, nothing out of the ordinary.

The uniformed officers are peering inside the closet, the bathroom.

Keller slides open the desk drawer. Inside is a sketch pad.

She extracts it, cracking the spine. A jolt runs through her. The artist is talented but the images are disturbing. On one page, a monster looms over a boy who is walking alone on a street at night. In another, a man is falling to the ground, what appears to be blood and brain matter projecting out of the top of his skull.

She flips through the pages. Chief McCray looks over her shoulder and whistles when he sees the drawings.

"Violent," is all he says.

Keller doesn't respond. They are indeed violent.

"We may have found a future mass shooter," the Santa Cruz chief chimes in, peering at the sketches.

"I don't think so," Keller says, still flipping through the drawings. "They're mostly of self-harm." She points to one of a figure hanging from a noose with a chair kicked over at the feet. Another of a faceless person standing on the edge of what looks like the Golden Gate Bridge.

"This kid's hurting." The sketches alone reveal this. But Keller also knows what the boy saw. His father killing himself after discovering the boy's mother with another man.

One of the uniforms reports they've found nothing. Not even alcohol or gummies, a rarity in any dorm search.

"We need to talk to the roommate and the RA," Santa Cruz's chief says. The officer nods, scurries out of the dorm. Keller wonders if there *is* a roommate given that one side of the room appears uninhabited.

Keller continues examining the sketch pad. The picture on the last page grabs her by the collar.

It's a familiar face. The handsome mug of Dr. David Maldonado. But the sketch artist has drawn devil horns on his forehead and there's a slash through his face.

Like the rip of a knife.

CHAPTER TWENTY-EIGHT

THE GOFFMANS

Alice looks at the bloody sweatshirt that sits on the passenger seat of her car. As soon as she parked in the visitor spot in front of the campus police station she felt a wave of overwhelming anxiety, a sense of impending doom.

She's suffered panic attacks enough over the years to understand that she's not dying—that her shortness of breath, the pain in her chest, the tingling in her hands, are physical manifestations of the maelstrom going on in her head. The questions that kept her up all night: Where is Felix? Why hasn't he called? Whose sweatshirt was in his laundry? And why is it covered with blood?

She starts the breathing exercise the counselor taught her long ago. She began having panic attacks in the early days of her marriage, when her teenage husband was prone to punching holes in the wall. It was the unpredictability of it all—how he could go from smiling and joking to putting a fist through drywall without warning. His fist eventually moved from the wall to Alice. When his aim turned to her little boy, Alice did the only courageous thing she's ever done in her life. She scooped up Felix in her arms, walked to the bus station, and headed west.

Though the panic attacks have subsided over the years, they've never completely gone away. They remain unpredictable, like her ex's rage.

Continuing her deep, measured breaths, she repeats a mantra, "This too shall pass," over and over again. She feels like she's drowning, the water rising and about to swallow her. Alice's mind flits to the student who died this week: Natasha Belov. Was this how she felt trapped in that sea cave?

Alice squeezes her eyes shut. *This too shall pass, this too shall pass, this too shall pass.*

At long last, her heart rate slows and her thoughts begin to clear.

She needs to get out of the car, go into the police station, and turn the bloody sweatshirt over to Chief McCray. It might be connected to the disappearance of the kids. It might help find Felix and his friends.

But her thoughts jump to the file she absconded from the dean's office. The one he's been asking about. The one that told lies about her Felix.

This too shall pass.

As if in a trance, she climbs out of the car, walks to the back of the vehicle, and opens the trunk. There, she throws the blood-covered hoodie next to the file and slams the lid shut.

CHAPTER TWENTY-NINE

THE KELLERS

It's now early afternoon. Twenty hours missing.

Keller's ASAC texted that he's taking command at the SCU campus police station, that he's created a formal task force, that he's called in more agents. It's not surprising. Once it became clear this wasn't just college kids being college kids—and Cynthia Roosevelt started making calls to Washington—there was no way they'd allow a temp agent to run point.

Her phone vibrates in her pocket. She scans the face of the device. It's Cody Carpenter's mom. She takes in a deep breath, answers.

"Hi, um, this is Zoe Carpenter. You left me a message. I'm just out of an emergency surgery and—"

"Thank you for calling back."

"You said it's about Cody. Is everything okay?" She sounds flustered, unnerved. Of course she is. A call from the FBI rattles anyone. But this is also about her son.

"We're trying to locate Cody. When is the last time you heard from him?"

"Not for a couple days. What's going on? Is he okay?"

"He's a person of interest in an ongoing investigation," Keller says.

"He's a *what*?"

Keller deliberates how much to reveal. It's always a careful balance in interviews, the give and take. "There was an attack on a man named David Maldonado, who's visiting the area." Keller pauses. "Parents Weekend for his daughter at Santa Clara University."

"Oh dear god."

Keller waits. The pregnant pause.

"Cody wouldn't. He . . ." Her voice breaks. "My son has been depressed. I've been considering having him withdraw from school. Take a break. He's been through, well, a lot."

"Dr. Maldonado told us what happened."

Keller notices that the woman hasn't asked if David Maldonado is all right.

"Do you have any idea where we might find your son?"

"It's Saturday . . . the dorm? Or library. He hasn't made many friends yet." Her voice wavers. "There was a problem with his roommate, who moved out."

"He's not in the dorm. The computer records show he entered on Thursday night, but he was seen Friday in Santa Clara and there's no record of him returning. Do you have a locator on his phone?"

"Hold on." There's a rustling sound like she's checking her phone. Then what sounds like a gasp.

"What is it?"

"He sent me a text when I was in surgery." Her voice is pure panic.

"It says he loves me. He's sorry."

"Do you have a locator on his phone?" Keller repeats.

Another pause. "He's turned it off."

Keller can't help but think about the boy's sketches. The images of suicide.

"Is there anywhere he likes to go? Somewhere to clear his head?"

"Oh . . . Oh god. He sent photos of him at a place. Where he said he goes to get away from everything." Another pause. "I just sent them to you."

Keller pulls the phone from her ear, opens the text. And feels a chill skitter through her. It's a photo of sunrise over a body of water, two legs swinging over a ledge. Her mind returns to the sketchbook. The figure standing on the brink.

Of the Golden Gate Bridge.

CHAPTER THIRTY

"Any word from your contact?" Keller says breathlessly into the microphone connected to her helmet. She's feeling the weightlessness as the chopper soars through the sky. McCray called in a favor and got a Santa Cruz SAR team to get them to the Golden Gate Bridge—a drive that would've taken an hour and a half in traffic. They'll touch ground in less than twenty minutes. She's had a few flights in Bureau helicopters, but it still makes her anxious.

"Do they see him?" she asks. Cody Carpenter sent his mother what can only reasonably be interpreted as a goodbye note.

McCray shakes his head. "Bridge patrol is searching," he says, his voice distorted in her headset.

The helicopter whizzes through the sky and Keller hopes they're not too late.

McCray is tapping on his phone with intensity. She wonders if he's explaining to someone, the dean of Santa Clara University, perhaps, where he's going, what he's doing. He's in tricky jurisdictional territory. Facilitating the meet at UC Santa Cruz with another campus police department was justifiably within his authority. But charging to San Francisco clearly is not.

Keller's in murky waters herself. She texted her mentor Stan for guidance and, in minimalist Stan fashion, he replied with only a section of the federal criminal code: 18 U.S.C. § 115. She'll look it up later. If Stan is wrong and it means saving a kid, she'll take whatever heat comes her way. Better to ask for forgiveness than permission, as her husband is prone to say.

"If he's there, they'll find him," McCray's voice breaks through the static of the headset. "When I worked in the city back in the day, they'd get about forty jumpers a year. They have a lot of experience . . ."

Keller swallows hard at the bleak statistics.

As if reading her thoughts, McCray says, "My buddy's with the California Highway Patrol and has talked down dozens of people. Saved a lot of lives. They know what they're doing."

"How many didn't he talk down?" Keller wonders out loud.

Soon, Keller can see the magnificent suspension bridge spanning the strait connecting the San Francisco Bay and the Pacific Ocean. The chopper touches down in an area not far from the bridge.

They're met on the ground by a man in a windbreaker and khakis. He and McCray greet each other like old friends. He introduces himself as Anush Rohani-Shukla with the CHP.

"Thanks for coming," McCray says.

"For you, of course. How's the babysitting job at the university going?"

McCray replies, "*Me* babysitting? You seen your girlfriend? I have shoes that are older."

Banter out of the way, the discussion turns all business.

"The patrol made rounds. They haven't seen anyone. They

had a guy last night who took the leap but got caught in the suicide barrier. He's in bad shape—that net's like landing on a cheese grater. But he'll live. He was in his forties and doesn't match your guy."

Rohani-Shukla calls over two young men who wear yellow reflective vests. He asks Keller to show them the photo Cody Carpenter's mother sent to see if they recognize the specific area.

Keller's heart is thumping, adrenaline tearing through her, as the officers debate locales.

One of them says, "I think it's near lamp sixty-eight, they've been doing some construction over there."

Another says, "I think it's on the east side. We kicked a kid out of that area a few weeks ago. He wasn't a jumper, an artist drawing the bay. I can't swear it was your guy, but . . ."

Within minutes, two groups have deployed to two different areas on the bridge. Rohani-Shukla, McCray, and one member of the security patrol go to the area where a kid was seen drawing. It's the most likely locale and it makes sense to send the more experienced team there. Keller isn't trained in suicide prevention, after all. She and the other patrolman rush to the second location.

The young patrolman is serious; his job demands it, she supposes. He takes her to a small area near lamp 68—they appear to map the bridge based on numbered lampposts. It's midafternoon and crawling with foot traffic. Tourists taking selfies. Joggers. Moms pushing strollers. And six lanes of traffic whizzing on the other side of steel barriers. Ominous blue signs are posted along the route: CRISIS COUNSELING. THERE IS HOPE. MAKE THE CALL. Emergency phones punctuate the pathway. It's heartbreaking. She's heard of places like this—a forest in Japan, a sea cliff in Australia—that seem to summon the hopeless who see no other way to escape their pain.

Keller dares a glance over the edge. She feels a current cleave through her at the 250-foot drop into oblivion. It's amazing anyone survives.

The officer stops at a trash can, one of those large concrete cylindrical bins. Behind it is a hinged metal gate. It's padlocked and opens to a pathway largely concealed by overgrown weeds. Keller imagines an eighteen-year-old kid climbing over. The officer unlocks the gate and they head down the slope.

The sudden chime of her phone startles her. She answers the call. It's Cody's mother. She's hysterical, her words tumbling out so fast and frantic they're difficult to comprehend. Cody just sent her a text saying he loves her, but he wants to join his dad. Keller's gut roils: Maybe Cody saw them coming down the hill. He could already be gone.

"We're doing everything we can to find him," she tells Cody's mother.

As she hangs up she spots a figure through the brush below. "I think he's here," she says to the young officer.

The officer talks into his radio, a static-laden voice responds.

"He wasn't at the other location. They're on their way," the officer says. "Wait— What are you doing? We need to wait for—"

Keller is already a dozen yards ahead of him, moving quickly.

She turns back to him. "The kid just texted his mom goodbye. He knows we're here. There's no time."

She doesn't wait for the officer's reply.

She moves slowly down the hill; one wrong step and she could go sliding into the abyss.

"Is the protective net under here?" she asks the officer as he follows.

"It should be. But there are gaps."

Of course there are.

She passes some type of storage shack and heads down another path. Beams jut out where the land and bridge meet. She looks out at the water, recognizing the spot from Cody's photo.

Then she hears a voice.

"Don't come any closer."

CHAPTER THIRTY-ONE

Cody Carpenter wears a Yankees cap under a hoodie, and even from twenty feet away Keller can see the dark circles under his eyes, like he's been here all night. He sits on the ledge, his feet dangling just like in the photo. And the worst part, there's a straight drop down. No security net. One of the gaps.

The bridge patrol officer stands behind her. Even without turning around, she can feel panic radiating off the young officer. They're on their own.

"Hey there," Keller calls out. "Everything okay?"

The boy's head turns. "I said don't come closer." His voice sounds detached.

Keller freezes in place.

She takes a quick look over her shoulder, hoping McCray and the others are close. Not yet. Though people are on the slope above: bystanders capturing the scene on their phones. Outrageous. But there's no way to chase them off.

"I'm Sarah," she says gently.

Cody Carpenter doesn't respond.

She needs to buy time until the others—the ones trained for this—arrive. "I like your hat. You from New York?" she asks. "We just moved here from the city. The weather's better here, for sure. But they don't know how to make pizza."

Keller doesn't know that, but she's guessing it's right. Cody is from Englewood, New Jersey, a commuter town for New York City, but he'll know a good slice of pie.

Still nothing.

When the boy stares back at the water, Keller shuffles a single step closer. She'll take this inch by inch if needed.

"Have you been here all night? You must be hungry. Maybe we can go get something to eat, talk."

"Go away," he says.

There's a resolve in his voice, a clench in his jaw. Building rapport isn't going to work.

He leans slightly forward. This isn't going well.

She needs to take a different approach. In a split second she decides to be direct.

"Dr. Maldonado's going to be okay, Cody."

The boy's head pivots around in surprise at her use of his name. At the reference to Maldonado.

"Just a few scrapes and bruises, a mild concussion. We know you didn't mean to—"

"You don't know anything." His voice is steady, unemotional.

"I'm with the FBI and I spoke to Dr. Maldonado. He won't press charges. Said it's his own fault. We can fix this." Not entirely true, but desperate times . . .

Cody has doe eyes that make him look particularly vulnerable. Her heart aches for him. He watched his father blow his head off while his mom was sneaking off with another man. It doesn't justify whatever he had in store for David Maldonado. But it makes it understandable.

The boy looks out at the water again. He is oddly vacant, like he's dissociated from what's happening.

Keller creeps another step closer.

"I talked to your mom," Keller says. "She's so worried. She said there's nothing that can't be fixed."

"*I* can't be fixed," Cody says.

Keller's mind returns to the sketch notepad. The monsters—the intrusive thoughts—haunting this boy.

"I just want the pain to stop," he says.

"I know," Keller says. She inches closer. "But can I tell you something?"

The kid doesn't respond. Keller is feeling a bit hopeless herself. She's not equipped to do this. But she doesn't dare look behind her to see if the others have arrived to help, doesn't dare take a break in this conversation.

"There have been a lot of people who survived the fall."

Cody's jaw pulses.

Keller lowers her voice, hoping he won't notice she's edging closer.

"And all of them—every single one—said that in the millisecond of flight they had the same thought."

He closes his eyes, not noticing she's so close she could almost touch him now.

"They said that in that fleeting moment they realized that all of the things that had brought them to where you are right now—all of their problems—could be fixed, except for one." Keller pauses, so close now that the ledge is making her queasy.

He doesn't move. Is he listening to her?

"They couldn't fix the decision to jump." Keller waits a beat. "But you can."

Cody sits for a long while, says nothing. Then he abruptly stands, his toes touching the ledge. He takes out his wallet, throws it into the grass. Does the same with his phone.

Keller's heart is jackhammering.

He swivels his head to stare directly at Keller. A look of peace spreads over his face. "You tell David Maldonado this is his fault. Tell him that—"

Before Cody finishes the sentence, she dives for the boy and tackles him football-style from the side, bear-hugging him as she hauls him backward, praying she's propelled them far enough from the ledge.

When Cody realizes what's happening, he thrashes about. They start to slide down the embankment, still tangled together, and Keller feels sheer terror that he might pull them both over.

Then she feels hands gripping her arms. Sees more hands securing the kid. Dragging them both from the ledge.

"Nooooo." The boy is crying and it nearly levels her. As the others put the kid's hands in flex cuffs behind his back, Keller doesn't weaken her embrace. A tear escapes her eye.

"You and your mom are gonna get through this," she whispers.

And she prays this time she's speaking the truth.

CHAPTER THIRTY-TWO

STELLA MALDONADO

Stella claws the metal grille separating their compartment from the driver's section of the van.

"We shouldn't . . . they may be out there, they may come back," Libby says, her voice quavering.

"Do what you want, but I'm not dying in this stupid fucking van," Stella shout-whispers back. She means it: She's not dying here. She's flooded with fear, but no way is she going out like this.

Felix sawed the duct tape securing his wrists on some jagged metal under the side bench in the van, then freed the rest of them. They pulled the tape from over their eyes, wincing as it stung their skin. The interior holds only two benches—it's essentially a stripped metal box. They were lined up on the grimy floor for hours? Days? In the darkness, the haze, it's impossible to tell.

Stella continues yanking at the grille as Felix and Blane slam their shoulders into the back doors, but they're locked and solid.

Mark's on the floor. His breaths are shallow, his shirt covered in red, but he's alive. Stella flashes to the roadside. Where they were frozen in shock at the sight of the gun. Where Mark bravely lunged for the weapon. The awful *pop*.

How did it all come to this? Her mind blazes through the what-ifs. What if she hadn't convinced the others to come to the bonfire? What if she hadn't pressured them to take the psychedelics her new friend supplied? Felix and Libby were reluctant, but Stella used her power over Felix to convince him; he's such a lapdog. And she knew Libby wouldn't be left out. Her mind flickers to the scene in the firelight. When Blane and Mark arrived at Panther Beach, half baked themselves . . . their faces twisted in anger when they saw Stella's friend.

"I can't believe this! You know what she posted about me?" Mark's face, a combination of hurt and anger. Things have been hard for him after everybody found out about his father.

But worse was Felix, the look of betrayal. "Wait, what? It wasn't just Mark that was accused in those posts," he said. "How could you?"

She has the image, almost dreamlike, of Blane and Mark taking off, then Libby and Felix disappearing down the beach into the darkness—Libby's dream-come-true, as she'd been pining for Felix since the first capstone meeting. Libby had been jealous that Felix obviously was into Stella, not her.

Stella doesn't remember much else. The blur of the fire. The sound of laughter. The sound of her own scream.

What if, what if, what if.

The screech of metal on metal brings her back to the present. The back door of the van is buckled, a gap is widening, maybe big enough for them to squeeze through.

"We need to move," Felix says.

He kicks at the door, the opening bigger, then squeezes through the hole. Blane is saying something to Mark, who is whimpering on the floor. Blane helps Mark to his feet, puts Mark's arm around his shoulder to try to help him through.

Libby's already outside, Stella close behind.

Where are they? A dirt road surrounded by woodland.

Felix is tugging on the door again, trying to widen the gap. Mark wails in pain as Blane guides him through the opening. Mark collapses to the ground, blood staining the gravel. Felix pulls him upright.

Stella's heart is galloping. But she's feeling a gush of euphoria. They're going to get out of this. They're going to survive.

Her jubilation vaporizes when she sees the gun trained on them.

CHAPTER THIRTY-THREE

THE KELLERS

When Keller arrives at the Santa Clara University police station, she's struck by the size of the media encampment. Outside the parking garage, she's forced to walk a gauntlet of questions:

Does the FBI have any leads on the missing students?

Do you believe the man at the bridge is behind the disappearances?

Why did he attack one of the parents?

Some are saying what you did on the bridge was reckless . . . How do you respond?

How's it feel to be a hero?

She ignores them all. Stan taught her years ago to pretend not to hear the questions. On-screen the audience can't tell. And saying *no comment* only fuels the fire. She's surprised by the speed at which they've gathered information. They know she's with the Bureau. Know about the attack on Dr. Maldonado. About the rescue on the Golden Gate Bridge. She has plenty of criticisms of the media, but she'll grant them one thing: They're tenacious. The problem is that sometimes tenacity gets in the way of the facts.

The number of news vans and satellite trucks and primping TV reporters is matched only by the variety of law enforcement types crowding the station house. The story of five missing college students—whom social media have given their own hashtag, #TheFive—is getting a frenzied quality Keller has seen only a few times in her career.

The conference room is now too small to contain the law enforcement masses, and the task force is occupying the bullpen of the station. When she enters, there's a smattering of slow claps that sound more like sarcasm than praise. A lean man with a military-style buzz cut takes note of her arrival. He comes over, sticks out his hand. "Richard Peters. Nice to meet you in person." Her new boss, the ASAC of the San Jose office.

"Trouble appears to follow you, Special Agent Keller," he says. "And internet fame." He holds up his phone and she understands. The clickbait headline reads: *Hero agent saves suspect in missing college student investigation.*

She considers apologizing for the spectacle, but says nothing. One of Bob's big rules: Don't apologize when you've done nothing wrong. Shoot, she needs to call Bob before he sees the news in his feed.

ASAC Peters continues: "The director called—after he got *another* call from State. So I need to take point."

"Whatever I can do to help," Keller says. It's not out of line, given the media attention and VIP parents of the missing students.

Like Peters, she'd trust her own people before anyone else in a crisis. Regardless of reputation and references.

Still, what Peters says next surprises her: "We need you to take a lower profile."

A polite way of saying she's being sidelined. "Understood," she says, knowing fighting it is pointless. "What can I do to help?"

He thinks on this. "The geofence data you wanted. Apparently there's a problem."

"Yeah?"

Peters explains that Google rejected their request for location data on phones in the vicinity of the spot where the students' phones last pinged.

"They used to provide baseline reports without a warrant, so we assumed they would turn it over, particularly given the urgency, but they've changed their policy."

Keller isn't surprised. Geofence data requests have become controversial, with privacy advocates saying the government shouldn't have access to the location of private citizens without probable cause they committed a crime.

"I can run point on getting a warrant," she says as enthusiastically as she can muster.

Peters excuses himself without saying more, then stands at the head of the room and waits for the rumbling of the fledgling task force to die down.

He starts by identifying the task force subgroups: one on CCTV capture and analysis, one to coordinate ground searches, one to handle electronic forensics, one to handle the parents. He then reiterates the BOLO on The Five, the Mystery Machine van, and Blane Roosevelt's father. Says the perp or perps have made no contact, no demands. Reminds them the clock is ticking.

"We also have a rumor-control team. To that end, the university and Bureau have issued statements that private citizens should refrain from taking to social media. That any false information or accusations will be prosecuted to the extent permitted by law. We don't want what happened in Idaho to happen here." He's referring to the murders of several college students a few years ago. Social-media sleuths fueled rumors, even accused innocent people of the crime, before the police arrested the alleged perp.

"The dean is losing his shit because it's Parents Weekend and he's already had a student die this week." Peters rolls his eyes.

Keller feels someone edging next to her. It's the student intern, Annie Hafeez. Her twinkling eyes hold Keller's for a moment, then she nudges her head to the side to signal Keller to follow, and walks off.

Keller decides to humor her. She waits a moment, then threads through the crowd, following Annie's swaying black hair. The intern steps into a tiny office. It probably was a broom closet until it was cleared out for interns. Photos of the young woman's family are pinned to the wall: An older couple. Annie with two other young women who must be her sisters. Three photos of a golden retriever.

"I have more intel," Annie says. "I couldn't find the posts on Rizz about Mark Wong. They must've been pulled down. But I talked to some friends and—"

"You really shouldn't be . . ." Keller lets the admonishment fade. "Did you tell your supervisor?"

"No," Annie says. "Well, I tried. He told me to get coffee and was otherwise too busy gossiping about you going viral with all the bridge videos." Her eyes are alight now. "I googled you and I saw those big cases you handled, and—"

Keller holds up a hand. She follows a few simple rules in her career: no showboating, no gossip, no complaining. Also: Loose lips sink ships. She raises her brows, signaling Annie to get to it.

"My friend Gigi is friends with the RA of the dorm."

"Campisi Hall?"

"Yeah, and she knows all the gossip and drama in the dorm."

Keller waits for her to continue.

"That kid Felix Goffman is a freak."

Keller furrows her brow. That's contrary to everything she's learned about the son of the dean's secretary. Though most of what she's learned is from the interview notes with his mom. And mothers don't always see their sons with clarity.

"Apparently he was, like, obsessed with Stella. Was basically stalking her or something."

"Stella Maldonado?"

Annie nods.

"And get this," Annie says. "Libby was into Felix and she's furious that Stella doesn't even like him but leads him on for the fun of it."

It's interesting college-kid drama but it doesn't explain much. It's consistent with the interview of Libby's parents: Stella and Libby in a fight, Stella breaking Libby's phone.

They're interrupted by the sound of people running past the office door. Curious, they head back to the bullpen and the room, full minutes ago, is nearly empty, save for a guy in a campus police uniform.

"Where is everyone?" Keller asks.

"They found Blane Roosevelt's father."

CHAPTER THIRTY-FOUR

On any other day, Keller would rush out of the station house and join the rest of the team tracking down a person of interest in a time-sensitive investigation. Blane Roosevelt's father, who by all accounts shouldn't have been anywhere near SCU, is one of the last people seen with Blane before he vanished. But Keller wasn't invited, purposefully so. And she's been ordered to keep a low profile, to stand down. Work on getting the geofence data. She can't disobey a direct order on her first day. Or can she?

She decides, *no*. She needs this assignment. For Pops. For Bob. Besides, her gut tells her that Blane Roosevelt's father—a disgruntled ex-husband and bitter novelist—has nothing to do with the disappearance of The Five. He should be interviewed, for sure. But the response from her ASAC and the newly forged task force, so many bodies rushing to wherever they've found him, seems disproportionate. Killing a mosquito with a sledgehammer . . . another Stan-ism.

Fate in the form of text messages confirms she's making the

right decision. They're from the AUSA who is dealing with Google's legal investigations specialist on the geofence request.

They say we need warrant for each phone

Keller texts back:

So let's get them

When he doesn't reply right away, she calls the guy.

"It's not that simple," he says. "Recent case law is against us. We can't just get a list of all phones in a particular area without probable cause for each particular phone. Those days are over."

"This could break the case," Keller says. "If we know who was in the same area as the students when their phones last pinged, it could identify the perp or witnesses."

"Sorry, I can't take this to a judge," he says.

To hell with that.

CHAPTER THIRTY-FIVE

Keller's not one to go over someone's head, but the circumstances warranted it. She reached out to Stan and, as is his way, he made it happen. Less than two hours later, she stands under the impressive portico of Olympic Country Club. When Stan told her to meet the assistant U.S. attorney there, she didn't know what to make of it. Government lawyers don't tend to make enough to belong to hundred-grand-a-year clubs. But then she understood: They're there to see a judge.

In the entryway, there's a cocksure-looking man in his early thirties. He wears a suit, standing out from the old-money casual wear of the members scuttling around the club.

Keller approaches. "Cameron?" she says.

He nods, shakes her hand dismissively.

"Apologies for interrupting your weekend," Keller says. A breach of Bob's no-apologies rule, but sometimes it helps build rapport.

"It's fine. My boss said Letko was too scared to try to get a warrant, which is typical," he says, referring to the original AUSA assigned to get the data from Google. "Time to send in the big dog."

Keller has met cocky prosecutors before. The job yields a lot of power and it can go to your head. She's also concluded over the years that the cocky ones tend to be the least effective. They often charge in without all the facts, tend to lack empathy for victims, treat the system like it's a big game.

"We're meeting the judge here?" Keller asks.

He nods, like it's a dumb question.

"Judge Henry?" Keller asks. Libby Akana's father, a judge himself, told Keller that Judge Henry would sign whatever papers they put in front of him.

"I wish. The duty judge for emergencies this weekend is Romero. *Linda* is a card-carrying member of the ACLU."

Keller doesn't like how he uses the judge's first name, but says nothing. She's also annoyed that if he'd consulted her before rushing the warrant, they might've gotten the papers in front of Ken Akana's friend Judge Henry.

A man in golf attire materializes and leads them through the club and outside. The course spans out into the distance. Lush greens and sand traps and lakes. They're taken by golf cart along a sidewalk that carves a path through the green and then onto the rolling course. Rounding a hill, they see a petite woman taking a swing. The ball soars into the air.

The cart stops and the player—a woman less than five feet tall but somehow giant at the same time—scrutinizes them.

The lawyer says to Keller, "*I* do the talking." He gets out of the cart and approaches the judge, Keller following after him.

"Your Honor, Assistant U.S. Attorney Cameron Greene. I understand your clerk advised that we were coming."

The judge's mouth pinches shut. "The warrant."

"Yes. We apologize for the interruption, but it's urgent. The data could help us find five missing college students who could be in great peril."

The judge snaps her fingers at the man driving the golf cart and he hurries over and hands the judge a sheaf of papers. As she reads, her brow crinkles.

"I can't sign this."

"Your Honor?"

"You know how many of these geofence warrants I got last year? It's out of control."

"Your Honor, respectfully, this is a matter of life and death and . . ."

"'A matter of life and death'! Why didn't you say so?"

"Your Honor, I—"

"Do you know what the Fourth Amendment requires?" she interrupts. "Does it say, go ahead, search away, do whatever you want if it's a matter of life and death?"

He cricks his neck, his bravado from moments ago fading in the wind.

"Well," the judge says, "does it say that? Is that what the Fourth Amendment says?"

"The Fourth Amendment requires probable cause of criminal activity."

"And . . . ?"

He's silent, like he's not sure what she's prodding him to say.

So the judge says it for him: "And *particularity*. The Constitution requires probable cause that is particularized to the person to be searched or items to be seized. Show me where in this"—she waves the warrant papers in the air—"you describe with particularity the persons to be searched or places to be seized. It's a fishing expedition. You don't know that *anyone* who was located in the geofence has committed *any* crime. You don't even know who they are."

Keller watches a bead of sweat roll down the AUSA's forehead.

"And let's put aside the Fourth Amendment," the judge continues. "Where's the basis for federal jurisdiction? All I've heard is that there are some missing persons. Last I looked, that's not a federal matter."

AUSA Greene is silent, like he's had the shit kicked out of him. And he has.

"Who are you?" Judge Romero says to Keller, finally acknowledging her.

"Special Agent Sarah Keller."

The judge shakes her head, disappointed. "Mr. Greene thinks he can get a warrant based on little more than 'life and death.' So what's the Bureau have to say about all this?"

Despite the dressing down, Keller likes this judge.

"Your Honor, if I can respond to both of your questions, starting with jurisdiction?" She remembers Stan's text.

"Title eighteen section one-fifteen prohibits assault, kidnapping, or murder—or conspiracy to do those acts—on the immediate family members of government officials. One of the missing students is the son of a government official, so there is a clear basis for jurisdiction. The conspiracy might involve the other students, so they're covered as well."

Keller can't swear on it, but she thinks she sees the corners of the judge's mouth rise a trace.

"But that doesn't solve the Fourth Amendment problems."

"I understand the court's concern with the overuse of geofence warrants. But this one is narrowly tailored, particularized."

"Not in these papers it's not," the judge says, flailing the affidavit in support of the warrant around again.

"Given the urgency of this matter, Mr. Greene didn't have time to incorporate information we have gathered as this investigation progressed."

The judge rests on her golf club, possibly amused.

"We have consent for the location data for the missing students' phones and an additional phone one of the students borrowed from a friend. The devices were last located within a fifty-yard radius of a section of Rancho San Antonio County Park. Given the students' disappearance, it is probable that anyone in that remote area at the time their phones went dark could be the perpetrator. We believe that the geofence will capture only a small number of phones within that discrete time and place, so this is not one of those cases where we'd rake in hundreds of other devices."

The judge frowns, looks out at her next hole. Then says: "Put what you just said in an amended warrant, and I'll direct my clerk to enter my electronic signature."

"Thank you, Your Honor," Keller says.

Cameron Greene, the prosecutor who insisted on doing all the talking, says nothing all the way back to the clubhouse.

CHAPTER THIRTY-SIX

On the drive home from the country club, Keller's mind churns. Maybe they'll get lucky with the geofence data from the warrant, but that's still going to take a little time. Results tomorrow at the earliest.

Until then, what are they missing? The kids' phones all last pinged at Rancho San Antonio. It's crazy not a single CCTV camera caught the van. She wonders if the video forensics team missed something, an camera at a gas station or Ring doorbell or ATM camera. She checks the time on the dash. It's six o'clock.

What the hell. A second set of eyes can't hurt. She resets the GPS and follows it down the 280 to the park. Her mind continues to whirl as she drives, trying to make sense of the mess of dead ends. Finally, she takes the exit. The park is five minutes out. She's not paying any attention to the dot on the GPS now. Instead, she's studying the landscape. For any businesses, any homes, that might have cameras.

She tugs up a service road and through a narrow lane with trees on either side. Could any hunters have set up some cameras they use to track game? Unlikely. Hunting wouldn't be allowed in the conservation area. How about campers or people who put dashcams on their vehicles? Needle in a haystack. And it's likely someone would've already come forward, given the growing media attention on the case.

She pulls into Rancho San Antonio. A smattering of cars and trucks and campers fill the parking lot. A few hikers are making it back to their vehicles. In the distance, figures stride up the hill, probably for a view of the sunset. There are signs identifying the various hiking paths and landmarks. But none of them appears to have a trail camera.

She considers getting out of her car, taking one of the paths. But it's a waste of time. McCray's team has canvassed the area. And she needs some family time, dinner with Bob and the kids, to recharge. She circles the lot, then makes her way out.

She accelerates on the desolate road, speeding well past the limit. Her thoughts return again to the weirdness of this case: five missing college students. She could understand one. Even two. But five? What is she missing?

She spies a large warehouse looming in the distance. It's too far, she thinks, to have any cameras capture vehicles traversing this road. She wonders what type of facility it is. Storage perhaps. Maybe an Amazon warehouse filled with products. That seems to be confirmed when she sees a line of semitrucks heading out of the facility. Maybe they're on a schedule.

She taps the brakes.

If so, maybe one of the truckers saw something? Saw the Mystery Machine.

Unlikely.

But something makes her yank the wheel to the left, turning onto the service road leading to the warehouse.

CHAPTER THIRTY-SEVEN

It's not an Amazon warehouse. Keller realizes this after she passes truck after truck with the purple-and-orange FedEx logo on their sides.

She stops at a security checkpoint outside the fenced facility. The guard perks up when he sees her FBI credentials. He speaks into a phone with someone and Keller is quickly granted entry.

She's met by a man in a short-sleeve button-up shirt. He wears one of those pocket protectors, like nerds in eighties movies.

"George G. Peacoat," he says, sticking out his hand. He has a Southern accent. She can't place it, but it reminds her of something. The voice of a character from one of those Pixar movies the kids used to watch over and over.

"What can I do you for, Special Agent . . . ?"

"Keller," she replies.

She explains that she's working the missing SCU student investigation. He's of course heard of it like everyone else.

"Do you have any cameras at the facility that could reach out to the service road?"

"We do not," he says with law enforcement efficiency.

Keller sighs.

"I can do you one better," he adds with a grin.

She stares at him, waits.

"Six hundred and fifty-two vehicles leave this facility every day, departing on the hour, twenty-four-seven, each with state-of-the-art dash and interior cams to ensure the safety of our drivers and the communities we serve."

He says this like it's a promotional video for FedEx, but she's liking this guy and his intensity. The pride in his work.

"Do you know where and what time we're talking about?" he asks.

She tells him.

"Come with me."

Keller follows as he treks down a corridor, and they stop in a room that has lockers. He opens one, hands her a hard hat and a safety vest.

She doesn't question it, and slips on the vest, dons the helmet.

Wearing the same gear himself, Peacoat pushes through two large swinging doors, and Keller marvels at the massive warehouse. It's loud with the roar of a maze of conveyor belts and industrial fans and other machinery as employees in purple jumpsuits unload, sort, and inspect thousands of boxes and packages that make their way along the complex lines.

"Impressive," Keller says over the noise.

Peacoat gives her a satisfied nod.

On the other side of the facility, they pass through another set of doors and back into an office space. Keller is surprised at how quiet it is, given the deafening rumble on the other side of the doors.

"We have video from all the trucks leaving the facility," Peacoat says as they continue walking at a fast clip. "Maybe they caught something in your timeframe."

"That would be great. But we don't have time for a lot of paperwork and—"

"When Corporate assigned me here," Peacoat interrupts, "I said, 'This is *my* domain.'" He looks intently at Keller. "Kids are missing. We don't need no darn paperwork."

He leads her to a security center where a woman sits at a workstation in front of an array of monitors.

"Everybody thinks we're just glorified mail carriers," Peacoat says. "But we are one of the most efficient operations in the U.S. of A., including our great armed forces." He instructs the tech to pull up the truck video recordings from Friday night.

As they wait, Peacoat speaks into a walkie-talkie, responding to questions from the floor.

"I appreciate you doing this," Keller says. "I know this is out of the ordinary."

Peacoat shakes his head in disagreement. "If you could see the things I've seen."

Keller tries not to smile. It's driving her crazy, the guy's voice. She's thinking it's a character from the movie *Cars*.

"We get weapons, venomous snakes, drugs, and that was just last week. And we have a good relationship with the Bureau. You know Trudy Banks at the San Francisco field office?"

Keller shakes her head. "I'm from the New York office, here on temporary assignment."

"Brought in the big guns because of the missing kids," he speculates.

"Something like that," she says.

Soon, the woman working the computer has pulled up video

from the trucks that left the facility last Friday between 7 and 9 p.m., before and after the missing students' phones went dead.

"We had some hazmat last month, had to clear the entire facility. Thought it was ricin powder. Turned out to be flour. Some special type from Italy." Peacoat smiles, shows his crooked teeth. "Being shipped to a baker shop. I told my team: Always do the legwork before you waste the feds' time."

He's interrupted when the tech calls out that she's found something. Keller and Peacoat watch the screen.

At 8:07 p.m., the Mystery Machine passes the intersection, its image caught by a FedEx truck. The video is clear, but the van is driving fast, racing toward the park.

"Can you slow that down?" Keller asks.

The tech nods like she's already on it and plays back the video in slow motion.

In the driver's seat is a familiar face: Blane Roosevelt. Next to him on the passenger side, Mark Wong. The video doesn't show the rest of the interior. Are the other students in back?

Keller gets closer to the monitor, examines the two young men. They're stone-faced, serious. Did someone in the back of the van have a gun on them, forcing them to drive to Rancho San Antonio? Or were they heading there of their own volition? The two boys were known as pranksters, party guys, so their serious expressions seem out of character.

"This is about twenty minutes before their phones last pinged. Can you find other trucks that were at that same intersection, say, a little *after* the phones went dead?"

The woman at the workstation nods, starts tapping on the keyboard.

This is a break, Keller knows. And with—what did Peacoat say?—some six hundred trucks leaving this facility every day, they're going to need a team to come here and go through a massive amount of video data.

"What in tarnation . . ." Peacoat says, breaking Keller's thoughts.

She looks at the screen. It's the Mystery Machine, racing away from the park.

The tech has zoomed in on the driver again. But it's not Blane and Mark in the front seats. Now it's a single person whose face is concealed by a mask—one of those pullover Halloween masks made of plastic with eyeholes.

Peacoat continues: "Is that a . . ."

"Yeah, it's a Smurf mask."

CHAPTER THIRTY-EIGHT

THE ROOSEVELTS

"What the fuck, Hank?"

They sit in the back of Cynthia Roosevelt's bullet-resistant SUV, her ex-husband looking like a chastened schoolboy. Smelling like a Dumpster after his bender, then brief stint in custody.

"I don't need this."

"What you need is a shower."

"I appreciate you picking me up. But what is it you want, Cynthia?"

"I want to find our son."

"You think I don't?"

She wants to say that maybe he shouldn't have gone on a bender, maybe he shouldn't have lied about not coming to Parents Weekend, wasted everyone's time thinking he was involved with the students disappearing. It took them all of a half hour to get footage from that fleabag motel to confirm he was there when the kids' phones last pinged.

"Why are you in Santa Clara?" Cynthia asks. "What's going on?"

He hesitates. "I got laid off. From the college. I was just feeling lost. I wanted to see Blane."

"Well, maybe don't fuck your TA."

"That's not why they didn't renew my contract. It has nothing to do with—" He stops, as if knowing it's pointless. "Did you ever ask yourself why I did it?"

Cynthia shakes her head. "Because you're a selfish asshole. That's why."

"Whatever you say."

"Oh don't even," she says. "Fine, humor me. Why did you feel the need to fuck a twenty-two-year-old?"

"She's thirty. A grown woman."

Cynthia puffs a sarcastic laugh through her nose. He's unbelievable. Even now, he's justifying.

"And you want to know why? Try having someone look disappointed at you every day. From the moment you wake up until you go to bed. Someone who's embarrassed of you." Hank looks away.

Perfect, he's blaming *her.* That's rich. But they don't have time for this. She feels a dull ache in her chest. A strange stew of anger and sadness. Deep down she knows what happened to their marriage isn't only his fault. "Look, we need to focus on Blane. Did you see anything on Friday night? Did he say anything?"

"No. He was in a hurry. Didn't want his *mother* mad at him for being late."

Cynthia represses the urge to respond to the jab.

"We spoke for less than five minutes. I told the cops everything already."

"Tell me."

He tells her how he was already in Santa Clara on Friday when they spoke on the phone. That he thought he and Blane could spend a little time together while Cynthia was working, since she's *always* working. That Blane had fallen off his skateboard but wasn't hurt. That he was in a hurry to get to the dinner. That Blane got a text—one that Hank assumed was from Cynthia—and seemed flustered and rushed off.

"We agreed to meet after. He was going to call me. He never did."

"You saw nothing?" Of course he didn't. He's useless.

"I'm sorry."

Cynthia releases a breath. "Here's what we're going to do. My team has secured a safe house nearby. You're going to stay there by your phone in case he calls you."

He doesn't respond but he doesn't protest either.

"You are *not* to talk to the media or leave that house. These internet people and reporters are already on a tear with that spectacle at the motel."

"You're worried I'll embarrass you," he says.

She doesn't say he already has. That idiot lead agent—what's his name?—created a media frenzy by storming the motel with at least a dozen other agents. The raid has been all over the news.

Worse, Cynthia's chief of staff showed her a viral video of Hank blinking into the sunlight as he's perp-walked out of the shitty motel. Paul says TikTok has been blowing up with conspiracy theories, people tracking down Hank's former students, combing through his novels, accusing Hank of killing Blane and the others.

"I'm not embarrassed," she lies. "We just need to stop the flow of misinformation. It's hurting the investigation, diverting resources."

Hank then does something she's never seen before in all their years together. He starts crying. Bawling, really. "I'm worried, Cynth, that—he's hurt or—" He's gulping for breaths.

Cynthia straightens her spine. She didn't cry when her ambassador father died. Didn't cry when Blane was abducted. Didn't cry one time during the divorce. And she's not crying now. Because they're going to find her son. Because she knows that Blane comes from *her* stock and he won't go down without a fight.

CHAPTER THIRTY-NINE

THE KELLERS

Keller opens the front door and is hit with the smell of cooked meat.

The twins call out from the kitchen, "Mommy!" A sound that always fills her up with something warm, something that takes away any darkness that clings to her from the job.

Heather and Michael bound into the entryway. Their faces are tomato-red from the beach.

"It's Taco Tuesday!" Michael says.

Bob materializes, and his bald head also glows red.

"You know it's Saturday, not Tuesday?"

Bob grins. "It's Tuesday somewhere."

"I don't think that's how it works and—" She stops herself. "How's Pops feeling?"

"Starving," Bob replies. "We waited for you. Let's get a move on." He grabs Heather's hips and they start a conga line. Michael latches on and he gestures for Keller to join. Keller shakes her head, but she reaches down and joins the procession.

The dining room table is set for a feast. Music floats in the background from a portable Bluetooth speaker Bob brought in his luggage.

At the table, Pops looks much better than when they arrived. A sparkle in his eyes. Skin less ashen. The magic of Bob. And the kids. She kisses Pops on the head and then takes her seat.

After they say grace, Heather passes the bowl of ground beef to Pops, who takes a scoop and jams it into a taco shell.

"You had an eventful first day," Pops says. "Already famous."

"You're famous, Mommy?" Heather asks, wonderment in her voice.

"No, silly. Pops is just playing. Right, Grandpa?"

Pops winks at Keller, passes the meat down the line.

Bob has disappeared into the kitchen, and when he returns he holds a tray of frozen drinks. Margs for Keller and Bob; frozen lemonades for Pops and the kids.

Pops is not pleased. "I can handle a cocktail."

"Not according to your nurse," Bob says.

Pops shakes his head.

"And I already confiscated your secret bottle of Jack," Bob adds, "so don't *even*."

Pops narrows his eyes, but his lips curl up ever so slightly at the edges. "How'd you know about my stash?"

"I spent my teenage years siphoning it. I was always amazed you didn't notice how watered down your booze tasted."

Pops gives a mischievous smile, eyes the twins. "Teenage years will be here before you know it. My revenge is coming."

"Dad," Bob says, changing the subject, "Janet texted, said she may be in town for work Monday. She's trying to come in a day early to see everyone."

"Aunt Janet's coming tomorrow?" Heather says. Bob's sister is another ray of light. And a fountain of gifts for the kids.

"I said she's going to *try*," Bob says, tempering expectations. Janet is the epitome of the cool aunt, but also has an erratic work schedule, traveling most of the year.

After dinner, Keller and Bob sit on the bed in Janet's old room, the kids and Pops down for the night. Bob still has some toothpaste caked on the corner of his mouth. She thumbs it away, gives him a kiss.

Bob hasn't asked about her day yet. They're simpatico that way. He knows she'll talk when she's ready. Knows she needs some family time to decompress. But she also senses that something's bothering him. Something other than his father's condition.

"Everything okay?" Keller asks at last.

"You know you're all over the internet." He pauses, then adds, "Again."

She nods. "My new ASAC made that clear. Sidelined me over it."

His face softens. "I'm sorry."

How did she find this man? He doesn't try to make it better, doesn't try to fix things, he just says the two perfect words. And listens. But there's something wrong, she knows him well enough to understand this much.

"Seriously, what's wrong?" she says.

He hesitates.

"Robert Jerel Keller . . ." she says. He's gotten unrelenting grief over his middle name. It's some weird combination of two family names. She can't remember the details. Just that his friends love to tease him about the name Jerel. And Keller uses it when she's mock scolding him.

"I watched the videos from the bridge. If they hadn't grabbed you . . . you and the kid could've gone over."

"The videos make it look scarier than it was. I was totally safe."

A lie, but sometimes you have to.

His mouth turns downward. Bob isn't a fool.

"I need you to be more careful. *We* need you to be more careful." He swallows hard, like there's a lump in his throat. "We need you, G-woman."

Keller experienced life-threatening injuries on her first brush with internet fame: a cold case involving a workplace slaying at a Blockbuster video when she was pregnant with the twins. She can't put Bob through that again.

"I promise," she says.

He nods. That's it. Given the silence in her home growing up, so many grievances stewing but never resolved, she always marvels at Bob's ability to draw her out, listen, then move on.

"Any closer to finding the students?" he asks.

Keller shakes her head.

"One of the fathers, the writer, has been all over the news."

"Dead end."

They found Blane Roosevelt's father at a low-end motel. Drunk and out of it, and quickly cleared of any involvement in the disappearance of The Five.

Keller tells him about Blane's mother, the high-powered State Department official with a bounty on her head. About the Maldonados—Stella's father being attacked, or more accurately, chased-with-intent-to-scare by a disturbed young man caught in the cross fire of infidelity. The one she had to save on the bridge.

And she tells Bob about her detour on the way home to the FedEx facility and the video of someone in a Smurf mask driving the Mystery Machine away from where the students' phones last pinged.

"Wait, so the frat has a van painted like the one from *Scooby-Doo*?" An admiring look spreads across Bob's face. "And nice find with the truck videos," he adds.

"I'm not sure my new ASAC thinks so."

She reported the lead to Peters. He reminded her that he'd asked her to keep a lower profile, but he seemed to forgive the transgression since it provided a lead. She imagines the video-forensic arm of the task force wasn't thrilled with Keller since they'd concluded there were no cameras in the area to mine for clues. Peters likely has them working all night at the FedEx facility.

"You think whoever is in the Smurf mask abducted the kids?" Bob asks.

"Or it's one of the kids themselves."

So many leads, so many dead ends. It's rare for a case to identify multiple potential perps in such a short period. Even rarer for so many leads to go nowhere. Most violent crimes are solved relatively quickly. Typically, criminals confess. Keller's instructor at the academy said prisons would be half empty if people just exercised their Fifth Amendment right to remain silent. Even if there was no confession, it usually didn't take Sherlock Holmes to solve a serious crime. If you're the victim of violence, you probably know the perpetrator. Husbands or boyfriends, typically.

And they're usually no match for DNA, modern criminology, cell data, Ring cameras.

"So other than your *Scooby-Doo* van and Smurf video, you have nothing?" Bob asks.

Keller nods, feeling a heaviness infuse her body. "And the longer the students are gone, the less likely they'll survive."

CHAPTER FORTY

MARK WONG

Mark's shoulder burns like he's been poked by a cattle prod. He's been shot. Fucking shot! It's his own fault. He tried to be a hero, save them all. But he should've known he was too big, too clumsy, too slow to save anyone. When they busted out of the van, he thought they might escape. But that hope was short-lived. They're back inside, the duct tape securing their wrists and ankles even tighter. The captors drove around for a long while, but now they're parked.

What the hell are these weirdos doing with them? Ransom? Kidnapping shit? Blane's mom is some big shot. That has to be it. But this duo—in blue Smurf masks they must've found in the van, left over from Alpha Kappa's Smurf party—don't look like kidnappers. They talk in whispers, but it's clear they're arguing about something. Maybe over whether he and the others live or die.

He thought life couldn't be more of a shit show. After that chick posted about his father on Rizz, freaking everyone out. He should've known the hot junior wasn't into a freshman. But she *was* into him. Touching his arm, laughing at his jokes, the deep eye contact, making him feel like he was the only person in the room amid the antics of the fraternity party. She nearly spit out her beer when he did the funny *Flashdance* parody: galloping in place while the crowd sang "Maniac" and sprayed beer all over him from the keg hose. He stole the bit from the movie *Tommy Boy*, which was fitting because that's what everyone calls him. It's something he learned as a kid after his dad's arrest: Make yourself the clown before they clown you.

He thinks of that party, Blane stumbling over. Shirtless as always. Like the rest of the pledge class, Blane idolizes Matthew McConaughey in all his ripped ab glory. Blane introduces himself to the junior girl, taps cups with Mark in toast of nothing. Or maybe in honor of a girl showing interest in Mark.

"How's pledging going?" she asks them both.

Blane, in his recently acquired California accent, says, "It's a'ight."

"Even the hazing?"

She seems to be fishing. Something the pledge master warned them about. It only takes one report to shut down the house. The brothers are like la Cosa Nostra—they have a code, omertà.

"Nah, just funny shit. Nothing like the movies and rumors," Blane says.

"What do you mean?" she asks. She's tipsy, but seems more curious than trying to entrap.

Blane smiles. "Like, they set a weekly quota for how many phone numbers we need to get from girls—it's designed to increase our confidence, our game." He grins. "And the other stuff is more comical than anything: The other night they made Urkel hang out with the furries to teach him about accepting our differences." Blane says this with a hint of sarcasm.

She laughs. *"What?"*

"You know, the furries—they dress up in animal costumes and have, like, sex parties where they hook up wearing the outfits. They have meetings every Tuesday at Hungry Hound." Blane takes out his phone, shows her a photo of the pledge they call Urkel buried in a group of furries.

Mark adds, "He said they were really cool. And why not? Everybody's got kinks."

"Really?" she says to Mark. "What's your kink?" There's a seductive tenor in her voice.

"I'm gonna jump," Blane tells them, his eyes flashing at Mark.

Later, Mark and the junior girl sit amid the light of a fire someone started in a metal drum on the patio of Hangover.

She talks about her father, who's overprotective of her, emotionally unavailable to her mother. Both her parents were raised in hard circumstances in Bulgaria, where they were taught that life and love were transactional, she says. And her dad's business requires him to associate with dangerous men.

The thing about alcohol is that it not only makes you lose your inhibitions, it hinders your judgment. That's what leads Mark to share his own sob story, thinking it might help them connect. And he tells her a secret he's kept from everyone. About his father.

It takes only a moment to realize the disclosure was a mistake. How she edges her chair away from his. How she quickly takes off.

Back in the house he finds Blane sitting on the couch playing *Street Fighter 7* next to his Big, both focused intently on the game.

"Where'd she go, bro?" Blane asks, his eyes flitting from the television to Mark. He lowers the controller, seeming to sense something went south. He examines Mark for a moment then abandons the game, comes over, puts a hand on Mark's shoulder.

He's a good friend, Blane.

"It's for the best," Shaggy interjects, eyes still fixed on the television screen.

"Why's that?" Mark asks.

"'Cause I've heard about that girl; she's crashy, bro."

"Crashy?" Mark says.

"Crazy *and* trashy."

SUNDAY

CHAPTER FORTY-ONE

THE KELLERS

Keller wakes from an uneasy sleep to the sound of her phone vibrating on the nightstand. It takes her a moment to realize they aren't back home in New York. That disoriented feeling when you travel. But she remembers she's not traveling. She's a Bay Area resident for the indefinite future. She feels a twinge of anxiety thinking about her less-than-illustrious start: already an internet meme from the Golden Gate Bridge incident, already sidelined by her new boss. But there's something far more pressing: five missing students whose chances for a happy ending diminish with every passing second.

The phone continues to rattle. She sees it's a call from her ASAC, 3:40 a.m. Probably not good news. Good news can wait until morning.

"Agent Keller," she answers, trying to sound awake, though she's not fooling anyone. Bob isn't snoring, thank goodness.

"It's Peters. We need all hands on deck."

She doesn't reply, processing.

"We found the van."

The *Scooby-Doo* van. By the tone of his voice, this isn't good news.

An hour later, Keller lingers at the periphery of the patch of gravel off Highway 17. The two-lane road has no streetlights and is illuminated by only the headlamps of the cluster of vehicles crammed to the side. Flares burn in the distance, warning drivers to slow as they approach the scene. On either side of the road are stands of evergreens. A thick stench of smoke clogs the air. Burning rubber and plastic.

The van, once a tribute to a beloved cartoon, is now a smoldering pile of metal. Torched.

Keller sees campus police chief Jay McCray, also on the periphery, and walks over to him.

"Bodies?" she asks.

"No, thank god."

She looks out at her ASAC, who's talking to a small group.

McCray continues: "Burned to destroy any evidence."

"What the hell is going on?" Keller says, as much to herself as to McCray.

He shakes his head.

"I was surprised to get the call from Peters," Keller says. "He'd made it pretty clear that my help isn't, um, needed."

"Same," McCray says. Then adds: "But they need us for the search. They're shorthanded with the other search team still scouring the park." McCray looks out at the trees lining the road.

Keller understands. Since the van was torched, maybe The Five are in the area. Or their bodies are. Her heart sinks at the thought.

"So, Blane Roosevelt's father was a dead end?" she asks.

"I only know what I've seen on TV," he says. "I'm not exactly in the loop."

"No ransom demands to any of the parents?" Keller asks. This is one instance where she'd welcome a demand. It would increase the odds the students are alive. Dead hostages aren't valuable.

McCray shakes his head again. He may not be in the loop, but he's tight with members of Peters's new task force. Campus officers under his command. Old friends on the Santa Clara PD. From the Bureau's San Jose office. "No demands—unless the parents are keeping it from us."

He glances toward the tall woman. The State Department official, Blane Roosevelt's mom. She's talking to Peters, her index finger stabbing the air, punctuating whatever she's saying. Keller doesn't see any of the other parents.

"They found blood?" Keller asks. Peters mentioned it on their call, though he still hasn't come over.

"Yeah. On the ground near the van."

"Another 'oh shit moment,'" Keller says, repeating the phrase McCray used when they first met. His instinct that the disappearance wasn't just kids being kids was spot-on.

Trucks arrive with those portable streetlamps. An agent appears to be organizing a grid, assembling the search team, which will include Keller and McCray and about a dozen agents and local cops. There's already a table set up with flashlights and reflective vests. A K-9 unit arrives.

Keller surveys the search area. The trees along the roadside are thick, so drones will be ineffective. Hence the manual search plan. Another Bureau agent shepherds them over to the makeshift command center, where they're told to await instructions.

Keller doesn't mind doing grunt work. An investigation is a

team sport. Sometimes you're the star player, sometimes you're on the bench, sometimes you're the water boy. She's the new person at the office, hasn't even met most of her colleagues. But it does seem like a waste to bench someone who spent the day gathering evidence, however useless it turned out to be. Sometimes the little nugget that meant nothing initially breaks a case wide open when another piece of the puzzle emerges.

"That was clever, finding the FedEx footage," McCray says.

"Thanks."

He adds, "I'm just waiting for the reporters to get wind of the video and start calling him the Smurf Bandit."

"I was thinking they'd say the kids were Smurf-napped."

They're mercifully interrupted by someone calling Keller's name.

She catches Peters waving her over, an impatient *get over here* gesture. Next to him stands Cynthia Roosevelt, hands on her hips.

"Good luck," McCray says.

Cynthia has moved away by the time Keller gets there. Peters doesn't look happy and his team members are all studying their shoes.

"We need you on the investigation," Peters says. "Not on the search," he clarifies. There's no enthusiasm in his voice. But Keller isn't going to question it.

Peters rubs a hand over his face, gives a tired nod. He then pulls out his phone, taps on it. "Start here," he says.

Keller hears her phone ping. The text has a pin for an address.

"CCTV video that needs review," Peters says.

She nods, decides to push her luck: "The chief of campus police knows this terrain, do you mind if"—she glances over at Jay McCray, who has a search vest on over his collared shirt—"if he rides shotgun with me?" She doesn't give Peters her father's speech about the need for local counsel.

"Fine," he says.

Keller heads toward Jay as someone sidles up next to her. It's Cynthia Roosevelt.

"I saw you on the news at the bridge," Roosevelt says. "And I understand you found the only viable clue, a video of the possible kidnapper."

Keller doesn't reply.

"Like I just told your boss: Never send in a man to do a woman's job." She turns, faces Keller. Her voice is steady but her eyes look shattered. "Now go find my son."

With that, Roosevelt is whisked away in a black SUV.

Keller looks over as flashlight beams wink in and out of the trees lining the road. She catches up to Jay before he disappears.

"Peters cleared me to have you help chase down some leads, if you're game."

"You don't gotta ask me twice," he says. "Besides, those kids aren't out there." He looks toward the trees.

"What makes you so sure?"

"The trail of blood they found, it stops well before the tree line."

"Like they got into another vehicle," Keller says.

He nods.

"Run with me to Starbucks?" she asks.

He gives her a skeptical look. "I could use a coffee as much as the next person, but . . ."

Keller says, "I'll explain on the drive."

It's 5:15 a.m. when they arrive, and there's already a long line in the Starbucks drive-thru. It's a place off the highway in Santa Clara that's open twenty-four hours.

Keller parks, gets out of the car, stretches her back. Jay seems wide awake, which is somehow annoying but comforting at the same time.

"We don't have those in New York," Keller says, admiring the drive-thru.

She points to a Volvo parked nearby. Two people inside: Libby Akana's parents. She texted them, asking to meet here. Unsurprisingly, they were awake at this ungodly hour and readily agreed to come to the Starbucks where someone slashed their tires.

When the judge and his wife see Keller and McCray, they climb out.

They look like a pile of devastation.

Keller greets them with hugs. What else can you do in circumstances like this? McCray, less comfortably, follows suit.

Inside, Jay orders coffees for the group while Keller and the parents collapse into chairs at one of the wobbly circular tables.

"They finally released the CCTV?" Judge Akana says. He's not a large man, but he's somehow imposing.

Keller nods, decides against trying to explain the delay. She looks over, and Jay is holding one of those cardboard drink carriers, talking to the manager of the Starbucks, a young guy with acne wearing a green apron. The one agents pressured to get access to the video footage, but who resisted until he got approval from Corporate. He must've been given the green light tonight after running it through the company's army of lawyers. Not everybody is a George G. Peacoat from FedEx who doesn't bow to the almighty Corporate.

The judge examines his phone, as if willing it to bring good news. Amy Akana seems distant, out of it.

When Judge Akana puts his phone back on the table, Keller catches the wallpaper screen. It shows a boy and girl at the beach.

The boy has white zinc cream on his nose, floaties on his upper arms, and is hugging his big sister. The girl has pigtails and is holding an inflatable inner tube. Keller feels a ripple of sadness, thinking about her twins in their beach gear, imagining what these parents are going through.

Jay comes over. Removes the cups from the tray and places one in front of each of them. "They're allowing us to review the footage without a warrant, but required that we come on-site. Because of some legal issues, they haven't had time to get approval to send a digital copy."

Judge Akana says nothing, stands, and he and his wife follow McCray over to the manager. The kid bows his head at the parents, surely knowing why they're here.

Behind the counter, there's a door that leads to a break room and a tiny office. The rich, earthy smell of roasted coffee beans permeates everything. They crowd into the office and the manager sits down at the desk, pulls up video footage on a desktop computer.

Judge Akana and his wife watch the video from Friday: their car pulling up to the coffee shop before their world turned upside down. They get out of the vehicle, dutifully lock the doors. The camera switches to the inside, where they head to the restrooms. The teen manager clicks to the shot from outside again. A man in an N95 mask enters the frame. He looks around. Then removes something from his pocket. He ducks low at the rear of the vehicle. Then he emerges and walks to the other side of the car, ducks down again.

"Do you recognize him?" McCray asks.

Keller watches both of them. The judge is squinting at the screen, head already shaking. Amy Akana looks less certain but says nothing.

Keller asks the manager to play the clip again. And again.

Judge Akana shakes his head, clearly frustrated. "I've never seen that man before in my life. Can I take a photo of this to send to my security team?"

The Starbucks manager looks conflicted. He says, "Um, I'd need authorization from Corporate, so I can't approve that." The guy thinks for a moment. "But I really need to use the restroom, so I'll be right back."

Once the manager extracts himself, Judge Akana raises his phone and takes a photo of the screen. He then sends a text to someone.

Keller studies the judge's wife. She's staring blankly at the monitor.

"We can get the video enhanced," McCray says. "The perp's wearing a mask, but there's probably enough of his face to run it through facial recognition."

"You don't need to do that," Amy Akana says.

They all look at her.

"I know who he is."

This sucks the air out of the room.

"But I need a moment alone with my husband."

CHAPTER FORTY-TWO

THE AKANAS

Amy doesn't know when she first started resenting her husband. Was it during the endless days and nights in the hospital waiting room and cafeteria while Ken was off being Super Judge? Was it the silence at the dinner table? Ken prioritizing his grief over her own?

She told herself that she wasn't being fair. One of them had to make a living while the other became a full-time caregiver for Timmy. And Ken gave up something far more precious than a career. He lost time with their son. Even if that time was brutal and heartbreaking and exhausting. It was still time with Timmy.

But God love him, Ken is taking action now. He was up all night sending emails, calling in favors, making sure every single resource was used to find their daughter. It's not fair. Amy knows there are poor kids in marginalized communities who get a single overworked detective and an inevitable banker's box in a cold-case closet.

Right now, though, she selfishly doesn't care. She's let Libby down these past few years and she's not going to do it now.

Libby. Oh, Libby. The perfect child. She represses a sob, knowing, that was an unfair expectation. Particularly since Amy was hardly a perfect mother. And certainly not a perfect wife.

Ken storms out of the back office of the Starbucks after she tells him why their tires were slashed. After collecting herself, she finds the FBI agent and campus police chief sitting at a table waiting. Ken isn't with them.

The FBI agent, Keller, gives her a sympathetic look. "Who was that man in the video, Mrs. Akana?"

"His name is Bruce Lockwood. He's a police officer I met at the hospital where my son was being treated."

Amy explains her son's illness, the long days and nights at the hospital. Meeting a cop who was there dealing with the aftermath of a teenager's overdose. She noticed how kind he was to the parents. Explains how she saw him another night, a few weeks later, in the hospital cafeteria. How he had an easy way about him. He knew who Ken was. Joked that her husband had freed some of his collars.

She admits that she began to look forward to those occasional encounters. On a particularly bad day with Timmy, she ran into him again. Ken was working late as usual. Timmy was sleeping. No harm in getting a meal outside the hospital for a change, she'd thought. Better than eating alone—again. And the rest took its inevitable course.

Until she tried to break it off.

"He became possessive. Unwilling to let go. I had to block him on my phone. Then he started following me." She pauses, takes in a breath. "I had nowhere to go. I couldn't get a restraining order because it would humiliate Ken. I couldn't do that to him."

"You're sure it's Bruce Lockwood on the video?"

Amy nods again.

"Did you tell him you were coming to Santa Clara?" Keller asks. "We're a long way from LA."

"No, the last time I saw him was the Saturday before we left. He approached me at the supermarket, of all places. He must have been following me. I told him to leave me alone or I'd be forced to call the police. To tell my husband."

"Did you post anything on social media that you'd be here? Tell anyone he knows you were coming?"

"I don't use social because of Ken's job. And no, Bruce doesn't know any of our friends."

"Have you had any contact with him since you've been in Santa Clara?"

Amy looks down at the table. "After our tires were slashed, I texted him. Told him he needed to stop. That it's over." Her lower lip quivers. She takes in a breath like she's steadying herself. Like she's forcing herself to push through. For her daughter.

"What did he say?"

"He called me. Apologized, begged me to come back to him. Swore he'd be better, pleaded that we belonged together."

"Do you think he could've taken Libby? Or the others?"

"Two days ago, I would've said that's crazy. But now . . ."

"Did you notice anyone following you from LA?"

Amy shakes her head. She feels like she's on the verge of collapse.

Soon, they walk Amy to her car. Ken sits in the driver's seat. She expects a clenched jaw, searing anger. But he seems more dazed than anything.

"I know that was hard, but you did the right thing telling us," Keller says as Amy gets inside the vehicle.

Ken says nothing, just starts the engine. Before he pulls out, there's a tap on the window. He lowers it, looks at the FBI agent who is staring inside the car.

"You said only three of your tires were slashed," she says. "Which one was left alone?"

"The front passenger tire."

Amy watches as the agent walks over to that side of the car, squats like she's examining the wheel well.

When she stands back up, she displays a small rectangular metallic box in her hand.

Then Amy understands and her heart plummets.

A GPS tracker.

CHAPTER FORTY-THREE

THE KELLERS

It's just past eight in the morning and Keller is fighting fatigue. She's getting too old to operate on only a few hours of sleep. She and McCray chug along the 101 to East Palo Alto.

"You always this bright-eyed so early?" she asks.

McCray smiles like he's heard this before.

Keller continues, "Have you ever had so many leads so fast, but not one of them pans out?"

McCray thinks on this. "Before I joined the university, I contemplated working with a cold-case squad as a kind of retirement gig—those officers live and breathe dead-end leads."

"I've had a cold case, fifteen years cold, and it was a doozy." She doesn't mention it nearly killed her, something Bob won't let her forget. She shakes the memory, says, "You're pretty young to retire."

"That's what my wife said when I put in my papers and was home all day driving her crazy. I met with the cold-case detectives and they said most of their time is spent running down leads that go nowhere. I decided I'd had enough frustration in my life, so it wasn't for me. Then I heard SCU's chief was retiring, and I liked the idea of being around young people, helping them navigate their inevitable mistakes."

Keller likes that idea too.

On the drive, they rehash their dead ends: The Maldonados—a cheating husband who got more than he anticipated when his paramour's husband killed himself and his son fixated on revenge. Nothing. The Roosevelts—a bitter divorce, a cheating husband, and a son abducted nearly a decade ago. Nada. The Akanas—a more sympathetic infidelity story, but again, nothing so far. They've got a BOLO out for Bruce Lockwood, the cop who's stalking Amy Akana. Is he the key to what happened to the students? Obsession does strange things to people. But it doesn't add up. Why would he take five students? Libby Akana, maybe, but four others? No, Lockwood's obsession seems limited to Amy Akana.

"How's the geofence data coming?" McCray asks. "If we know who was at the park when the phones went dark, it could break this wide open."

"The judge signed the warrant yesterday. Just waiting on our friends at Google. I'm told we should get the results today, tomorrow at the latest."

Until the electronic data comes in, they'll have to rely on shoe leather.

Keller checks the GPS. Fifteen minutes until they arrive at the halfway house where Mark Wong's father lives.

"This guy have a history of violence?" McCray asks, probably wondering if they need backup.

"Only if you're a thirteen-year-old girl."

"Lovely."

Keller shakes her head. Andrew Wong is anything but lovely. According to his file, nearly a dozen girls he coached over the years on the swim team came forward, but he was convicted of only two assaults. Keller hasn't had a lot of experience with sexual predators. One of the benefits of working financial crimes. What she does know dumbfounds her. She's convinced it's some type of brain disorder. They're hardwired to be attracted to kids. Worse, they tend to have an insatiable appetite—a singular focus—on finding ways to abuse the most innocent. They pick careers to be near victims: coaches, scout leaders. Like a famous bank robber said when asked why he chose banks: because that's where the money is.

Keller believes that pedophiles are incurable—they are certainly among the few criminal types who don't "age out" of crime. You don't see many eighty-year-old bank robbers. Keller isn't a law-and-order maniac; she understands that often crime is the result of poverty, a lack of opportunity. If she had her way, drug offenders crowding prisons would be released. Incarceration would be reserved for the violent. But sex offenders, particularly child sex offenders, would receive the same life sentence they've given their victims.

But the law doesn't reflect Keller's worldview: Andrew Wong did less than ten years.

She asks, "His parole officer ever get back to you?"

"Nope. I get it, they're overworked and it's the weekend, but I said it was urgent, so I'd at least expect a call." McCray shakes his head.

They pull up to the ramshackle house in East Palo Alto. The neighborhood is like many that have slid into a decline: lopsided porches, rusted chain-link fences, overgrown yards.

In the common area, they're met with nervous stares from

recent inhabitants of various correctional institutions. It's easy to tell which ones were inside for a long stretch. The way they watch their surroundings, the way they carry themselves. Like elk tiptoeing in mountain lion territory. Years of having to be on alert.

The house's director says Andy Wong isn't there. He's allowed to go on a walk in the morning before his shift at the moving company, a job he secured through an organization that helps ex-cons find work. He's approved to go to Bay Road, but not past the intersection of Bay and University.

"You're welcome to wait," the director says.

Keller looks around the drab house. She gestures at Jay that they'll find Wong themselves, and he nods agreement. They're risking Wong returning and taking off when the others tell him the FBI was looking for him. But Keller thinks that's low-risk. It's a manageable area to find him in. And Wong's file says he was a model inmate. As they leave, the director says that Wong often goes to the convenience store on Gloria Way, so they'll start there.

Five minutes later, they pull to the curb. The small market is crowded with teenagers, peculiar for a Sunday morning. McCray jumps out of the car to check out the store but returns quickly.

"Just a bunch of squirrely middle-schoolers," he says. "Some of them are wearing soccer uniforms, must be a game nearby."

Keller gets a pit in her gut. Middle-school kids. She searches her phone quickly. "We're near a school."

Jay gives her a look like he's thinking the same thing: How on earth could a child sex offender be placed in a halfway house near a school?

She finds the school on her maps app and drives faster than she should in the residential neighborhood.

That's when she sees him. Sitting on a bench at a bus stop. Watching a group of young girls stroll to the soccer field. They stare at their phones and laugh and are oblivious.

"You've got to be kidding," Keller says. She feels rage erupting in her chest and brings the car to a screeching halt in front of the bench.

She and McCray step out.

Andrew Wong sees them.

And he runs.

So much for being a model inmate.

She and Jay exchange an exasperated look: *Really?*

She yells for Jay to take the car and sprints after Wong.

Ahead, Wong cuts left onto a side street. By the time Keller makes the corner, he's scrambling over a six-foot fence surrounding someone's backyard. Keller continues after him, cursing herself for skipping the gym the last few weeks. It's been hard with work and shuttling the children around and preparing for the move, but she didn't think she was *this* out of shape.

A dog barks as she gets closer, and she watches the mangy mutt snap at Wong's ass as he clumsily heaves himself over the fence on the other side of the yard. Now well behind, Keller veers through the alley to intercept him.

But Wong has disappeared. She stops, bends over, hands on her thighs, catching her breath. That's when he darts out from a cluster of trash cans, and she's off again. She tries to head him off, but he's gaining ground.

Wong makes it to a busy street. He's running toward a crosswalk where vehicles are stopped at the light. If he crosses and Keller doesn't make it before the light turns green, there's no way she'll catch him. Her breaths are coming in rasps now, but she pushes herself to make it before that light changes.

She's too late.

But then something bizarre happens: Andrew Wong doesn't head to the other side of the street but instead dives into the flatbed of a tow truck.

Keller sprints toward the truck, bellows "FBI! Stop!" But the driver can't hear her above the noise of traffic.

The truck is moving fast, disappearing.

Wong is getting away.

It's then that she sees the tow truck's brake lights glow red.

She races along the side of the street behind the truck and watches as the driver's door flies open. A heavyset guy stomps to the back of his truck.

Keller's getting closer, about to yell for the driver to stop Wong. But she doesn't need to. He yanks Wong out of the flatbed by the back of his shirt collar. When Keller reaches the truck, Wong is face down on the ground. When he tries to spring to his feet, the driver puts a heavy work boot on his back.

Jay pulls up, flies out of the car.

Keller's perspiring, her breath shallow from the chase. She holds up her badge and thanks the driver.

He nods and gets in his truck and drives away like it's any other Sunday.

"I didn't do anything!" Wong says as McCray hoists him to his feet.

"Where are they?" Keller says. "It will go much better for you if you tell us now."

"Where are who? What are you—"

"Where's your son? Where's Mark?" Keller demands.

"Mark?" Wong asks, seeming genuinely confused. "I have no idea."

The worst part? She believes him.

CHAPTER FORTY-FOUR

At the East Palo Alto City Jail, the officers working the security line joke with McCray about intruding on their turf, ask about his family, let him breeze through the checkpoints. They're not as friendly to Keller, but she still gets the McCray treatment. It took the East Palo Alto cops less than an hour to process Wong after McCray called them in. A parole violation was the cleanest way to detain him for questioning.

In a dirty interview room, Keller and McCray eye Wong, who slouches at a small table. Wong's handcuffs are secured to a steel bar on the tabletop.

McCray puts his cell phone on the table, recording the meeting. He states the date and time, identifies who's present.

"You are speaking to us without counsel, Mr. Wong," Keller says. "Is that by your free choice?"

"Yes."

"Just so we're all clear, I want to remind you of your rights." Keller then recites the *Miranda* warning and Wong says he understands.

"I think this is all one big misunderstanding," Wong says.

Keller frowns.

"That neighborhood," Wong continues, "it isn't, well, the greatest. I didn't know you were the police. I got scared, which is why I ran."

Keller feels a nerve in her face twitch. "That doesn't explain why you were sitting on that bench leering at underage girls," she says. "That violates your conditions of release."

"I wasn't—I had no idea they would be there. I'm permitted to go on walks and I stayed within the boundary. It's Sunday, I didn't know kids would be in the area. I avoid anywhere near kids."

McCray jumps in now: "That sounds like something you need to take up with the judge. We don't have time to—"

"You asked if I've seen my son," Wong says.

Keller now understands why he was willing to talk. Andrew Wong wants to leverage anything he might know to get himself out of this jam.

"We're listening," Keller says.

"Perhaps if you can explain to the prosecutor that this was all a misunderstanding, I might have some . . . some information about Mark."

McCray blows out a breath. Keller knows why. It's one of the sad realities of law enforcement. The system doesn't work unless deals are cut with monsters.

Yet, she's not sure she can stomach a trade with this oily man who molested young girls—who, even after being imprisoned for ten years, found himself on a bench ogling girls with ponytails and braces.

McCray asks Keller to step outside the room with him for a moment.

"This guy . . ." she says.

"Your call."

"*My* call?" She offers a wry smile. "I wanted this to be yours."

McCray sighs again. "I don't think they're going to send him back to prison for sitting on that bench, running from us. His story is a lie, but a plausible one."

Keller agrees. "What if he's playing us?" she says.

"Always a risk."

She bunches her lips. "Fine."

Back in the room, McCray turns his phone back on record, says, "We don't have authority to make any commitments. I'm just a campus cop and Agent Keller would have to run this through a bureaucracy to give you any firm commitment. But if you're asking for my word that I'll support you with your PO, with the prosecutor, I can do that. That should be enough for this to go away. But only if you're not B.S.-ing us."

Wong's mouth tightens. "I need it in writing."

"Then I'm afraid we're done," McCray says. He stands. Keller does too, joining the bluff.

It doesn't take long before Wong blinks. "Wait."

They both turn but don't sit back down.

"I need you to say on the recording you'll support me. That this was a misunderstanding."

McCray says, "I've told you what I can commit to. You have my word."

More thinking. Then a nod and: "Mark came to see me."

"When?" Keller says.

"On Friday."

The day the students went missing.

"Last Friday?" Keller confirms.

"Yeah. I don't work on Fridays. He showed up at the house that afternoon."

"What did he want?"

Wong swallows. "He said he needs a lawyer. He wanted to know about my lawyer."

"What did he need a lawyer for?"

"He didn't say."

McCray gives an exaggerated sigh.

"I swear," Wong says. "I asked. He just said he needed some advice."

"What did you tell him?"

"I told him I don't have a lawyer. My private lawyer from my trial burned through all my money and the jury came back in twenty minutes guilty on all counts. I wouldn't recommend that idiot to anyone. And my appeal lawyer was a public defender."

"Did Mark tell you anything, anything at all, about why he needed a lawyer? Why he'd come see you after—how long? Ten years, right?"

He shakes his head. "I said I'd like him back in my life. I'd like to get to know him."

"What did he say?"

"Nothing. He just said it was a mistake coming and took off."

They press Wong on the details, but his story stays the same. Keller believes him: If he was lying, he'd go all-in and make it more salacious than this cryptic encounter in which Mark needed a lawyer.

Outside the jailhouse, Keller says, "I think he was telling the truth. You?"

McCray nods.

"So are you going to keep your word to him?" Keller asks.

McCray looks at her and reveals both hands, each with fingers crossed.

CHAPTER FORTY-FIVE

"This is getting pretty damn frustrating," Keller says to McCray. It's lunchtime already and they're sitting in a booth at In-N-Out Burger, waiting for their number to be called. Then it is.

"This is about to make you feel better," McCray says. He stands, heads to the counter, and retrieves their trays of burgers and fries. In-N-Out was McCray's idea, but Bob has been raving about the chain forever.

She feels guilty experiencing it without him. But duty calls. And between the sleep deprivation and her aggravation over this case, she could use some salt and grease and Coca-Cola in her system.

Still, she decides to send Bob a photo of her food with a question mark.

She watches the dancing dots. A GIF appears with a character from South Park and the caption, *I forgive you.*

She holds the burger in her hands and takes a bite. And damn!

"I can't believe you've never been here," McCray says. "I thought your husband's from the area."

"This is the first time we've been back to the area since my kids were born. It's hard to travel with kids, and my job . . ."

"How old are your children?" McCray asks.

"Nine. Twins—Heather and Michael."

McCray smiles. "Nine to twelve were magic years for mine." He looks somewhere faraway. "Thirteen to eighteen, not so much, but they come back to you."

"How old are they?"

McCray dips a french fry in ketchup. "Thirty-four and thirty-seven, which is hard to believe."

"What do they do?"

"One is the COO of a tech company in the Silicon Valley. She obviously got her mother's brain." He smiles. "My son is more of a free spirit. He worked in finance in your fair city for two years after graduating from Columbia but now owns a bar in Prague." More pride.

"Wow, smart kids."

"Yeah, again, thank their mom."

"What's your wife do?"

"Neurosurgeon."

"Seriously, a brain surgeon?"

He nods, allows a small grin. "We got married young, before she knew any better."

"That explains it," Keller says, grinning back.

"What brings you to the West Coast? I hear the New York field office is the pinnacle," he says.

She tells him about Bob's father. About her hardship transfer. How she worries about disrupting the twins' lives.

"I wouldn't fret too much about the kids. They're at a good age for a change. And they'll remember this time with their grandfather and experiencing Northern California. It's beautiful here."

She appreciates the encouragement from someone who's been there, done that.

"But take some advice from an old-timer," he says, pausing for effect. "The cliché about your children is true: The days are long, but the years short." The sentiment is interrupted by the chime of a text. He scans his phone. "No luck tracking Amy Akana's stalker yet. They're coming up short on everything. And they're starting to sound desperate."

"Television cameras have that effect," Keller says.

Back at the campus station thirty minutes later, McCray goes to check in with his team, and Keller decides to close the loop on the only parent she hasn't interviewed herself: Alice Goffman.

Jay spoke with Alice the night the students disappeared, but that was before they knew the kids left campus like they'd been summoned, before a masked subject was videoed in a van one of them had borrowed, before Annie the Intern heard rumors that Felix was called a stalker in an anonymous post. It could be a waste of time, but it's not like she has any solid leads.

Keller tries Goffman's cell phone, but she doesn't pick up. Unusual, since you'd think all the parents are waiting anxiously by the phone for any breaking news. She starts to tap out a text to Goffman, but is interrupted by a peppy voice.

"Agent Sarah!"

Keller glances up.

Annie Hafeez has a big smile. Is the intern ever not smiling?

"Working on a Sunday," Keller says.

"It's my day off, but I'm still searching for clues online, like you asked."

Keller gives an appreciative nod.

Annie adds, "But I'm available for *anything*. You name it, I can do it. I'm ready to go."

"Unless you know how to find Felix Goffman's mom, I think I'm covered." Keller smiles.

Annie's head rattles like she can't believe what Keller just said. She starts thumbing her phone then walks over, shows Keller the screen.

Several posts. The Rizz site again:

Libby's parents spotted in Half Moon Bay

Blane's father released from feebs custody, mother picked him up from station

Mark's father in custody in E. Palo Alto

"People are tracking them? Why?" Keller asks, dumbfounded. This app is a menace.

Annie shrugs. "It's fun, I guess. My friend Annalise—I know that's funny, Annie and Annalise—said there're, like, crazy rumors flying. She even heard you're bringing in psychics to help. And the TikTokers are going *cra-zy*." Annie looks around, cups her hand like she's about to tell a secret. "Just between us, Annalise is kind of naïve. Can you believe when she first met me she said, 'I never met a Muslim before,' like I was from outer space or something? She was like, 'You don't drink or smoke?' And I was like—"

"Has anyone on Rizz tracked Alice Goffman?" Keller interrupts.

Annie looks back down at her phone, checks the app: "She went into the campus church less than an hour ago."

CHAPTER FORTY-SIX

THE GOFFMANS

Alice sits beneath the beautiful painted ceiling of the campus church, staring up at the statue of St. Clare of Assisi, flanked on either side by Mary and Joseph. Services ended hours ago and she's the only one in the small mission.

She prays for her Felix to return safely. For all the kids to come home.

She hasn't been able to sleep.

She needs to talk to a priest. Needs guidance.

Needs to confess.

A smartly dressed young man appears in the church. He wears dark-framed glasses, offers a compassionate smile.

She closes her eyes, continues to pray for Felix's safe return, for a sign of what she's supposed to do.

"Ms. Goffman?"

Her eyes pop open, surprised.

The man with the glasses is sitting in one of the creaky wooden chairs near her.

"I'm Shay Zable. I'm with the *San Francisco Daily.*"

"I'm sorry, I have no comment." There's been a throng of reporters outside her apartment building. Knocking on her door. Calling her cell phone. A woman who said she hosts a podcast also stopped Alice on the street. The CSS has tried to keep them all away from campus at least, set up a designated area for the press, warned that trespassers would be prosecuted. But apparently the warning wasn't enough for this young journalist.

"I understand your reluctance to talk to the press," he says. "But this is your opportunity to set things straight. Rumors are flying. I don't know if you use social media, but there's a lot of speculation and allegations about your son."

Alice feels tears welling. She didn't think she had any left.

"And I'm sorry to approach you here." He looks around the church. "Honestly, I didn't want to. My boss . . . It's my first real job after graduating. My mom worked hard to put me through school. It was just the two of us and I need to do well."

Alice is sympathetic, but the police have advised the parents not to speak to reporters or internet people, explained that it can end up hurting an investigation more than helping.

"My story isn't going to be about the disappearances," he continues, still trying to convince her. "Directly, anyway. It's about the misinformation. How social-media sleuths are impeding the investigation. For instance, there are rumors Felix was stalking one of the missing students. That maybe he—"

"Felix would never. They're his friends."

"That's exactly the kind of thing I would report. Set the record straight."

Alice feels her panic returning, like she can't get enough air.

"There are rumors that he had problems in high school. That he was bullied."

She's definitely not out of tears because more start pouring now. "He's always been a sweet boy, and the universe isn't always kind to sweet boys."

"Do you think he did something? That maybe the others knew, so he had to . . ."

"Never," Alice says. But her mind flashes to the sweatshirt. Covered in red. "He's never hurt anyone. When he was a little boy he'd carry bugs outside rather than kill them."

"They're saying he's responsible. You can clear things up, tell them about the real Felix."

"I'm sorry . . ." She squeezes her eyes shut, hopes when she opens them the reporter will be gone. That she'll get a sign on what she should do.

"Listen," the reporter says, his tone not so friendly now. "If you don't talk to me. I'm gonna have to report that your son is a murderer."

Alice's chest shudders, she keeps her eyes closed. She begins to hyperventilate.

And then she receives the sign she's been looking for. A woman's voice:

"And *I'll* have to report that you're an unethical journalist committing libel."

Alice opens her eyes. It's the FBI agent, and she's thrust her badge in the reporter's face.

"Not to mention obstructing a federal investigation."

The reporter swallows hard and scurries out.

Alice now knows what she has to do.

CHAPTER FORTY-SEVEN

THE KELLERS

After scaring off the reporter, Keller eyes Alice Goffman. She's understandably a mess: unruly hair, bags under her red-rimmed eyes, wrinkled blouse.

Alice gets up from her seat in the small church, says, "I have something I need to show you."

Keller follows her out of the church and to the employee lot for the dean's office. Alice says nothing, just opens the trunk of her Honda. She retrieves a manila folder, hands it to Keller.

"What's this?"

"It's from a site the kids all use. Someone reported it to our office."

Keller opens the file, sees a header for Rizz. The posts rumored to exist, the ones Annie hasn't been able to find. Maybe someone took screenshots before the posts were pulled down:

CREEP LIST

I'm tired of everyone covering for them. These are the campus predators.

Mark Wong (like father, like son)

Felix Goffman (stalker)

Prof. Turlington (again . . .)

Keller feels her heart trip. She flips to a second printout:

CREEP LIST

You know the creeps. Here's who is enabling them.

Libby Akana

Stella Maldonado

Blane Roosevelt

"Why did you—" Keller stops herself. The answer is obvious. Alice secreted the report from the office because it named her son.

"Did you talk to him about it?"

"Yes. He said it's a lie. Said whoever posted them pulled them down."

The rumored Rizz posts exist. They reference every single one of The Five. Plus a professor. Who wrote the posts? Do they have anything to do with the missing students? Keller's stomach churns.

But the real gut punch comes when Alice retrieves something else from the trunk. A sweatshirt. Alice holds out the garment gingerly so the front faces Keller.

It's covered in a large stain. The color of blood.

CHAPTER FORTY-EIGHT

THE MALDONADOS

David still feels like crap. Muscles sore, monster headache. But at least he's out of that low-end hospital. They should be ashamed of themselves. Hospitals should be temples of the gods, but that one? A disgrace.

He sits at a high-top table on the patio at the Ritz. Nina hasn't spoken to him since they've been back. The task force head told them to stay near a phone, but otherwise keep out of the way. The stunning view of the sun glinting off the ocean is a contrast to the dark worry set in his bones about Stella.

"Ouch," a voice says. "What happened to you?"

David turns and sees her. Blonde. Early thirties. Pretty.

It takes him a beat to realize she's referring to the bandage on his head, covering the gash from when he took the fall.

"Long story."

"I'll bet. Mind if I sit?" She holds a cocktail, gestures to the open spot at his table.

He looks around. Hesitates. But maybe some company will

distract him from thinking about Stella, about Cody Carpenter, about Nina. Keep him from losing his mind.

She asks him why he's in town, where he's from. He deflects to questions about her.

She says she's just flown in from Florida for a bachelorette party. Her brother's fiancée, whom she can't stand, is from the area.

"She's an actress." She rolls her eyes.

A lot of David's patients are actresses, but he doesn't mention it.

"I can't believe he's marrying her." She shakes her head, gazes out to the ocean.

They sit in the silence, her hair blowing in the breeze, the heavy scent of her floral perfume wafting through the air.

"You married?" she asks at last.

"Yes," he says. He's not sure for how much longer, but for now it's true.

"Happily?"

Avoiding the question, he replies, "How about you? Married?"

She guffaws. "Do I look married?"

"What's married look like?"

She gestures to his bandage.

"You're young to be so cynical."

"You're old not to be."

She's so pretty. But this is not the time. As much as he likes holding the attention of a beautiful woman, trying to keep his mind off Stella, it isn't working. He needs to go.

He makes an exaggerated show of looking at his watch. "It was nice to meet you." He steps down from the tall chair.

"Was it something I said?"

"No, I've just got a lot going on."

"I've heard."

It's then he sees the phone on her lap. It's set at an unusual angle, like she's been recording him.

"Do you think Cody Carpenter did something to The Five?"

"Are you videoing—" He stops, turns, and heads toward the door to the hotel.

"Or do you think this is your daughter punishing you?" she calls out. "A hoax?"

He picks up his pace.

"David! Do you blame yourself?"

His heart is thrumming. But it breaks at her next words:

"Well, you *should* blame yourself."

CHAPTER FORTY-NINE

THE KELLERS

The task force predictably was frenzied over the new leads. Agents took turns questioning Alice Goffman in the interrogation room, techs raced to analyze the sweatshirt, government lawyers pressured the Rizz site to reveal who posted the Creep Lists. In the tumult, Keller decided to focus on the most unusual aspect of the Rizz posts: the allegation that a professor was a campus predator.

She knocks on the door of the small home. It has a 1970s vibe, but Keller doesn't know anything about architecture. It's a modest house for a full professor—a PhD, according to his bio on the SCU website—a testament to housing prices in the area. She worries for a moment that she shouldn't have come alone, should've coordinated with the task force. But McCray warned that SCU requires faculty interviews to go through the dean's office. And once the dean is contacted, McCray said, university lawyers will be involved. Wagons circled.

A man in his late thirties answers the door. He's bookish and wears a collared shirt and khakis.

Keller can hear a crying baby inside. The man has that frazzled look Keller recognizes from early parenting. For a brief moment she wonders how the young mother from the airplane is doing.

"Professor Turlington?"

"Yes," he says suspiciously. "Can I help you?"

Keller displays her badge, and he turns and looks over his shoulder into the house. "I've got it, honey," he calls out like he doesn't want his wife to overhear. "You're here about the missing students?"

"That's right," Keller says. "Why did you think it's about the students . . . ?"

"Well, why else would an FBI agent be at my door?"

She gives him a *fair enough* expression.

"I'd like to help, but I didn't have any of the students in my classes."

Keller already knows this; McCray checked for her. "Did you know any of them? Outside of classes, I mean."

He shakes his head. The kind of definitive gesture that has the ring of truth.

"Look, I want to help," the professor continues, "but as you can hear, we have our hands full. Twins."

Keller smiles. "I know too well—I have twins. When one is happy, the other . . ."

He nods politely, but it's clear he wants to get back to it.

"One quick thing," Keller says. She opens a file folder that contains copies of the Creep List posts.

When Professor Turlington sees the first printout—the logo for Rizz at the top of the page—he appears crestfallen.

"You've seen this?"

He exhales, looks at the ground.

Keller waits for him to explain.

"I didn't see it, but I heard about it." He swallows. "You know what's worse than being formally accused of something?"

"What's that?"

"Being the target of a whisper network after a faceless online report with no accuser, no details, no nothing. Just vague accusations." He swallows. He's trying to hold it together, but he's upset. "I teach government. And I try to teach these kids about why we have a right to confront our accusers in the Constitution. Try to teach them what happened in common-law England when defendants were deprived of the right to cross-examine those whose words were used against them. How it was so harmful our founders thought it important enough to include in the Bill of Rights, even before the internet and social media."

"So it's not true?" Keller asks, more to gauge his reaction than his answer.

"What? That I'm a 'creep'?" He uses air quotes. "That I'm 'problematic'? Make students 'uncomfortable'?" He accentuates each word with disdain.

Again, she doesn't know why. But he's convincing her. Then again, people who abuse their power are often convincing.

"Here's the thing," she says. "Whoever posted that about you on Rizz also referred to the missing students."

This gets his attention. Like he's connecting the dots, didn't realize previously that the posts mentioned The Five. That's plausible if he really didn't see the posts.

The front door opens. A young woman pushes her head out.

"Everything okay, honey?" she asks.

"Yeah," he says. "I'll be right in. It's about the missing students."

She gives Keller a weak smile, then ducks back inside.

"Any idea who might have posted this about you?"

"I assume you've identified who it is from Rizz," he says.

"Not yet. The good folks at Rizz aren't going to just hand that information over. According to the site, they will fight disclosing the identities of their users. A court battle will take some time." She looks him in the eyes for a long beat. "You have any idea who posted the Creep Lists?"

"I don't have an idea," he tells her. "I *know* who did it."

CHAPTER FIFTY

Keller sits on the sofa in the living room that has all the accoutrements of new parenthood: a blanket spread out on the floor, a portable crib in the corner, one of those automatic swings.

She holds one of the twins as the professor's wife, Jill, holds the other. After the professor dropped the grenade that he knew who made the Rizz posts, there was no way Keller was leaving without having a deeper conversation with him, and not on the front porch.

"You're good with her," Jill says.

"Lots of practice," Keller replies.

When both babies conk out, Keller follows Jill to the nursery. The room has hundreds of butterflies painted on the walls. Not stickers, but intricate hand-painted butterflies.

Keller and Jill each embark on the perilous endeavor of lowering the babies to the mattress without waking them.

Success.

In the hallway, Keller says, "I love the butterflies."

"Jonathan hired someone to paint the nursery. He calls me his little butterfly."

She's sweet, this woman.

"I'll try not to keep him too long," Keller says, a not-so-subtle hint that she wants to question her husband alone.

Jill gives another faint smile. Before Keller heads back to the living room, Jill says, "He's a good man. The false accusations, they really hurt him . . ." She lets the rest die.

In the living room, Keller finds Professor Turlington on the sofa, leaning forward anxiously.

"Thank you," he says.

Keller isn't sure what he means. Helping with the kids, perhaps. But maybe it's more: not treating him as guilty before proven innocent in front of his young wife, who obviously doesn't need more stress in her life.

"Why do you think Natasha Belov made the posts?" Keller asks. The professor was sure that the young woman, who died of an accidental drowning less than a week ago, was behind the Rizz accusations.

Professor Turlington releases a breath. "She skipped nearly all the classes in my course last year. I'm not a hard-ass, I know they're kids, but they're here to learn. So I have a policy: Four unexcused absences and you fail. On her third absence, I called Natasha to my office, warned her. And she said she was going through something personal. I said I could help her get some campus resources, but I have to stick to the policy."

"And I take it she didn't like that?"

"To the contrary, she said she understood. That she'd make sure not to miss another class. That she'd reach out to CAPS, the school's counseling office. I came home and I told Jill that I was Super Professor." He shakes his head.

"And then she missed the fourth class," Keller says, seeing where this is headed.

He nods. "I reached out to her, said that I was disappointed, but—contrary to my own policy—would give her one last chance. But she then missed *another* class. I had to draw the line."

"And then what happened?"

"An anonymous report against me." He looks down at his lap. "It said I pressured a student for sex, stalked and harassed her."

"What happened?"

"The university conducted an investigation."

Keller waits.

"They were somehow able to trace the report to Natasha, they didn't tell me how. There were rumors spreading—it's a small campus."

"What happened?"

"Natasha denied it all. And I was exonerated."

"But you still thought she was behind the anonymous report?"

"The inquiry concluded that she likely made the report, angry at me, but then denied it for fear of getting in trouble for making a false accusation. I started this year thinking it was behind me. But then . . . Rizz." He takes in a breath. "I get added to this 'creep list' anonymously. The post was pulled down quickly, but not before the rumors started."

"Did you try to talk to Natasha Belov about any of this?"

"Are you kidding? No way was I going near her. It could've looked like I was trying to intimidate her, or worse."

Keller nods. "Any idea why she'd do this to you?"

"I have *no* idea. I was nothing but supportive. And the worst part: When she disappeared last week, until they realized it was an accidental drowning, there were more rumors that I had something to do with it. Can you imagine?"

Keller cannot, particularly if he's telling the truth.

"I don't want to speak ill of the dead. But she was a disturbed young woman."

Keller doesn't respond. She's feeling defeated, suspecting this is another dead end.

At the same time, if Natasha Belov posted the Creep Lists, she is somehow connected to The Five. Keller needs to find the link.

CHAPTER FIFTY-ONE

BLANE ROOSEVELT

"Did you know if you're a pilot and survive a plane crash you're, like, in super high demand from airlines and can get paid more than other pilots?" Blane says, adding, "Assuming you didn't cause the crash."

They're in the dark—suffering the oppressive heat of the steel cargo hold of a U-Haul truck—and he can't see the others. But he imagines their expressions: part bewilderment, part exhaustion, part traumatic stress.

"It's because of statistics," Blane continues, though he has no idea if any of this is true. "Because it's statistically improbable that a pilot would be in more than one plane crash. It's what my mom used to tell me when I got scared someone was going to take me again." He coughs a small laugh. "I guess she lied."

No one says anything. He's never talked to them about what happened during those four days when he was ten, but they surely already know. The internet ensures that there are no secrets anymore.

"What's some bullshit your parents told you?" Blane asks, if only trying to lighten the mood. Keep their spirits up and alert in case they have another opportunity for escape. They're tied up, but he managed to bite through the tape over his mouth and they spent what felt like hours doing awkward Twister moves to tug off each other's gags and blindfolds with their teeth.

Mark speaks first, his voice weak. "Lies our parents told us? Um, you really want to start with me . . . ?" Blane smiles at Mark's morbid reference to his father, a child molester.

Stella releases a laugh and the others join in.

"Yeah, you win, buddy," Blane says. "Stella? What's the biggest lie your parents told you?"

She's quiet, like she's thinking about this. Stella has been the strongest of them all so far. Other than Mark going for the gun, she's been the most defiant with their captors, the last one of them to cry. The first to start plotting their escape. They were so close when they pried their way out of the Mystery Machine. So they thought. Until they saw the gun, until the pair moved them into the U-Haul. Still, that the captors felt the need to switch vehicles is a good thing, Blane thinks. It could mean the police are looking for the van, know they've been taken. Or maybe their captors just needed a vehicle that was more secure.

Stella breaks the quiet. "My father said he wouldn't do it again." She waits. "Wouldn't cheat on my mom. On his family."

It's quiet for a long time. Blane thinks he hears a sob from Stella's direction. No matter how much they drive us crazy, parents are our weak spots.

"My parents' biggest lie?" Libby chimes in now: "That they loved me as much as they loved my brother."

There's another heavy silence. The strange reality that they may not get out of this has smothered any efforts to console.

"You're up, Felix," Blane says, genuinely curious. Of them all, Felix seems to have no parental resentments. He's been quiet, like always. He's not a talker, Felix Goffman.

Felix speaks: "My mom said high school would be different. That I wouldn't be the weird kid anymore." There's the sound of him exhaling. "When that didn't work out, she said it would be college. It started out well enough. I met you all."

He doesn't continue about how it ended up: the Creep Lists.

"Fuck, this is getting depressing," Mark grunts. "I'm starting to wish that asshole who shot me had better aim."

Light laughter fills the chamber.

Mark continues. "Let's cut the shit with the pity party. Answer this: What's the first thing you're gonna do when we get out of this?"

More quiet. Blane expects the obvious answers: a hot shower, a great meal, a stiff drink.

But Stella surprises him: "I'll hug my parents. Even my shit dad."

Mark doesn't respond, but one by one the rest of them say:

"Same."

"Same."

"Same."

CHAPTER FIFTY-TWO

THE KELLERS

"I need to know everything I can about Natasha Belov," Keller says into the phone. "Was she friendly with any of The Five? Did she have classes with them, date any of them? And when will we get her autopsy report?"

"Okay," McCray says in a measured drawl, clearly trying to slow Keller's racing thoughts.

Keller takes the hint. She needs to slow down. Investigators need to proceed deliberately, methodically, and not get worked up. That only leads to tunnel vision, mistakes, rushes to judgment that result in innocents behind bars. Not to mention, investigation hours wasted.

"Before she drowned, my office had some interactions with Natasha, mostly the usual college kid stuff, alcohol and the like," McCray says. "I've also pulled her university file. She's from a prominent family in Bulgaria. She spent her last two years of high school attending boarding school in New Hampshire and was a strong student with no disciplinary problems. Her first year at SCU was reportedly successful: lots of friends, good grades." McCray pauses. "But by the end of her sophomore year, things turned."

"Something happened?"

"We don't know. Her roommate from last year thought it was drugs. Natasha started partying really hard—not just booze. Most of her friends distanced themselves since she was getting out of control. She started partying off campus with a rougher crowd. She nearly flunked out, and everyone was surprised she returned this year. She was on academic probation and she skipped most of her classes this quarter."

Keller processes this. She's seen the devastating effects of drugs on certain people. It's such a roulette wheel. Lots of folks can use drugs recreationally. A line of coke here, some Adderall there. But for others, that first taste becomes a driving force in their lives.

McCray continues. "After she was reported missing we did a wellness check at her apartment, spoke to some students. She didn't have many friends left at SCU. That's why it took so long for anyone to notice she was missing."

"Because she was always missing . . ."

McCray releases a breath into the phone, like he's disappointed with himself.

"Who reported her missing?"

"It was an anonymous report."

"Anonymous? That's unusual, isn't it?"

"At the time, we just thought it was another student who was out partying with Natasha and didn't want to get in trouble."

"What did they say?"

"The officer who took the call said it sounded like a young woman. Said she saw Natasha high or extremely drunk on Panther Beach last Tuesday night."

"When was the call?"

"Thursday. I should've taken it more seriously. Her folks were furious we didn't alert the media right away, have a larger search team sweeping the beach. We probably would've found her sooner if we had, but the coroner thinks she likely drowned late Tuesday night. When the tide filled the cave."

"I need to talk to the coroner."

McCray pauses like he's going to protest, say it's a waste of time since the preliminary report rendered this an accident. Instead, he says, "Trapman is an odd duck. Not sure he'll meet with us on a weekend, but I'll try."

Twenty minutes later, Keller receives a text, the pin for a location. Then another:

Meet you there. Prepare yourself.

On the drive, Keller's thoughts race as she tries to fit the puzzle pieces together, make the pixels come into focus. Natasha Belov died just a few days before the students disappeared. If Belov was the author of the Creep List posts, and the inclusion of Professor Turlington suggests that she was, she also accused The Five of being creeps.

She arrives at Grant Park thirty minutes later. Before she's out of the car, McCray has materialized in the lot.

"The coroner's here?" Keller asks, scanning the tree line, the late afternoon sun gilding the green leaves with gold. "Camping or something?"

McCray gestures with his head for Keller to follow.

Soon they veer off the path and into a clearing. The place is crawling with bearded men wearing ragged uniforms and carrying what look like old-time rifles.

"Please tell me this isn't a Civil War reenactment," Keller says.

McCray holds the faintest of smiles.

At the edge of the campsite, two men stand guard in front of a large tent.

"I need to see Trapman," McCray says, no-nonsense.

One of the guards says, "The colonel isn't taking visitors."

Keller retrieves her badge, not in the mood. But McCray puts a hand on her arm.

"We have information on General Pemberton's movement in Vicksburg," McCray says. "It's urgent we see the colonel—this could be the turning point in the battle."

The two guys think on this, then step to the side, allowing them to pass.

Keller gives McCray a look.

McCray shrugs. "I was an American history major."

They're met by another uniformed officer at the tent entrance who opens the flap to allow them inside.

In the back, a man in a uniform decorated with several medals sits in front of a table studying one of those battlefield boards.

These guys really go all in.

"Jay?" the man says.

"Sorry to interrupt you on the weekend when you're—" McCray gestures around the tent. "We're working the missing student case and the Bureau wanted to speak with you."

Keller shakes his hand, introduces herself. "You performed the autopsy of Natasha Belov?"

Trapman gives her a curious expression, like the name doesn't register.

"The student who drowned," Keller adds.

"Oh yes," Trapman says.

"Your preliminary conclusion was that it was an accidental drowning?"

"That's right. She had saltwater in her lungs. No bodily trauma or signs of foul play."

"She'd been missing three days before she was found. A body submerged in water that long is often decomposed," Keller says, testing his conclusion about bodily trauma. She's seen a floater before and they're usually bloated and unrecognizable, making it difficult to detect perimortem trauma.

As if reading her thoughts, Trapman says, "The sea cave where she was found is only submerged for brief periods each day when the tide rises. We surmised that she must've been exploring the cave and got trapped by high tide. We've had a couple deaths in the caves over the years. Same thing. People don't understand it can turn from safe into death trap in a matter of minutes. She was found in the very back of the cavern, tucked in a space between some rocks. That's why she didn't get sucked out to sea, or we might never have seen her again. But she only spent brief periods submerged."

"Did you find anything on the body?"

"She'd tucked her phone in her underwear; it was protected in one of those waterproof beach cases."

"Anything else?"

"We found a small baggie wedged in the phone case, consistent with the type used for controlled substances. We're awaiting tox but our theory is she was high, wandered into the cave before the tide shifted, and got trapped. We ruled out foul play because she was alone. If anyone was with her, they would've been goners too."

A semireasonable conclusion.

"Where's her phone?"

"It was bagged. Santa Cruz PD should have it, unless they released her effects to the family."

"Was there anything out of the ordinary? Anything that stood out to you?"

He thinks on this. "One thing was a little odd."

She waits.

"She had residue of a red compound in her hair and on her clothes."

"Blood?" Keller asks.

"No. If I had to guess, red dye." He pushes up the glasses on his nose.

Keller's mind leaps to the sweatshirt Felix Goffman's mother found in his laundry. It was covered in red. It matches, even if it doesn't make sense. But nothing in this damn case makes sense.

She thanks Trapman for his time.

"If you're ever interested in participating in reenactments," Trapman says, "we could use more women. We can't seem to get many interested."

"Shocker," Keller whispers to McCray as they duck out of the tent.

CHAPTER FIFTY-THREE

FELIX GOFFMAN

Felix sits in the back of the U-Haul, listening to the hum of the spinning tires. His hands and ankles are still bound, but Blane managed to help remove the tape covering their mouths, their eyes. It doesn't matter much because it's dark in the windowless cabin and Felix has barely spoken in the seeming hours they've been trapped in the truck. Even now, he's the quiet one. He's always been that way. He barely spoke well into elementary school. He doesn't remember why, it was just who he was. But when the kids started calling him Quiet Boy and his teachers expressed concern, his poor mom stayed up nights worrying. She'd asked one of the professors at SCU if he had any advice, and he helped her find specialists and therapists for Felix. SCU gradually became a safe haven for Felix and his mom.

The professionals never put their finger on it. Felix did well on standardized tests, seemed otherwise physically and emotionally healthy. He just didn't talk. Until one day, out of nowhere, he did. He remembers this because his mom let out a scream.

But the legacy of Quiet Boy carried over to middle school, where kids can be particularly cruel. The words *freak* and *creeper* were recurrent.

Mom thought high school would be better. He'd shot up in height and he was what some might call conventionally handsome. But it's a strange thing, a reputation. Once you get one, it's like a tin can tied to your leg, rattling after you. In the cruel politics of high school, he made few friends, usually new kids or other loners who dropped him as soon as someone better came along.

He entered college with low expectations. By then, he was used to being alone. But then he met his capstone group. Blane and Mark would joke around with him and bring him to frat parties and make him laugh. Stella would hop on him for piggyback rides and play drinking games and make him feel like one of the cool kids. And Libby looked at him in that earnest way of hers and somehow made him feel wanted.

They didn't ditch him when the Creep Lists came out, when someone called him a stalker. Stella even said, "I'd love for you to stalk me," and traced her finger under his chin, which gave him goose bumps.

Blane and Mark, who were also on the list, laughed it all off, though he wasn't sure it was genuine.

And Libby said she was contacting Rizz and demanding they take it down. He didn't know what she said, but the post miraculously disappeared. Though nothing ever really disappears.

The four were his first true friends. And they were worth protecting.

Which is why he did what he did.

CHAPTER FIFTY-FOUR

THE KELLERS

Back at the station, Keller and McCray report in to the task force, try to make sense of their limited clues. The bullpen is overrun by Bureau agents and local law enforcement, so they camp out in McCray's large office; the task force might have largely marginalized the pair, but it's still McCray's station house.

"They released all of Natasha Belov's effects to her family? Before the final coroner's report?" Keller says.

"My contact at Santa Cruz PD said it's protocol. No signs of foul play. And her family was heading out of the country and wanted her things."

"Shoddy. They shouldn't have released Natasha's phone, they shouldn't—"

Keller's interrupted by the chime of a FaceTime call. Bob's smiling profile pic appears on the screen.

"Do you mind if I take this?" Keller asks McCray. "In case it's about my father-in-law?" The concern for Pops is true enough. But after this long day, she just needs a dose of Bob.

"Of course. Want me to step out?" He gestures to the door.

"No need, assuming you don't mind witnessing some embarrassing marital talk."

"I have plenty of experience with that."

Keller answers and a woman's voice comes through the phone. "Hey-ee," she says.

"Janet! You made it!"

Bob's sister gives a Cheshire cat grin. "I couldn't miss seeing you and the kids." She glances at someone off-screen. "And Dad and this goon."

Bob's head appears in the frame. They couldn't look more different: Janet, a stylish Asian woman with severe bangs; Bob, a bald white guy in need of a shave.

Keller says, "I have my colleague here and don't have much time to talk." She directs her phone at McCray, who waves.

"Well, hell-o," Janet says playfully. "Is he single?"

Keller shakes her head in apology at McCray, and she swears he's blushing.

"I'm so sorry, I won't be home until late," Keller says. "How long are you here?"

"I head out after my meetings tomorrow. But no worries. I totally understand. I've been watching the news . . ." She doesn't need to explain more. "But we can chat in the morning. Or maybe we'll be up when you get home."

"You're staying at the house?" Keller says, surprised, thinking Janet would prefer one of the expensive hotels her clients put her up in. "We took your room. We can go down to the basement with the kids and—"

"Don't be silly. I love the old sofa. Brings back my teenage years of coming home late and passing out. And I couldn't subject you to Bob's old room, given all the ungodly things he did down there. Frankly, I can't believe you let your children near that room. If you had a blacklight it would—"

"All right," Bob cuts in. "We'll let you get back to work. Nice to meet you, Jay," he says loudly. "You both be careful out there." It's a line he stole from an old TV cop show.

"Sorry about that," she says to Jay.

"What a lovely family," is all he says.

There's a knock on the door. Annie the Intern peers through the glass.

McCray waves her inside.

"Hi, um, I found something and I think it could be important."

"What is it?" McCray says.

Keller holds back a smile. The intern and her infectious enthusiasm remind Keller of a young detective named Atticus she worked with, who was taken from the world too soon.

"So, I've been going through Rizz like Agent Sarah, I mean, Special Agent Keller asked." She gestures at the computer on McCray's desk, silently asking permission to use it. McCray gets out of his chair, and Annie takes his seat and pecks on the keys. "Then my dad called and wanted to know what's for dinner and I said, 'How would I know? Make your own dinner.'" She tucks a strand of hair behind her ear. "And my sister is in the background and she says something about all the TikTokers reporting on the case and wants to know what's happening." Annie looks up from the screen and gives them a serious look. "Of course, I told her this is official police business and I can't tell her anything."

Keller considers pushing her along, asking her to get to the point, but she realizes it will be faster to let the young woman go through her process.

"But then I get to thinking. I've been focused on only the sites, not TikTok or podcasts, so I go in *deep*." She taps the keys one last time, then displays her hands at the screen: voilà. She beams. "I love working on this. I think, like, I've found what I'm supposed to do with my life."

A voice comes from the computer speaker: "Is the disappearance a hoax?"

On the screen, a young guy—he can't be more than fifteen—faces the camera. He has shoulder-length brown hair under large headphones, one of those microphones with a foam-covered head close to his face. "I'm Ziggy de la Cruz, and this is *The Treehouse* podcast."

After some intro music and opening credits, the young host continues: "We've all been following the story of the missing college students—five kids who vanished into thin air over Parents Weekend at Santa Clara University in Northern California." The host pauses. "Social media has gone crazy with theories—they were kidnapped by a foreign government, they were sold to sex traffickers, they were murdered and dumped in the woods by a serial killer." He pauses again. "But what if there's no foul play here? What if this is one—big—joke?"

Keller and McCray tap eyes for a beat and continue watching.

"In a *Treehouse* exclusive, one of our listeners alerted us to videos posted on the popular site PrankStool that may shed light on what happened to The Five. Over the past few months, fraternity pledges Blane Roosevelt and Mark Wong apparently have posted several videos of pranks they've pulled in their brief time at the university. PrankStool has a policy that they will never disclose who posts, or pull down something once posted. So, the videos don't disclose who made or posted them other than the screen name TommyBoy2029. But one of our listeners recognized Roosevelt and Wong in one of the segments. Take a look for yourself."

The screen shows headline links for different videos:

Telling College Students They Look Like My Hot Cousin

Sniffing Strangers & Telling Them They Stink

Asking Sorority Girls Football Questions

Under each headline is a frozen screenshot of the video. A cursor moves on the screen and highlights one of the links. A video then fast-forwards, freezing on a quick shot of two smiling faces: Mark Wong and Blane Roosevelt.

The host continues: "TommyBoy2029 posted a video that raises questions of whether the disappearance of The Five is an elaborate hoax."

Another link appears on the screen, a video titled *She Thinks She Killed Her Friend Prank*. The video buffers and then begins.

It shows a bonfire burning on a dark beach.

"Look what we have here," a voice says from off-camera. "I don't know what they took or how much they drank, but I want some of *that* shit."

The screen pans the perimeter of the bonfire where two young women are passed out. It's impossible to make out their faces.

The unseen narrator continues: "Tonight, we find out what happens if you think you killed your friend."

A hand on the video displays what looks like a travel-size shampoo bottle. The video zooms in and the label comes into focus: STAGE BLOOD by a company called Ben Nye. "Leftovers from an epic Halloween frat party." The bottle is jostled back and forth in the way products are displayed in Instagram reels. There's more snickering off-camera.

Then, the camera shifts to show the back of a heavyset guy, who's laughing like he's inebriated, stumbling over to one of the passed-out girls. He turns, his head out of the frame, his hand displaying the bottle of stage blood again. Then he pours the red liquid over the front of the girl's sweatshirt. He stops, then drips some in her hair.

Keller's heart skips. "That pink hoodie, I think it's the one Felix Goffman's mom found in his things."

The guy with the fake blood, still laughing, then picks up a rock, one about the size of a baked potato. He walks over to the second passed-out girl. Her face is covered by her long auburn hair. The guy carefully opens her hand. The girl stirs, and the boy—Keller's convinced it's Mark Wong—freezes. When the girl settles, Mark finishes uncurling her hand and places the rock in it.

Off-screen, another guy whispers loudly, "Someone's coming."

The heavyset guy quickly squirts what's left in the bottle on the rock and scurries away.

The video time jumps. The camera is positioned low now, like it's on a dune or grass, and zoomed in. It's quiet, then Mark and whoever was filming—undoubtedly Blane Roosevelt—erupt in laughter as the girl with the rock in her hand comes to.

She staggers to her feet and releases the rock, unclear what the hell is going on. Then she sees the other girl with the fake blood all over her and releases a scream worthy of a horror movie. The terrified girl's face is out of the frame, but Keller is fairly sure that it's Stella Maldonado.

A voice from the dark calls out. "What's going—?" The outline of a male form on the other side of the bonfire appears.

The video then jostles as Blane and Mark take off away from the beach, laughing like idiot drunks.

The screen goes dark.

It's quiet in McCray's office now.

At last, McCray asks, "What's it mean?"

"I don't know," Keller says. "But look at the date and time it was posted."

The video shows that TommyBoy2029 posted it at 11:39 p.m. last Tuesday: the last time Natasha Belov was seen alive at Panther Beach.

The heavy silence is interrupted by the ring of McCray's phone, then the look of anguish on his face as he listens to the caller.

"Judge Akana, you need to wait for us to get there. You are *not* to go in." McCray's tone is steady but desperate.

McCray motions to Keller, says, "We need to go now." Phone pressed to his ear, he races out of the office, Keller at his heels.

CHAPTER FIFTY-FIVE

THE AKANAS

How many worst days can a person have in their lifetime?

Ken ponders this question as he paces down El Camino Real headed back to the motel. The campus police chief arranged for the room, which was paid for by the university. The chief said the move was to give Ken and Amy some privacy—to get them away from the press stationed outside their original hotel. But Ken suspects it's also a precaution until the police take Bruce Lockwood into custody. Question him about stalking Amy, the tracker on the car, his whereabouts when Libby and her friends disappeared.

As a judge, Ken has presided over cases prosecuting stalkers. Most are cowards. Insecure little men. Or individuals with untreated mental illness. What's always stood out to him is that they honestly don't think what they are doing is wrong. That if they just try hard enough, their undying love will be reciprocated. But when they finally understand that isn't the case, things can get dangerous.

Ken's wearing the ridiculous baseball cap and sunglasses, the cheap disguise he bought at the convenience store, but a couple of students have their phones pointed at him. He'd better get back. He ducked out of the motel for a few minutes to get some air. The room is stifling. From the warm breeze blowing from the ancient air conditioner. From the heavy silence.

He makes it back to the motel parking lot, and the question chases after him: How many worst days can a person have? He's had at least five. One, the day the doctor delivered Timmy's cancer diagnosis. Two, the day Timmy took his last breath. Three, the day, last Friday, he and Amy pulled up to strobing police lights at Rancho San Antonio County Park. Four, Saturday, when the FBI gave its grim report that all signs pointed to foul play. Five, today, when Amy told him about the affair.

His blood curdles at the thought of the love of his life with another man. The thought of the man harassing Amy and her dealing with the threat on her own.

Something that can only be described as rage settles in his chest. But he needs to push it down. Remain calm. No drama. But maybe that's what pushed Amy away. That he'd leaned too much into his No Drama Akana persona. No drama meant not having to face the devastation. By pushing down his bottomless grief over Timmy, he left Amy to bear hers alone.

He walks toward the staircase. The motel is like ones he's seen in movies—two stories, with the rooms accessible from outside.

Before he heads up, he spots something unsettling. Something that makes him fear that today will be the sixth worst day of his life.

An F-150 truck in the parking lot. With an LA Police decal on the back window. The truck described in the BOLO for Bruce Lockwood.

CHAPTER FIFTY-SIX

Ken Akana grips the phone, presses it tightly to his ear.

"You are *not* to go in," Chief McCray commands.

He hears Chief McCray say something in the background, then his voice is back in Ken's ear again. "I have a team only five minutes out," the police chief says.

Ken's heart hammers. They're close. And he knows the chief is right. But Amy . . .

He stabs the disconnect button and hurries quietly up the concrete stairs to the second floor, to the door of their room. The window is open a crack—he'd opened it earlier—but the drapes are drawn now.

He crouches low, puts his ear to the opening. Hears Amy's voice, steady but pleading:

"I'll go with you. You don't need the gun."

"We can finally be together now, out in the open," the male voice says.

"Yes." It's weak and unconvincing.

"And I can help you find your daughter."

"Did you have anything to do with . . . ?"

"What? Of course not. Why would you—I'm a *police* officer. Of course I wouldn't."

"Okay," Amy says, "help me find her, let's go."

"I want to wait for your husband."

"But I told you, our marriage is over. We're through. He's not coming here."

Ken's heart is shattering into pieces—she's trying to protect him.

"I know he's staying here. I saw you check in together. He and I just need to have a talk."

"About what?" Amy's tone is desperate.

"That's between us men."

"You don't need to do that. I don't want him. I only want you."

A siren wails from down the street. Ken jerks to the side as the drapes fly open.

"Goddammit," Lockwood says. "We need to go."

Ken catches sight of distant spinning red and blue lights. The police are close, but they won't make it in time.

The door bursts open.

Amy comes out of the room, Lockwood right behind her, his hand clutching her upper arm. Amy's eyes widen when she sees Ken.

Ken waves for her to get out of the way, to run. Fear blazes in her eyes but she does it, yanks her arm away hard and takes off.

Ken doesn't wait for Lockwood to comprehend, to go after her, to take a shot.

He launches himself into Lockwood, propelled by white-hot fury, summoning every ounce of his strength. He rams into the man, throwing his weight into it, grabbing his midsection, and hoisting him up and over the thin metal railing.

CHAPTER FIFTY-SEVEN

LIBBY AKANA

The first time Libby ever saw Stella Maldonado was at the campus swimming pool. She wore a tiny bikini and brimmed with confidence. This girl wasn't pretending—faking it like Libby had been doing for so long.

She watched as Stella rolled her eyes at the boys who were showing off, doing cannonballs and acting like idiots, trying to get her attention.

The girls too took note when Stella emerged out of the pool dripping, like a scene from some nineties movie.

Libby wore a cover-up and hadn't gone in the water since the group of shirtless frat boys planted their flag in a cluster of lounge chairs. She pretended not to notice when Stella took a chair next to hers. Libby nearly looked behind her when this girl—this effortlessly cool girl—spoke.

"Hey, don't you live in Campisi?"

"Yes. I'm Libby," she said, the way her dad taught her. Firm eye contact and a thrust of her hand for a shake.

She thought she'd blown it when Stella smirked, took her hand, mirrored her stiff tone, and said, "Stella Maldonado."

There was no other idle chitchat—the *where are you from? what's your major?* talk. Instead, Stella just said, "I have some vodka in my room."

Libby was taken aback. She didn't drink in high school . . . well, maybe a beer she nursed at parties. But she also didn't hesitate to head to this cool girl's room.

Libby Akana's first act of rebellion.

And over the next week—drunk on vodka, intoxicated by living on her own without the cloud of her brother's illness, inebriated by the spell of the cool girl—Libby felt euphoric.

She'll never forget those early days at SCU.

She didn't think things could be more perfect. Until she met the tall, quiet boy who appeared at her first capstone meeting. Felix Goffman with his soft voice and old-fashioned name.

Libby thought it was kismet when Stella was assigned to the same group.

She was infatuated. With them both. Before then, she'd never thought of herself as a follower. But follow she did.

And she wasn't the only one. Felix followed Stella too, hung on her every word, positioned himself to be near her at the dining hall, at parties, at study group.

They were a love triangle, even though none of them had hooked up. Libby and Felix were under the spell of the exotic girl from the Upper East Side with her talk of speakeasies, summers in the Hamptons, parties in Brooklyn.

The three were inseparable. But things started to change. Felix sulked when Stella would disappear at a party to make out with a guy—or a girl. Libby sulked because Felix was sulking.

And Stella was oblivious to it all. Oblivious that she was the sun they orbited. Oblivious to the green-eyed monster growing in Libby, oblivious to her anger that Felix was entranced by Stella. Then Stella began to pull away, become a follower herself, in the throes of an obsession herself. With a junior she met at Rave in a Cave. Someone Stella talked about the same way Libby and Felix spoke of Stella:

She's so cool. Totally herself.

She's so wild. She poured a beer on this guy who got too handsy.

She's so brave. She shoved this girl who called me a bitch.

Then: "My friend said she could score some psychedelics. She says it's the only way to really open your mind. Want to come?"

"I'm not sure," Libby had said. It was a big leap from vodka to psychedelics. But she was losing Stella, losing Felix. Since meeting this friend, Stella barely responded to any of Libby's texts. Seemed to be avoiding her. So this invitation was big. *Big!*

"Suit yourself, Libs. Felix?"

"Ah, yeah, okay. I'm all for opening my mind."

Stella kissed him on the cheek and that sealed the deal.

"Okay," Libby said, "I'm in."

"You're going to love her. I've told her all about you guys."

The plan was set. Tuesday night at Panther Beach.

Libby spent the entire week with her stomach in knots. She plotted how to back out without disappointing Stella. Then she decided that, maybe with her mind opened, she could tell Felix how she felt about him. Maybe she'd overcome the fear of him saying, *I'm sorry, I don't think of you that way.*

Maybe the drugs would give her the courage she needed.

Tuesday night, they ran into Blane and Mark in the common area of the dorm.

"Bonfire party? We're in."

When the four of them arrived, Stella was the only one on the beach, dancing to her earbuds. She looked like a snake being charmed, the way she moved in the firelight.

Libby remembers Blane and Mark's faces when Stella's friend—the girl Stella basically dropped Libby for—arrived. Libby isn't proud that she took pleasure when Mark said, "You? No way. I'm not partying with this chick."

Blane said, "She's crashy." They said the girl had made the posts about Mark's father. The posts about them all, the Creep Lists.

Stella defended her friend, said they were being dramatic. But Mark and Blane stormed off.

Libby and Felix, of course, took Stella's side. Libby isn't proud of that either, or that she drank too much of the cheap vodka and took the psychedelics. That she did indeed ask Felix to walk with her on the beach after Stella and her friend passed out. That she began to tell him how she felt, only to be interrupted by the sound of Stella's scream.

And right now, just a few nights later, she's not far from that very spot again.

But this time, she's being marched at gunpoint to a sea cave where she will die.

CHAPTER FIFTY-EIGHT

THE KELLERS

Keller walks up the steps at the front of the house. The porch light is out, windows dark. She'd hoped to see Bob's sister, but everyone must be asleep. It's nearly ten o'clock; she spent the better part of the evening at the campus station. The mood there was dark, deflated, particularly after the attempted abduction of Judge Akana's wife, the death of Bruce Lockwood, a now-disgraced fellow law enforcement officer.

Keller tries to shake the image of the pool of blood around Lockwood's head on the concrete of the motel parking lot. The shattered judge and his wife holding each other in the motel room.

After, the task force continued to brainstorm, share intel, and try to connect the dots. Her boss finally insisted she leave, get some rest. Keller resisted until he made it an order. Peters still hasn't taken to Keller.

She finds the key to the unfamiliar lock—there's a trick to it, Bob told her—and manages to get the door open.

From the foyer, she hears whispered voices. Sees a light burning from the living room. She finds Bob and Janet, cocktails in hand.

"Hey!" Janet says, already on her feet. She gives Keller a tight hug.

Bob rises too. "Did you ever get dinner?"

"No. Wasn't hungry after that burger, and we've been running nonstop."

Bob is adamant that she eat, and they all converge in the kitchen, where he heats up a serving of lasagna. He says he made it for Janet, since it's her favorite.

He pours her a glass of wine, tops off Janet's whiskey, as they sit at the kitchen table. They catch up on Janet's life: still single, and still loving it. Still too much travel for the firm, and still loving it. She coos about the kids.

"I can't believe how big they are. It's only been—what?—a year since I saw you in New York? They've grown so much."

Keller nods. She's trying to stay focused, to remain in the present, but her mind is elsewhere. With the bloody body in a motel parking lot. With five college students who are unlikely to have a happy ending.

"Any developments in the case?" Janet asks, perhaps sensing Keller's mind is there anyway.

"Mostly dead ends," Keller replies.

"Those poor parents," Janet says. "I don't have kids, but if I did, I'd make anyone who hurt them pay. Make them suffer the same fate . . . no, a worse fate."

"I told you she has a dark side," Bob says.

Janet punches him in the arm.

Likely sensing Keller's stress, Janet steers the conversation back to the twins. "It was so cute: Michael asked me why Bob and I don't look alike. It didn't dawn on him we were adopted."

Bob says, "She told him I got hit with an ugly stick. But honestly, how did he not put that together?"

"He's not always quick on the uptake," says Keller with a smile.

"Like his father," Janet adds.

"Truth," Bob says.

Later, Keller washes her face in the small bathroom. She excused herself, told Bob and Janet she was wiped out. Bob's always been a night owl from his years working with musicians when he was a recording engineer. Janet also likes the night. She's been known to go to clubs after midnight, keeping up with women half her age. Keller smiles, thinking about her son's question: Why don't Bob and Janet look alike? Beyond Michael's sweet obliviousness, it's funny because the siblings are so much alike in other ways: both aggressively positive, both kind, both spreading light wherever they go. Pops and Ruth should've written a parenting book.

Keller is exhausted but too wired to sleep. Not even the glass of wine made her drowsy. But she needs to be sharp tomorrow, so she gets into bed, turns off the lights.

And she lies there, hoping to drift off. But her mind churns backward through the day. Get to sleep, she tells herself. When it's plain that's not going to happen, she checks her email for any developments. A screen is the worst thing to put in front of your eyes if you're trying to sleep, but she can't help herself.

There's a message from that cocky AUSA who got taken down a few sizes by Judge Romero on the golf course. Keller sits up, clicks on the light. The geofence report must be in.

The report is short. It lists the time and date for the searches:

Friday night, 7 to 9 p.m., within a 50-yard radius of the parking lot of Rancho San Antonio County Park. The report has overlapping circles with blue dots inside them representing the phones within each area. Keller pinches the screen of her phone to zoom in on the smallest circle, the one with the most blue dots clustered together.

She feels a prickling of excitement when she sees only six phones in that area at that precise time, the phones within the "fence." Four from the missing students, either under their own names or their parents' accounts. The fifth, an account for Deepa Patel, Libby Akana's roommate. That's consistent with what they know: Stella smashed Libby's phone and Libby borrowed her roommate's.

But what gets Keller's adrenaline soaring is the outlier number. There's only one other phone in the smallest circle in the geofence at the time the kids disappeared.

Her heart bangs in her chest as she sees the account holder. It's registered to Natasha Belov.

CHAPTER FIFTY-NINE

Keller's mind is whirling, thoughts bouncing around in her skull. Natasha Belov's phone was within the same radius as The Five's phones when their devices were either shut off or destroyed. But this makes no sense: Natasha Belov's lifeless body was found in a sea cave *before* The Five went missing.

So how did her phone end up forty miles away three nights later? And the more important question: Who had Natasha's phone?

Keller recalls that Santa Cruz PD released it to Natasha's family.

For some reason, her mind hurtles to Janet's words from earlier that evening, and they hit Keller like a two-by-four:

"I don't have kids, but if I did, I'd make anyone who hurt them pay. Make them suffer the same fate . . ."

Keller makes a quick search on her phone, then rushes to the living room. Bob and Janet look startled.

"The sea caves at Panther Beach. You know how to find them?" Keller asks her husband.

"Ah, yeah, we'd go there as kids. Everything okay?"

"I need you to take me there now."

"Now? What's—"

"I'll explain on the way."

Bob tilts his head to the side.

Concern spreads over Janet's face. "Sarah, is everything all right, are you—"

"Can you watch the kids?" Keller interrupts. "I mean, be there in case they wake up or Pops needs something?"

"Of course. But—"

"We need to go *now*," Keller tells Bob.

"Whoa, slow down. What's the urgency? Why can't it wait until—"

"Because," she says, breathless, "it will be high tide in less than an hour."

CHAPTER SIXTY

THE FIVE

The water is up to their chests now, the sea cave dark, with only a ray of filtered moonlight coming through the small opening. They're just silhouettes in the darkness.

"We need to get out of here," Blane says. "Fuck it—I'd rather take my chances than die like this."

"There's only one path out," Libby says. She moves into the splinter of light. Her makeup, still smeared from the tape covering her eyes, bleeds down her face. "And he's out there. He'll shoot . . ."

Mark says nothing. His wound might be infected; he's taken a turn for the worse and is slumped against a rock.

"He can't shoot us all," Blane points out.

"But the waves," Libby says.

She's right, of course. All of their options are bad ones. Stay and risk drowning; leave and risk getting shot or sucked out to sea.

They've gone around and around and the decision has been

to sit tight, tread water, and hope by the end of high tide there's a gap at the top of the cave, enough air to survive.

"So we just wait to die?" Blane asks the group.

Another wave pounds the rocks and more water gushes into the cavern.

At last, Stella breaks the quiet: "I'm sorry."

This seems to awaken the group, if only because Stella isn't one for apologies.

Stella continues: "I told Natasha things—I didn't think she'd post about them on Rizz."

It's a moment before anyone responds.

Felix's voice pierces the gloom. "You told her I was a stalker? That's why she posted that? You said I—"

"I didn't mean it the way she posted about it. I didn't say 'stalker.'"

"Well, how'd you fucking mean it?" Felix says, his voice laced with pain.

"She told me she had a stalker, that she was being harassed. I told you guys what happened to her with him. So I joked that . . . I said you could be a bit—I don't know—smothering. I was only trying to connect with her about what she was going through with her real stalker."

"Whatever," Blane says. "But what the hell did Mark and I do to deserve her posting that he was a creep, posting about his father, saying I was an enabler of shit?"

"I didn't tell her any of that. She said she met you at a party. That Mark told her about his dad. That she overheard you both talking shit about her. Calling her *crashy*."

"So she accuses Mark of being a creep?"

"I told her to take the first post down. She actually got mad at me, and included *me* on the second post as one of the enablers."

"And you stayed friends with her," Blane says, his tone filled with disgust.

"She apologized. I told you guys she's been through some serious shit. She took the posts down."

"So what did *I* do, Stella?" Libby demands.

Stella is quiet a beat, then says, "I don't know. I told her you were, like, perfect and she—she seemed like she was jealous of that or something. I don't know. But I told her she needed to take down the Creep List posts. That it was uncool. That you were my friends. And she took them down. I thought if you got to know each other . . ."

Another stretch of silence continues as they process it all.

Then, Blane: "So it's your fault. If she hadn't posted the Creep Lists, we wouldn't have pulled the prank with the fake blood. She wouldn't have run off when she came to. She wouldn't have wandered into this cave and . . ."

"It's not Stella's fault," Felix interrupts. "It's mine."

Before anyone asks, Felix wades toward the cave's small opening. Another breaker pounds the rocks and he's pushed back. But he grabs the jagged wall and forces his way toward the moonlight.

"I'm going to make this right," he calls back to them. "I'm going to try to stop him. Just hang on."

Before he disappears, he says, "If something happens to me, tell my mom I love her."

CHAPTER SIXTY-ONE

THE KELLERS

"This is a bad idea, Sarah," Bob says, looking around the opening in the brush leading down a path to the sea caves. "You need to wait for the task force."

"That's what I'm doing. McCray is a few minutes out."

He side-eyes her. Waves crash in the distance and trees rustle in the strong wind. Bob is rarely tense, rarely uptight about anything, but in the moonlight she sees worry in his eyes.

Less than ten minutes until reinforcements arrive. But water is already filling the cave, if the internet tidal charts are right. They might already be too late.

Maybe she's wrong, maybe the kids aren't here. But the puzzle pieces finally fit.

Mark and Blane made the PrankStool video that shows Stella coming to, screaming when she sees Natasha Belov covered in what she must have thought was blood. Then someone else—Felix? Libby?—appears at the scene. Mark and Blane run off and the video goes dark.

Then what happened? The video doesn't answer that. But it was posted on Tuesday, the night Natasha was last seen, according to the time stamp on the PrankStool site.

Later that week, a young woman—Libby?—makes an anonymous tip that Natasha is missing.

Mark Wong visits his father, asks about getting a lawyer.

Libby and Stella are in a fight about something.

Then all the kids disappear the night of the Parents Weekend dinner.

Who would have a motive to take them all?

Someone seeking revenge for what The Five did—what they must've done to Natasha Belov that night on the beach. Someone who loved Natasha so much that they crave vengeance, want whoever caused her death to pay, to suffer the same way their daughter did by drowning in that sea cave.

Bob is quiet as he paces on the dunes.

"They're just kids," Keller adds. "I can't wait for too much longer."

"We have kids too, Sarah." It's the second time he's used her first name, a rarity. Usually it's G-woman, Agent Bad Ass, Hot Mama, or some such.

"And honestly," she says, trying to ease the tension, "when's the last time we got to go out alone on a date?"

A vehicle pulls into the lot near the opening and McCray appears. He holds a flashlight.

"It's nearly high tide, we can't wait," she says to McCray. But it's really for Bob.

"Sarah . . ." her husband says.

"You both wait here," McCray says. "I'll check it out."

Before Keller can protest, McCray starts down the path.

Keller faces Bob.

He shakes his head, angry. "Please don't do this."

"I'll be okay. The rest of the team will be here soon."

"I'm coming too, then."

"No," she says definitively. "You're not trained. And it will get me in trouble. And I need you here to show them the way." What she doesn't say is that she can't put both of them at risk. For the twins.

McCray has disappeared down the trail.

"Promise me you won't go into the cave," he says, relenting. "It's not just getting trapped in there that can kill you. People have been sucked out into the ocean by the riptide. I'm serious, Sarah."

Keller turns, looks toward the parking area above for any signs of the team. Looks for strobes or flashlights.

"I love you," she says, then she turns and runs down the path.

She catches up to McCray. He's stopped at a fork on the trail. He puts a finger over his lips like he's listening for something.

Keller's heart is thrumming. The tide is climbing high up the rocky shore.

McCray whispers into her ear: "I think I see someone over—"

His sentence is stopped short by the explosive sound of a gunshot.

CHAPTER SIXTY-TWO

"Stay with me!" Keller shouts into the wind.

She's holding back terror and tears as she applies pressure to McCray's chest. Blood seeps through her fingers.

McCray is still conscious. He's trying to say something. Keller is shaking, even though she's not cold.

McCray's eyes dart around like a trapped animal's. He's in shock.

"You're going to be okay. Focus on my voice, Jay."

His eyes widen, then he tries to sit up, but she keeps the pressure on, keeps him pressed to the ground.

That's when she feels what can only be the barrel of a gun against the back of her head.

Panic grips her. But at the same time, her training kicks in. She forces a calm, a detachment that enables her heartbeat to steady.

"Hands," a male voice commands.

"I can't, he's bleeding, he'll—"

Another *pop*, and sand bursts up from the ground near McCray's head.

Keller raises her hands. She gasps at the sight of the blood oozing from McCray's chest when the pressure is removed.

"Take out your gun. Slowly," the voice says.

With two fingers she retrieves her sidearm, her back still to the man. You should never give up your service weapon. But she has no choice. In the movies, she'd beat the shooter to the draw, twist around, and take him out. But this isn't the movies. She has a gun to her head while McCray bleeds out in the sand.

The gun is plucked from her hand.

Then she hears a woman's voice. "This has gone too far. You can't."

It takes Keller a moment to realize that the woman with the Eastern European accent isn't speaking to Keller, she's talking to the man with the gun.

"What choice do we have now?" he replies.

The female voice continues: "This—all of this—isn't bringing her back."

"They need to pay. For what they did to her."

The woman pleads now: "This man, this lady, had nothing to do with—"

"Mr. and Mrs. Belov," Keller says loudly, her back still turned. This silences the couple.

She takes the chance and slowly turns toward them, hands still raised.

When she turns, she sees the pair is wearing Smurf masks. The same disguise from the FedEx video.

Mr. Belov says something Keller can't make out, then rips off his mask, like he's beaten.

"The tide . . . there's still time," Keller pleads. "We can still save them. Make this right. It's not too late."

Mrs. Belov removes her mask, gives her husband a pleading look.

"He needs a doctor or he could die," Keller says, looking at McCray. She focuses her attention on Mrs. Belov. "You're right. This needs to stop."

She's praying the Bureau, the rest of the task force, will be there soon. She can see McCray writhing on the ground in her peripheral.

She should've listened to Bob. They should've waited for backup.

Natasha's father's expression is pure devastation. Mixed with something else: fury. He holds up a phone. "She recorded it. Her last moments."

Keller eyes the cell phone in the sparkly case.

Mr. Belov's voice breaks. He's still holding up the phone in one hand, his gun in the other. "Do you know what they did to my daughter?"

Natasha must have made a video recording, maybe for someone to find, maybe to text to her parents. A dying declaration.

"She was so happy before. So excited about going to college. Then . . ."

"Your wife is right, Mr. Belov," Keller says. "This won't bring her back."

"Maybe not." His jaw clenches. "But it will remove terrible people from this planet. Make them feel what she felt."

"They're kids, Mr. Belov."

"Kids who chased her into that cave to die."

"We don't know that."

His face contorts with anger. "*I* know that." He shakes the phone in his hand.

Keller's mind races. She could run, try to elude them in the darkness, but he'll shoot. He's proven that.

Mrs. Belov walks over to her husband, says something Keller can't hear, possibly pleading with him.

Keller's gut roils when the wife shakes her head violently and Mr. Belov pushes her aside. Keller sees resolve in his expression.

"I'm sorry," he says.

He raises the gun and directs it at Keller's center mass.

Before he shoots, a voice cuts through the night.

"Stop! They didn't hurt Natasha. Neither did my friends." A young man emerges from the darkness, looking exhausted.

Mr. Belov whirls around.

Standing with his hands raised is Felix Goffman. He's soaking wet.

"Get back," Mr. Belov says. He moves the gun back and forth between Keller and Felix.

"Just listen to me," he tells Natasha's father. "I . . . I was out of it the night Natasha died . . . alcohol and drugs," he admits. "I was walking on the beach and heard a scream, so I ran to the bonfire. I found her there, passed out, covered in what I thought was blood. I checked her pulse, I did my best anyway. I didn't know it was a prank, that the blood wasn't real. I didn't know she was passed out, I thought she was gone."

Mr. Belov glowers at Felix. Keller looks back at McCray; his eyes are still open and his chest heaves shallowly.

"I didn't want my friends to get in trouble!" Felix cries. "I thought it was just the drugs, everyone was out of their minds. So I carried her down the beach. Near the dunes. I thought she was already dead—"

"Lies."

"No," Felix says. "And my friends didn't know about this. I told them she ran off after the prank."

"You're lying. You harassed her! You threatened her. You *stalked* her!"

Felix appears confused. "No, I never—"

"Enough!" bellows Mr. Belov. "I found the texts on her phone. She saved them all. You sent my daughter thirty-seven texts on the day she died! You harassed her for more than a year! She *begged* you to stop bothering her."

Felix shakes his head, clearly alarmed. "No! Listen: I wasn't even a student here last year. I didn't even meet her until—"

"The news reports say you're a stalker, a creep. My daughter saved your contact as 'Dr. Creep.' Stop lying!"

Keller sees understanding dawn on Felix's face. "It wasn't me texting her," he says. "But I know who it was."

Mr. Belov aims his gun at Felix. Keller considers charging him, but Belov's wife now has Keller's own gun pointed at her.

"Who was it, then?" Belov asks, his chin rising up.

"I promise I'll tell you, I'll even *take* you to him. But you have to let my friends come out of the cave first."

Mr. Belov seems to ponder this. Then he walks up to Felix and puts the gun to his head. "You're going to take me to this person now."

Belov pushes Felix ahead of him, away from the cave. He tells his wife, "If the agent moves or any of them come out of the cave, shoot them. I'll return soon."

A distraught Mrs. Belov holds the gun weakly in her hand but nods.

"Be strong. For Natasha," he says.

Then Mr. Belov marches Felix into the darkness.

CHAPTER SIXTY-THREE

Mrs. Belov keeps the gun trained on Keller. The tremor in her grip tells Keller that the woman doesn't have the stomach to shoot her. That she should charge the grieving mother. If Keller doesn't get help soon, the students will die, and McCray needs immediate medical attention, if it's not already too late.

But the twins. Bob. She can't take the risk. The task force will be here any moment.

"It's not too late to save them," Keller says.

Mrs. Belov says, "Stop talking."

"The police are almost here. You won't escape. I'm not the only one who knows it was you who took the students."

"I said, stop—"

Mrs. Belov is stopped short by a large figure rushing her from an oblique angle. After a jarring collision and nearly zero struggle, Mrs. Belov lies pinned tight to the sand, Keller's service weapon flung out of her reach.

Keller's heart drops when she realizes who's straddling the woman.

Bob.

Bob!

It's then that a sea of bodies storms down from the bluff above. Before Keller can move, men and women in blue windbreakers are everywhere. Pulling Bob gently off Mrs. Belov, then securing the woman in cuffs.

Keller turns toward a sound, the blades of a helicopter slashing the air as it projects a searchlight beam onto the sea cave.

A voice murmurs in her ear: "Worst date night *ever.*"

She turns and throws her arms around Bob. But then she yanks away and reels in a panic: "McCray?"

"We've got a medic working on him, he's still conscious," her ASAC says, approaching them. Peters looks different, like the stress has chewed away a piece of him.

"The kids?" she asks, still frantic.

"They're on it." He angles his head at the rescue helicopter.

"Belov took Felix Goffman," Keller says.

"Do you know where?"

Keller shakes her head. "I need to talk to his wife."

Minutes later, Keller sits in the front seat of a police cruiser, her gaze on the woman handcuffed in the back.

"We need to find your husband, Mrs. Belov. For his own safety."

Iza Belov appears ravaged, like she hasn't slept in days. She stares ahead blankly.

Keller continues. "Is this what Natasha would want? Your husband taken down like a hunted animal?"

Finally, a reaction: Mrs. Belov's eyes meet Keller's. "Are they all right? The other students."

"They're out of the cave," Keller says. "But far from all right.

Right now, we need to know where your husband took Felix Goffman."

Mrs. Belov stares ahead blankly. "I knew when that boy was shot that first night . . ."

"Help us find your husband. So we can bring him back safe."

Bloodshot eyes look into Keller's. "When the police gave us Natasha's belongings, I told my husband not to go through her phone." She looks out the car window. "That there are some things we don't need to know. That these days a phone is more personal than a diary. But he wouldn't listen. He saw her texts and her web searches and her pictures. He saw videos of them that night. Saw a group text. That's when he changed. I kept thinking he'd let those kids go. But each day we held the students, he would find something else on her phone, something that would break his heart again."

Keller realizes that Mrs. Belov isn't going to tell her where to find her husband, if she even knows. "Why did you take the students?"

Belov lets out a strangled laugh. "He wanted them to feel what she felt when they chased her in that cave." She swallows. "I did too, at first. But then my head started to clear. I said we should let them go."

Keller imagines the scene: The Belovs summoning the students to the park using Natasha's phone. Maybe they hadn't intended at first to take the students; maybe they wanted to confront them, but then things spun out of control. Mark Wong was shot. Then they restrained The Five in the van and there was no turning back.

Mrs. Belov continues: "This morning, my husband found a file on Natasha's phone, a file that explained why she—why the drugs, the suicide attempt last summer, the distancing herself from her friends, from us."

"What did he find?" Keller asks.

"Texts. Hundreds and hundreds of them. Harassing her, stalking her. Threatening her."

Keller's heart is accelerating.

"Who?"

Mrs. Belov shakes her head again.

"My daughter didn't use his real name in her contacts. She called him 'Dr. Creep.'"

Keller frowns.

"He gave her a nickname too," Mrs. Belov spits the words. "He called Natasha his butterfly."

Keller feels a lightning bolt crack through her. She rushes out of the car and tells her ASAC that she thinks she knows where Ivan Belov took Felix.

CHAPTER SIXTY-FOUR

As they speed toward the small cul-de-sac, Keller wishes she could be at McCray's side at the hospital. At Pops's house with her family.

But she needs to catch the man who tried to steal five kids from their families.

She's uniquely familiar with the location where Mr. Belov has gone. Keller was there, mere hours ago, meeting the professor and his young wife and adorable babies.

She's instructed the team that they are *not* to go in guns blazing. The element of surprise is their best chance at catching Ivan Belov. At saving Felix Goffman, the professor, and his wife and twins.

As Peters drives, Keller reflects on her meeting with Professor Turlington. She believed the charismatic professor. That he'd been the victim of a seductive young woman everyone said had severe problems.

By all accounts, though, Natasha Belov had been a joyful kid, a vivacious student her first year. But something happened sophomore year—and it happened the quarter she took Turlington's government class. And maybe that's the way it goes: We instinctively believe these charismatic, accomplished men and demonize their accusers.

They reach Professor Turlington's street and Peters kills the headlights. It's after midnight, quiet. Not the kind of neighborhood where anyone comes out this late. They park a few doors down. Two tactical teams are in place: One will take entry from the front of the house, one from the rear.

Peters is coordinating it all on his radio. He gives her a look. "You're sure about this?"

She nods, double-checking the Kevlar vest Peters gave her.

They crouch-run to the front of the house where a team is already in stacked formation. The doorframe is splintered. Someone kicked it in before they arrived. She feels a shot of adrenaline rip through her.

They file silently into the house. Trailing the team, Keller hears voices. Someone shouting. Someone crying.

The lead raises his arm, closes his hand into a fist to signal for the team to come to a stop. Keller quietly makes her way to the front. The team lead shakes his head, gestures for her to get to the tail. But she peeks around the corner of the hall into the living room. The room strewn with the trappings of new parenthood, but also something horrific: the body of Felix Goffman, blood staining the carpet around his head.

Even worse, Ivan Belov has a gun pressed to the temple of Professor Turlington's wife, who is visibly trembling, all the color drained from her face.

"Admit what you did!" Belov shouts. "You texted my daughter thirty-seven times the day she died. She wouldn't have been on drugs or with those kids that night if you hadn't . . ."

"No, I didn't!" the professor shouts.

"I went through every single text. She told you she'd go to the police if you didn't leave her alone."

"I told you, I didn't do anything to your daughter," Professor Turlington whimpers.

Turlington's young wife is weeping now, making occasional gulping sounds like she's struggling to take in air, the gun still pressed firmly to her head.

"There's a tradition passed down from my grandfather, a famous vodka maker," Ivan Belov says. His tone is distant, detached. "When my Natasha was born, we buried a barrel of his best vodka. It was to stay there, to be excavated on her wedding day. The finest drink for her guests." He swallows. "Now we will drink it at her funeral." He pauses. "This is your last chance. To save your wife."

Keller's heart is galloping, but her hands are steady on her gun as she aims it at Belov. She tries to keep her thoughts clear, focusing on the best tactical move. How they can take Belov out without Mrs. Turlington being collateral damage. The curtains are drawn, so the team from the rear won't have a clean shot. And if Keller and her team charge in, the gun pressed to the woman's head might discharge as he's taken down.

"Okay," the professor says at last. "I'll tell you. Just don't hurt her."

Belov gives the professor a hateful stare.

"It's not what you think," the professor says. "We were— I never forced her. We were together. And when she called that night, I came to help her."

Keller feels her heart skip in her chest. The professor was at Panther Beach the night Natasha Belov got trapped in the cave and drowned.

"I was too late. I couldn't . . ."

Keller watches as Mr. Belov's face turns to stone. "You lie. She didn't call you."

"No . . . Please," the professor says.

Keller believes Belov's going to do it—she braces to take the shot—but then Belov raises his free hand, showing Turlington his dead daughter's phone.

Keller can't see the display, but a voice comes from the device. He's playing a video.

"Who's there?" a young woman's tremulous voice says from the phone.

There's the sound of wind blowing into the receiver.

"You guys aren't funny."

The voice stops. There's a long beat of silence.

The voice returns, higher-pitched in panic. "What are you—? Get away from me. Don't—"

Then there's a rustling sound like quick movement. Like she's running.

Mr. Belov says, "I thought it was the kids. But it was *you* . . ." He says this as if more to himself than to the professor.

The final pieces are aligning themselves in Keller's head: After the prank, Felix Goffman thought Natasha was dead and carried her to the dunes, not the cave. Natasha must've come to, disoriented, her mind still spinning from the psychedelics, vodka, and cruel prank.

The rest of the students were gone. Natasha was alone on the beach.

Then someone else appeared. Professor Turlington. He'd slipped out of his house and followed her, hiding in the shadows until he could get her alone. Fuming all the while because he thought Natasha made the Rizz posts renewing the allegations against him. Enraged because she rejected him and ignored his barrage of texts.

Natasha must have been terrified, knowing Turlington was dangerously obsessed. Knowing he'd silenced her before. In a last, desperate move, she put her phone on video-record. Then she ran, stumbling across the sand, tucking the phone into her waterproof case and hiding it.

Keller has just heard the final words of the young woman.

She knows what happened next: When Turlington caught Natasha on the beach, he silenced her for good. Drowned her, then dragged her body into the cave to make it appear to be an accident. Maybe it was he who reported the PrankStool video. Trying to place other people at the beach that night in case his staged scene didn't hold up.

Keller looks at Belov as he lowers the phone. He is going to shoot them both—make the professor watch his wife die first, feel that pain, then kill Turlington.

She can't wait any longer, she has to risk it.

"Drop the gun, Mr. Belov," she says, coming into the room, her weapon trained on Belov. She hears the team shuffle in behind her.

The grieving father doesn't react at first.

"Drop the gun," she repeats, louder. Then it happens in less than a heartbeat.

Belov shifts his gun and empties it into Professor Turlington.

Keller simultaneously discharges her firearm.

Belov falls to the floor. Next to the professor, next to Felix Goffman.

Agents burst through the back doors, kick Mr. Belov's gun away, confirm he's dead. That all three of them are. They hurry Professor Turlington's wife out of the house, retrieve the babies safely from the nursery.

Keller turns over her gun to Peters, per Bureau protocol when an agent uses deadly force. Then she goes outside, takes in the night air, and calls her husband. She feels an ache in her chest, a sudden need to see him and her children.

"It's over," she tells Bob. "I'm coming home."

GRADUATION WEEKEND

THREE YEARS LATER

CHAPTER SIXTY-FIVE

THE ROOSEVELTS

Cynthia steps out of the SUV, which has pulled to the front of the restaurant. She smiles at the DS agent holding her door. She thought they were up her ass before, but now that she's secretary of state, she can't escape her team of shadows.

The crowd outside the establishment—a Mexican restaurant Blane picked called Puesto—gawks. In D.C., no one bats an eye at a security detail. Any self-respecting hostess is fully versed on the protocol. But here, the masses, mostly tech geeks by the looks of tonight's diners, act like the pope has arrived.

She's led to a table in the back. She has a six-person detail just for this dinner, which is ridiculous. The threat has diminished since she was confirmed as secretary—they wouldn't dare take out such a high-level target. It would be an act of war. In these partisan times, her typical threats are people who disagree with the administration's policies. She doesn't fear a physical assault so much as a drink being thrown in her face or being spat upon.

She sees Blane and his buddy Mark screwing around at the

table. Blane didn't get the haircut for tomorrow morning's ceremony as promised, but she won't mention it. Or she'll try not to. Who's she kidding?

The boys stand when she arrives. Blane says "Mom" so cheerfully it's almost as if he's really happy to see her.

Sitting at the side of the table is his father. Hank offers a small smile and Cynthia returns it.

Hank stopped drinking after the kids were taken. And he started to resemble that confident young writer she'd met in college. He even finished the Great American Blank Page. His new book was released last year, and Cynthia made a surprise appearance at his *Politics & Prose* signing. After all, she loved him once. And she realized after what happened that if she wanted to have a good relationship with her son, she needed to mend things with her ex.

Seated, Blane pours her a margarita. He and Mark have had a few already, she thinks. It hasn't crossed his mind to go alcohol-free out of respect for his father. *Kids.*

"We considered skipping out on the dinner," Blane says with a grin. He still uses humor to cope with what happened after they missed the Parents Weekend dinner—and to deal with everything else, for that matter.

Cynthia gives him a withering gaze. The one she reserves for the yes-men surrounding the president.

"Got it. Still too soon . . ." he says sheepishly.

Over tacos and chips and guac, they talk about Hank's new book, his life. Reviews have been good. He just finished his next novel. He's in a serious relationship.

"I think you'd like her." He examines Cynthia, who is trying to pretend she agrees. "Okay, maybe that's going too far."

"So, Mark," she says, addressing Blane's friend, who's been quiet. She doesn't know if it's just awkwardness around parents or melancholy about graduating and having no family to celebrate the achievement. "Blane says you have a job lined up after graduation?"

Blane cuts in, says, "Yeah, swim coach . . ." As he's prone to do, her son laughs hard at his own joke. She and Hank pretend not to understand the reference to Mark's awful father.

To Cynthia's surprise, Mark laughs too. He and Blane are best friends for a reason.

"I'll be working in Silicon Valley. It's an AI startup—next-gen stuff."

"Those machines are gonna put me and other novelists out of business one day," Hank says. "Are you going to miss your partner in crime?" Hank adds, pointing his chin at Blane.

"We have the trip for the summer before I start my job and he starts grad school." The two are off to Europe. Cynthia may need to smooth over U.S. relations after that trip. She allows herself a smile at the thought. An unexpected feeling of nostalgia sweeps through her as she thinks about the trip she and Hank took after college—when life was full of hope and few responsibilities. Before becoming parents.

Blane is attending Georgetown to get his degree in IPOL. Cynthia is an occasional guest lecturer there, and she likes that he'll be back in D.C. She never imagined he'd leave California. Maybe being held captive in a van called the Mystery Machine or nearly drowning in a cave at Panther Beach changed that. Or maybe he just wants to be home.

When he got accepted at Georgetown, he told her he wanted to be like her. One of those rare times she got teary.

She looks out at the restaurant. Other than the businesspeople, it's filled with families on the cusp of sending their children out into the world. She reaches over and clutches Blane's hand, then reaches out for Hank's. And dammit if she doesn't feel a tear roll down her cheek.

CHAPTER SIXTY-SIX

THE GOFFMANS

Alice sits at her desk in the reception area of the dean's office listening to the phone buzz incessantly. She needs to pull it together. It's Saturday, but the dean ordered everyone in just in case he needs something for his big day—when he gets to crow onstage in his white gown and offer his wisdom to this year's graduates.

Finally she answers.

"Where have you been?" the dean says. "I've called several— Never mind. I need the speech printed again. And they were supposed to have gluten-free snacks for our commencement speaker."

Alice shakes her head. Their commencement speaker, some giant in the tech industry, has a rider that would make a rock star blush.

The dean continues: "You need to run over to Safeway and pick some up."

Alice doesn't respond, her eyes snagging for the hundredth time that morning on the photo of Felix perched on her desk.

Every graduation day is hard. Every day is hard, actually. She carries a ferocious sadness inside her. But today is worse: It would've been Felix on that stage. Felix in the gown, moving his tassel from right to left, tossing his cap high in the air.

The dean continues barking something. She says "Yes, sir" without comprehending his words and places the phone on its cradle.

She imagines Felix holding his diploma, posing for photos. His handsome face with a broad smile.

Many say he was a hero. Risking his life to save the other students. Saving the FBI agent. Others aren't so kind. The truth—the whole truth—is something she'll never know. The surviving students must've made a pact to keep the full story between them. They defended Felix when a few jackals on social media and podcasts and true-crime shows speculated the worst.

A sob escapes her. She can't seem to keep her thoughts straight.

The dean is at her desk now, his face stern.

"Alice?" he says. "Alice?"

He rips something off the printer, mutters about the commencement speaker's snacks.

Alice stands. She feels like she's in a trance. At the same time, something familiar is thrumming through her veins. The same feeling she had so long ago when she and Felix got on the bus with only the clothes on their backs and started anew.

She carefully unlocks the cabinet. Retrieves her handbag.

The dean is saying her name again. She doesn't bother to acknowledge him.

She grabs the photo of her son from her desk, the only thing she wants to take from this place. And she walks out, holding his picture against her heart.

Today won't be Felix's entry into a hopeful world, a fresh start.

But maybe it can be hers.

CHAPTER SIXTY-SEVEN

THE AKANAS

"Hurry," Amy says, tugging Ken's hand as they maneuver through the crowd at Stevens Stadium. She looks up at the masses. The bleachers are jammed with families of the graduates. Bright music from the marching band wafts through the air. Their flight from Heathrow was late, and they nearly missed the entire ceremony.

Ken pulls her to a stop.

"Hurry, we—"

He interrupts her with a kiss.

She marvels that this is the famously punctual, even persnickety, No Drama Akana. That's what they used to call him before he retired from the bench. Before he and Amy sold everything and became wanderers, going from one small town in Europe to the next.

Talking.

Holding hands.

Laughing. Finally laughing again.

They clumsily make their way along the crowded bleachers until someone generously makes room for them to sit. Otherwise, no one is paying them any mind. Just a few years ago all eyes would've been on them. Because Ken presided over the Rock Nelson trial. Or because they were the parents of one of The Five. Or because Ken had killed Amy's stalker. But internet fame is, thankfully, fleeting.

Ken folds her hand into his as they gaze down at the graduates below. They've missed the remarks of the dean, the valedictorian's speech, the commencement speaker. But that's okay, they made it in time for the grand finale, when the students walk across the stage.

Amy feels a lump rising in her throat. After everything they've been through, Libby is graduating.

"There she is!" Amy cries, spotting Libby in the procession line near the stage. Amy soaks in the vision of her daughter in her shiny gown, her hair draped over one shoulder. Since the trauma of her freshman year, Libby doesn't have the same sparkle. None of them are the same. But they found their way through.

When the announcer calls Libby's name, Amy and Ken jump to their feet. And Ken turns and kisses Amy again.

Later, in the chaos of everyone finding their graduates, Libby wades though the crowd. Ken races up to her, hugs her, and spins her around.

"Daaaad," Libby protests, but Amy can tell she likes it.

Ken asks his girls to pose for a picture.

As he fumbles with his phone, Libby says, "What's gotten into him?"

Amy smiles.

"No," Libby corrects, "what's gotten into *you*?"

"We're just, I don't know . . . *happy*."

Libby's smile reaches her eyes. Her posture straightens like a weight has been lifted. She looks over at her dad, who is talking to another parent.

"Mom," she says. "I have something to tell you."

Amy examines her daughter. She's holding Amy's gaze with those pretty eyes.

"Anything."

"I'm not going to law school."

This is a surprise. Her grand plan since she was a kid was to go to a good college, attend an Ivy League law school, and become a judge like her father. She's even been accepted to Yale.

"No?"

"I got a job."

Amy smiles.

"It's for St. Jude's."

Amy's throat thickens. She can't speak. The cancer center that not only provides the best treatment for kids but covers the expenses for families that need it.

"I want to help people—people like us."

Ken comes back over. "You ready to get some food?"

They both nod.

Amy finds her voice. It's laced with something she recognizes as pride. "Libby has some important news."

She tells him, and Ken gives her another whirling hug, and Libby laughs—a laugh Amy hasn't heard since before their family was overtaken by despair.

Yes, they really did find their way through.

CHAPTER SIXTY-EIGHT

THE MALDONADOS

"Get you a refill, ladies?"

Nina eyes the bartender, who holds the bottle of red. It's terrible wine, what she'd expect from the bar at the Embassy Suites. Yet it somehow tastes so good.

Stella responds for them both as she returns from taking a call in the lobby: "Keep 'em coming." Stella's cheeks are pink and her graduation gown is unzipped, the sash flung like a scarf. They shouldn't have another. They finished two bottles at dinner earlier. But looking out at the other families having nightcaps—merriment and relief in the air from the big day—Nina slides her glass closer to the barman.

He smiles. He's an all-American type who doesn't look much older than Stella. He fills their glasses. He pauses a beat at Stella's glass, then fills it to the top.

"Congratulations," he says to her with a wink.

"I love a heavy pourer," she flirts.

Nina takes a sip and studies her daughter. She's so grown-up, but also still just a kid.

"What did your father say when he called?" Nina asks.

She shrugs. "The usual. He's *sooo* sorry he missed it. He's *soooo* proud of me. Yada yada."

Nina smiles. Stella is too young to even know where *Yada yada* originated—an old TV show Nina and David used to love—though maybe like everything else, what is old is new again because of Netflix.

"He's so proud of you," Nina allows.

Nina and David split only a month after Parents Weekend. It had been a long time coming. It was hard enough to get over his infidelity, much less the attack by his paramour's son, what happened to Stella. Their divorce wasn't pretty, but they're both trying.

Nina heard through the hospital grapevine—from friends who sided with her in the split—that the boy, Cody Carpenter, got treatment. Was enrolled in community college and doing well. That family deserved something good to happen to them.

"He texted me last month really broken up about not coming," Nina says, not sure why she's defending David. "Chrissy bought the cruise tickets as a surprise. Nonrefundable, but he said he'd cancel if you were going to be upset."

"Yeah, he said the same thing to me," Stella says. "I was actually fine with it. I thought it might be awkward."

"I hope you didn't do that for me?"

"Honestly, for me. Chrissy is nice enough. But she's sooo dumb." Stella flips her hair, and in a baby-girl voice imitates her father's girlfriend: *"Stella, I'm obsessed with your outfit. Stella, I'm obsessed with your hair. Stella . . ."*

Nina represses a smile. She hasn't met Chrissy and is happy

David found someone. But she admittedly is taking joy in her daughter's mockery.

"What about you, Mom?"

"What about me?"

"You seeing anyone?"

"Not really."

"You should. You're still pretty hot."

Nina blushes, takes a swallow of wine. "You know that me and your father, for whatever our differences, *are* so proud. Your dad did the sappiest post on social media when you got into med school."

"I saw." Stella shakes her head, embarrassed for him. "Chrissy should really take away his phone."

They clink glasses again.

She watches as Stella examines her phone, thumbs a text to someone. It's nearly midnight and the parents are starting to clear out.

Nina drains her glass and says, "I think I need to call it a night." She pauses, hopes Stella will say the same thing.

Instead, Stella says, "Some people are getting together, so I'll probably . . ." She eyes the lobby door.

Nina resists the lecture. Resists protesting. Her daughter is a grown woman. A college graduate. Still, she says, "You'll share your location on your phone."

Stella releases an exasperated breath. "Yes, Mom."

"I love you," Nina says.

And she watches her beautiful daughter glide out of the hotel, the sash fluttering behind her.

CHAPTER SIXTY-NINE

THE KELLERS

Sarah Keller pulls her bag behind her, turning to see if Bob and the kids are keeping up. The Amtrak train to D.C. was delayed and she's going to be late for her appointment.

Michael and Heather wear backpacks and strut through D.C.'s Union Station, seeming to take no notice of the majestic great hall—New Yorkers, unimpressed with this lesser version of Grand Central. Bob grouses as he trails behind.

The front of the station has a line for cabs. To Keller's surprise, the lawn, usually a beautiful lush green, is covered with tents. Another sign of the times.

"Stan said he's circling around."

When her old boss and mentor makes it to the front of the station, Keller checks her watch. "I don't think I'm gonna make it."

"You go," Bob says. "We'll get an Uber to the hotel. I'll take the kids to the museums, and you can find us later."

She gives him a *you sure?* look.

"Go," he says. She kisses Bob and gives the kids—thirteen-year-olds not keen on hugs in public—a squeeze.

Inside the sedan, Stan greets her with a stiff nod, makes a show of looking at his watch. "You always like to make an entrance."

God, she misses him.

An hour later, they've made it through security at Quantico and are seated in the first row. Stan rarely makes an appearance at these things, so the Quantico folks are rolling out the red carpet.

Keller flashes back to when she participated in this very ceremony. The pride she felt finishing her grueling FBI training. How *patriotic* she felt. How full of purpose.

She didn't know then her real purpose would be to spend her life with a bald guy with a penchant for dad jokes and the two bright lights they created together.

Someone slips into the seat next to her. Keller smiles. "I'm so glad you made it," she says to Jay McCray.

"Not every day I get an invite to Quantico," he says. "And besides, my wife needed a break. My retirement hasn't suited her." He grins.

The associate deputy director—who obviously drew the short straw this year—appears at the podium. He gives a stock speech, likely the same one given to Keller so long ago, yet it somehow still manages to give her a lump in her throat. Then the graduating class materializes.

Keller and Annie Hafeez make eye contact as Annie walks across the podium. Her family—it looks like multiple generations of Hafeezes are here—clap politely.

Few good things came out of the case that brought Keller and Annie and McCray together. But helping a young woman find her purpose—making sure the Bureau took notice of an applicant with such promise—is something Keller will always be proud of.

At the end of the ceremony, she and everyone in the room stand as the graduates recite the Federal Bureau of Investigation's oath.

And Keller recites every single word.

CHAPTER SEVENTY

THE FOUR

The bonfire is an orange ball in the darkness. They haven't been together since that night they ran for their lives on this very beach.

They say little. They're no longer the capstone group. No longer The Five.

They link hands as before, but there's no terror now. Tonight they bow their heads, say a silent prayer—a tribute. To a young woman they let down. To a young man who made a mistake, then saved their lives. To their respective gods.

Then, they disappear into the night to begin their lives.

READER'S NOTE

A quick note about the setting and research for *Parents Weekend*. I need to make it abundantly clear that my depiction of Santa Clara University, its administration, and its faculty bears no resemblance to reality. This is a thriller, after all. The only thing accurately portrayed about SCU is its beautiful campus. I chose SCU as the setting for the book because my son is a student there, and I got the idea for the novel while at Parents Weekend. I think Santa Clara is one of the country's finest institutions, and my son has had an idyllic college experience. I hope the university won't hold his father's warped imagination against him.

On research, I managed to receive only a few emails about inaccuracies in my last novel, so I am hopeful, perhaps delusionally so, about *Parents Weekend*. A few people helped me try to get things right. Thanks to retired FBI Special Agent Jennifer Gant, who corrected my many mistakes and forgave me for leaving in others for dramatic effect. I am also grateful to Jay Gruber, the chief public safety officer at Georgetown University, for taking time to answer questions about university police procedures and for keeping young people safe during his impressive career.

I also owe a continuing debt to my friends at the best law firm in the country, Arnold & Porter, who not only have supported my novels but also helped me with complex legal questions, this time geofence search warrants.

All errors and embellishments—and outright blunders—are mine alone.

Two old friends also helped with research by sharing things about their lives. Thanks to Annie Hafeez Khalid for lending me her name and some of her background for one of my favorite characters, Annie the Intern. And to one of my oldest friends in Washington, who I will not name since he remains under a threat much like Cynthia Roosevelt, yet somehow hasn't let it dampen his love of a good laugh.

Last, back to those emails about my mistakes and inaccuracies. Please send all corrections and complaints about *Parents Weekend* care of author David Ellis at www.DavidEllis.com /contact/. (Kidding! Sorry, buddy.)

ACKNOWLEDGMENTS

This is always the hardest part: saying goodbye to characters I've lived with for so long and finding the words to adequately thank the many people who allowed you to meet them.

To Lisa Erbach Vance, the best literary agent in the business. I always thank Lisa first because she's responsible for this career I cherish. Thanks also to Natalie Rosselli, Kristen Pini, and the rest of the team at the Aaron M. Priest Literary Agency.

To my editors, Kelley Ragland, Catherine Richards, and Kelly Stone at Minotaur Books, St Martin's Publishing Group, for their expert pens, brilliant insights, and *extreme* patience.

To my marketing and PR team, Stephen Erickson, Kayla Janas, and Martin Quinn, for their hard work, creativity, and good humor.

To the rest of the team at Minotaur for helping make this book the best it could be. And to Elishia Merricks, Emily Dyer, and the rest of the team at Macmillan Audio for bringing the pages to life.

To my private editor, Ed Stackler, for once again being my secret weapon.

To my buddy and megatalent, Sarah Pekkanen, for helping me work through tricky parts of this story and for her friendship.

To the many writers who over the past year participated in my events, provided blurbs, or simply shared some laughs (and cocktails): The Paris Writers (Kimberly Belle, Cindy R. X. He, Christina McDonald, Kaira Rouda), Ethan Cross, Laura Dave, Lisa Gardner, Kimberley Howe, K. T. Nguyen, Jeneva Rose, and Ashley Winstead, to name a few. And to my pal David Ellis. It's rare to make fast friends at my age, particularly one who shares a similarly dark sense of humor.

To my family, of course: Trace, my smart, talented, beautiful wife. And to my children, Jake, Em, and Aiden, for making me proud.

To readers for giving precious hours of your lives reading my stories. It's one of the great honors of my life.

ABOUT THE AUTHOR

Julia Litvin

Alex Finlay is the bestselling author of several novels, including his latest bestseller, *If Something Happens to Me*. His work regularly appears on best-of-the-year lists and has been translated into twenty-five languages. Four of Alex's novels have been optioned or are in development for film or major streaming series. Alex lives in Washington, D.C., and Virginia.